SINS & SORROWS

Michael Tisdale

ISBN: 1548664758
ISBN 13: 9781548664756

For Kristine

DISTURBING THE PRIEST

Part One
The Road To Damascus

CHAPTER 1

The Indian sat alone, pondering the universe as he often did. Meditating on a high rock, taking in all the beauty of The Great Spirit. All the riches and food of plenty. His wife of five years who was unwavering, standing by his side. Even when he left the tribe to set out on his own, not wanting to be a part of the war with the white man. Great Spirit had shown him the devastation and agony that was forced upon his people, long before it actually came to pass. He was a man of visions among the elders, a shaman, respected. He would never forget the day when his visions and warnings would go unheeded. Chief Running Bird had stripped him of his position, and chose to walk blind into a battle that would result in the slaughter of many braves, women and children.

They were outnumbered by a vast margin, fighting for ignorant pride. Spirit had spoken through him but the words had fallen upon deaf ears, and thus, a once mighty tribe did not survive. Legacy, history, an entire way of life wiped away in a single afternoon. He could still hear the unreasonable speech from their angry leader. Spirit sent tears to fall from his eyes but still they would not listen.

Running Bird's words were still branded in his memory, "Black Jackal, take your squaw and make yourself scarce, for you have lied to your brothers. It is not Great Spirit that speaks through you, but fear and shame."

He gathered his belongings for an unknown journey as courageous young warriors readied their horses and sang the old song of war and death. Such hatred entrenched in their souls, that they did not harken the wise instruction of The Great Spirit, second guessing his power and knowledge, riding to their own untimely demise.

In his heart he was shaman, and would always be. The last survivor of a proud clan, too proud in the end. He returned to his home days later, to once again shed tears of despair for his brothers and way of life. He took supplies and returned to his woman, to start over in the world.

He would decide to return to his woman with fresh meat for dinner, to praise Spirit together as one, and lay in each other's arms as he intended to do for all eternity. She was a good woman, his Tameka. A good companion for Black Jackal. Understanding and true. The thought of her tender touch warmed his heart and he arose to leave from his sitting vigil there on that high rock, far above the bounty of endless green land. Life was good, regardless of those recent unexpected occurrences. Great Spirit must have had a reason, he would tell himself, and he would not question Spirit as his tribe had done, falling to a catastrophic end.

Black Jackal did arise and turned to leave, but in that moment his sight became unsure and his head felt weak. He moved back to a kneeling position, as he knew this was a sign that Spirit wished to show him something. On his knees he waited, and the images in his mind became clear. He was shaman, touched by Spirit, as only one in many were. His muscles relaxed, and he accepted the vision.

Black Jackal awoke some time later, on his face in the dust and dirt of the trail. Slowly he regained his faculties and once again felt blood coursing through his legs. On his feet he blinked and looked around him.

"Thank you, Noo Wen Tayo Great Spirit. It shall be done." he mumbled out loud, and began his journey home.

Tameka was a vision unto her herself, the most desirable squaw in the entire tribe to Black Jackal, and he considered himself blessed to call her his own, as she was to marry such an important leader in the shaman. She saw him as he made his way through the forest and into their small camp. He was strong and muscular, his skin bronzed by the sun, his hair long and black as the hawk's eyes. He appeared himself as a god amongst mortals. Yes, Tameka was thrilled whenever Black Jackal returned to her.

He was an honorable warrior and hunter. He would kill a mighty bison, and then kneel and pray, thanking Spirit for the sustenance, then apologizing to the beast itself, explaining why it had to be done, and what survival would come from its sacrifice. He would pray that Great Spirit would see his hunt, see his kill, and remember when it was time to walk with Spirit in the beyond. He was thorough, and reverent at all times upon the precious beautiful earth.

But this night he wore a serious face and his deep umber eyes roared with fire.

"Tameka, come to me." he bellowed, as she responded with haste.

"Yes, my husband."

He embraced her. "You have been gone for three moons." she said.

"Great Spirit has given me a vision." spoke Black Jackal, coming straight to business, as there was no other business greater than a vision from Great Spirit.

"A holy man will travel from afar to right a wrong and face a fierce evil."

"He comes *here*? When?"

"Soon." the Indian answered, "Soon. We have been charged by Spirit to help him. And...we shall help him."

CHAPTER 2

The priest enjoyed philosophical debates with the other holy men of the town, but only to a point. Their opinions were often unwarranted and without merit. When it likened to arguing with a wall, that was when he had had enough.

"What do you think of the Nazarene?" was the anticipated proposal those last few weeks. "Perhaps he is who he says he is" was not always the popular reply to that line of questioning. Often he would glance around the street, seeing the glory of God in all things; even the smallest examples were precious. His daughters were precious. It was the thoughts of his family that was interrupted that day by talk of them among his robed peers.

"Your eldest is acting strangely, my friend. We are...concerned, as you know. It has been noticed before."

"Sapphira my eldest, yes, she is strong willed and at times stubborn." the priest answered, "It will pass."

Now the conversation became more serious, more so than ramblings of the Nazarene.

"It *must* pass." stated one.

"I know of the measures that must be taken, my brothers. Do not wonder on whether I am aware...please."

"Make it so", continued the white-bearded elder, "and we will meet again in the temple on the Sabbath. Passover approaches and this inconvenience must be eradicated."

"Yes", he replied, "I understand."

The priest excused himself and made his way home on the sandy street of the village. His heart grew heavy, as he knew Sapphira was only making things worse out of sheer bullheadedness. Her speech and actions were testing not only his patience, but that of the town. Those priests were the authority of God in the flesh, and of much higher persuasion than he. Not by the measure of their service, but by simple seniority. Their dire tone was beginning to grow. Maybe he should depart from that place, he thought often, find the Nazarene and follow him. Tales told of healing and magic were met with fascination from some and disgust by others. Whispers that he may indeed be the Son of Almighty God, and as much chattering of his evil purpose, placed here as an agent of the Deceiver. And of course there were those who proposed that he was mad. He told himself that time would tell, and arrived at the front door of his humble abode.

Peeking his head inside he saw his greatest blessing from The Creator, his youngest daughter Penninah, digging in a bowl of flour and herbs with the utensil her mother had used before her.

"Penninah, how is supper coming along?"

She looked up with an angelic smile for her father and softly grunted, returning to her chore. Penninah was mute, and more often than not could be heard making odd noises and chirping sounds, or crying when she was sad.

They said it happened to children after witnessing a tragic event, and he prayed every day for her recovery. He would always tell her that she was his gift, and she would smile at him, and make a humming sound as if she were singing. Sometimes just a clicking noise from her throat, or again, sometimes just the smile. There was never any trouble from Penninah, his cherished little one.

"Where is your sister?"

Penninah glanced at him again, with a concerned look this time, and motioned with eyes away, towards the door. Then she frowned.

"These are trying times." the priest said to her. Somewhere within him he always hoped for a reply that never came. He loved her so.

Later that evening, as the priest and his pleasant, obedient daughter sat by a small fire after their supper, his oldest offspring approached from the darkness and stepped into the glow of the burning amber light. Her face was perfect, as a statue of a Roman goddess, a beautiful girl growing into a woman, her attractive appearance marred only by a stern look and down turned lips.

"Sapphira, where have you been?" the priest asked. A moment of silence ensued before she would speak to her worried father.

"What does it matter?"

"It matters."

"To *you*!"

"I am your father. Your every move matters to me. And it matters to the elders who are talking of the shame you are bringing upon our house...and what they are thinking of doing about it."

"I do not care!" Sapphira shot back, "I do not wish to live here any longer!"

"Please, Sapphira, why does an anger burn in your heart so that you would tempt the elders and risk your life? I cannot lose you."

"Like you lost mother?"

She had always known just where to stick the thorn into her father's side, and say the things that would hurt him the most.

"That was long ago. There is no fault with us and no reason for your bitterness. My heart overflows with love for you and you only care to spat at my feet."

Then again the silence. He despised quarreling with her, as it made his very soul cry out in pain. Those heated exchanges were becoming more frequent.

"I have met a man that will take me to Damascus." she stated in a blunt uproar, as if her mind were made up.

"Sapphira..."

"You will prosper without me here, alongside your grunting little monkey servant!"

The priest arose from his seat by the fire. "She is your dear sister and she has a name! I will not hear these words!"

"I am leaving!" She announced with a slight growl.

"No, I forbid it!"

Then Sapphira's eyes grew cold as she said, "You can pray for me, father, but that is all you can do. Your God is weak and repays your loyalty by taking your wife, and leaving you with a useless mute for a daughter, living in a hovel!"

"God..." the priest stammered, " God has *reasons* to test us."

"Perhaps there is no God after all, and YOU are a FOOL!" Sapphira lashed out with all the animosity she could muster, to shock her father, as she thought, into reality.

"They will stone you! Sapphira, please..."

"I am leaving!" And with that final threat, she stormed off into the night from where she appeared mere minutes earlier. The priest, feeling defeated, slumped back into his seat. Penninah, a helpless witness to the entire fight, rushed over to comfort him, laying her head on his shoulder and letting a light whimper escape.

"What can I do?" he asked of her, but knew there would be no answer. Her devotion was enough to console him.

There was no point in searching for Sapphira, through the deep forest and the thick brush surrounding the sleepy Hebrew town.

As he lay his head to rest, he thought to himself, perhaps her running away would not be such a terrible act after all. Perhaps, with all the judging eyes upon them, she would be safer with her freedom. Sending her out into a cruel world to escape death by her own people's hands, to an outsider would seem as madness. But here the difficult decisions were, facing them. She was a woman now for all intent and purpose. Maybe it would be for the best. He struggled with that notion, for how did God factor in, and how would he be perceived by The Heavenly Father, sending his sinful daughter away to escape his judgment? Maybe his daughter was right, and he had been a tyrant to her. He had taught her the scriptures, and raised her in the temple. But there they were at odds, still existing in the shadow of their loss, the death of their mother. His dear Abigail.

He would dream of her that night as he did most nights, hoping for a sign, or word of encouragement from her through his unconscious state. It was there that he could see her lovely face again, touch her and pretend that all was right. There were mornings that he wished to curse the dawn, for his nighttime world was much more bearable than the one he had to rise and face without her.

He did the best he could with the girls. Poor Penninah needed extra attention and care, and he feared that Sapphira was often left to her own devices. He would blame himself, regardless of his blame's validity. It fell on his shoulders to do right by them both whatever the cost, giving his very life for theirs if it came to that. One last look at Penninah slumbering at peace, and he allowed himself to wander, searching for Abigail in another realm.

Penninah, though, was not asleep. She waited until she heard the first signs of restful breathing from her father before rising as quiet as a field mouse, and tip-toeing through the door to look for Sapphira. She turned to see the priest in misery, and in her own way, had to do something to save her broken family. She walked to the edge of the forest, thought a quick prayer, and stepped inside. She made her way to a clearing, but upon discovering Sapphira meeting that man she spoke of, remained hidden for the moment.

He was an older gentleman in a long dark robe. He appeared much as the other men in the village yet he was much more handsome and alluring. She could see why Sapphira longed to be with him. She wondered if she herself would ever fall in love. No, she would conclude, she must remain and take care of father. No one would want a freakish mute, a 'monkey servant' as Sapphira had been mean enough to put it. Her sister could be so intolerable, and often her thoughtless words would cut her like a knife, much as they did father. It was different to see her happiness for a change, held in the arms of a man such as this. For a moment Penninah forgot herself, stepped back and broke a small fallen tree branch under her loose sandal, alerting the couple to her presence.

Sapphira's long kiss was interrupted by the inadvertent sound made by Penninah.

"Who is there?" called Sapphira into the unknown.

The tall long haired man with rugged features turned and repeated, "Yes, who is there? Come on out, child." As if he had already known, perplexing Sapphira for a second. Penninah moved from the woods with a ginger step, into the light. She was embarrassed that she had been discovered, but more frightened than anything.

"It is my sister, the one I told you about. Go home, monkey!" said Sapphira, rolling her eyes and letting out a sarcastic sigh, "Go home, Penninah."

The trembling child shook her head 'no' and motioned for Sapphira to come home with her.

"Go home, monkey!" she repeated.

Penninah began to cry, still motioning with her hands to her rebellious sister. The man smiled, and suggested, "Perhaps she wishes to accompany us on our journey...to Damascus."

In a rare moment of clarity, Sapphira turned to him and pleaded, "That would leave father all alone. He needs her."

"Suddenly you are concerned of your father's well being?" The man inquired, "She will be of more use to us. Come here. Penninah, is it?"

Penninah began a modest approach, unsure, and took one small step at a time.

"Yes...come to me, young one."

Even Sapphira knew this was not a good idea, but remained silent.

The priest awoke rather in an unexpected manner from a dream state, rubbed the sleep from his eyes, and gazed about his meager home, wondering why it was not daylight. When he focused more and his attention crossed over Penninah's empty bed, he leaped up and called her name. And again. Opening the door, he stepped into the street.

"Penninah!? Where are you?"

A fear overtook him as he remembered the terror he felt when his wife took a late night walk and never returned. They found her mauled remains four days later, attacked by a wild beast of some kind, what they assumed was a large vicious creature. Oh how he wept. The suffering was immense, and he wrestled with agonizing sorrow for weeks. He raised the two girls the best he knew how, still seeing his own failures in Sapphira's icy stares.

He stumbled out into the night, embarking on an immediate search. His scared little Penninah, who took her mother's disappearance harder than anyone it had seemed, and had never uttered a single vowel since. She was true and loving, but the painful memory still blazed deep within the quiet, odd girl.

Through the lush trees he ran, desperate then, as an unbroken horse fleeing its captive stable. Running, to find what? A haunting fear set in, and he could feel the blood moving in his own veins, quick as a raging waterfall over a ravine. His heart beat at a savage pace, pounding to awaken the sleeping and the dead.

He arrived in the clearing, stopping in his tracks at the disturbing sight before him.

Sapphira, and a strange man holding an unconscious Penninah in his arms. A blue glow emanating all around them. It was not of his earth that he knew, and he could smell the nefarious intention from those 100 yards of separation.

"No!" yelled the priest, "Creature, leave them be. In the name of God and all that is holy. I compel thee. Leave them and be on your way!"

It was then that he saw this demonic figure's sharpened teeth and lifeless black eyes, and knew what he was looking upon. It chilled him to his bone's marrow.

"You compel no one!" the vampirus proclaimed, "I do not fear you, priest. You are too late. As you have been your entire existence. I have taken these children for my own, for my own glorious purpose. "

"Who are you?" the priest cried, shouting over the growing breeze that had turned into wind.

"Who am I?" answered the monster, "Beyond this world I stand. Beyond time I stand. Beyond your wretched mortal reach I stand. Free. With the power from one whose glory is greater than even the will of your God."

"Blasphemer...they are mine." the priest called out, "They are... all that I have."

"Then you have *nothing*, priest!" The words that would tear his coil apart for the rest of his life came cold and emphatic. The light intensified into a bright and brilliant explosion, engulfing them until they appeared as three blackened silhouettes. The priest charged forward but was knocked back by an invisible force that rattled his chest cavity and sternum. He fell to the ground as the blinding light faded and they were gone. The wind calmed, and leaves cascaded about his prone body. He rose and rushed to the spot where his daughters had been and fell to his knees, distraught. He gathered handfuls of dirt and threw them skyward.

"Where are you? In the name of God, where have you taken them? Where?"

His arms outstretched and tears soaking his cheeks and beard, he was alone, pleading under his heavy breathing.

"I will...find you." He managed the threat from his lips before collapsing to the forest floor. "I will." he rolled over onto his back, under the huge blanket of stars above him.

"Why...why have you forsaken me, Father? Help me. I have been your servant in all things. I need the strength of your hand, now more than ever."

He knew they had not gone to Damascus. At least not the one that he knew.

CHAPTER 3

The priest opened his eyes, still laying in the scattered leaves in that damned clearing. He made it to his feet knowing what he had to do, and also knowing that he would not sleep much more after that evening's horrific events. He was truly alone, now that his entire family and reason for existing at all had been taken from him in a rapid blink. He brushed the soil from his poor man's attire and made his way back towards home. A spark had been lit inside this man of God's heart, but even he, in that moment, could not decipher between revenge or great purpose. Reaching his door, some early rising passerby gave him a good morning nod that was not returned. It was too late for pleasantries he feared, for now he had to go about accomplishing the impossible. And to do that, he would need more information than any earthbound human could provide.

The temple and its leaders possessed all the knowledge of the ages, from a slight biased point of view, to be kind. Bless them, he thought as his brain squirmed like a lizard, writhing inside his own skull. He would not approach the priests, for they would warn him of the endless dangers of this and the dangers of that, and lecture him on scripture that he had memorized since he was a boy. He needed what was forbidden to him, and he made up his mind then and there that nothing would stop him from acquiring knowledge, even if it meant stoning if discovered. What would they do if it were their children? Sit and read scripture? Pray on their knees, hoping God would just bring them back? Maybe they would think him mad, and stone him anyway on the spot. He had seen it done, after all.

He gathered a few light possessions in a sack, a change of garment and general everyday items, and stepped through his front door. He paused for a few seconds and settled on the notion that he may never again step through that door. That he would be leaving his home, where a lifetime of memories had been born and nurtured. It was where he had first made love to his sweet Abigail, following in the eyes of the Almighty, following their union of being. A deep sigh, and the next step led him away from that cherished place and onto a fateful journey into the unknown.

He could fail, but decided not to. So it was that the good yet heartbroken priest set off to find the most forbidden person he had ever heard tales of. Ariatta, the witch.

When he was young he had heard the whispers of the witch that lived in the heart of the dark forest, much farther than that clearing. He considered it a fantastical imagining to break up a constant monotony of work and worship. A myth no more. Yet the stories continued, and as he grew, years after becoming a man, he still heard the hushed musings of the wild woman.

They said that once she appeared in the center of town and brought a thunderous downpour that destroyed every field in an instant, cursing them all, before vanishing as quick as she had arrived. True or not, there was enough evidence to support at least the suspicion that a powerful witch did exist. He was not afraid. He traveled for what seemed like weeks but it did not dissuade him. This serpent of Satan would be his only hope, as ironic as that were. Yet he still stopped to ask the Lord's guidance, to lead him in his quest.

The nightfall fell on the fourth day as if the sun were moving faster than usual, hurrying to set beyond the far horizon. It was then that the priest saw the glimmer of a campfire. Could it be? He knew of no one who resided that length from civilization. Even that sounded odd to him now. That civilization itself or what was perceived as civilization could be questioned in its honesty. But he was far from it. He approached a small tent with remnants of smoldering ash in front, and low flickering candle light from inside.

"Come in." a raspy female voice invited from within. The priest, cautious, yet welcoming a breath of hospitality from anyone, moved the entrance flap aside and stepped into a mystic nest. Burning candles all around, surrounding what appeared as a woman, draped in thin cloth.

"I am the one you ssseek." she said, before he could process it all.

"You are..." the priest waited a beat before saying the name aloud, "Ariatta?"

"I am the one." came the seething reply. To the point, thought the priest, shedding his apprehension, for that was what he had come for.

"There was a man..." he began before being cut off.

"The man you follow isss far from here, and will be difficult to pursssue, for he possssessses the darknessss of Ba'al in hisss undead sssoul."

There was a time of silence after that, before she spoke again, almost hissing the syllables at him like a snake.

"He alssso posssessssesss your flessshh."

"My daughters."

"Go back to your homeland, priessst. They are lossst to you."

"There must be a way." he insisted.

"The Monsssster bendsss time itssself. He is beyond thisss realm even now."

"Where?"

The witch stared him down with devilish abandon, as if her eyes were burning him where they focused. "Thessse are mattersss that humansss are not to have undersssstanding."

"I must understand. Tell me all." the priest insisted.

"He travelsss through the dimensssions. Hisss ssstrength ssstreams from The Dark Lord to achieve thisss. But he can only move forward, and in cccertain...incrementsss."

"Then he has a destination."

"Yesss."

"Then I must be there upon his arrival."

The witch raised her head to look in the priest's face, her eyes glowing from beneath the thin drapery. "Imposssible."

"Nothing is impossible!" the priest disagreed.

With that, the witch turned her head away. "I cannot help you. I have revealed too mucchh to you already. And without payment of any kind."

"I will find him." the priest announced to her, and turned to leave.

"Wait", she called out, "Are you cccertain I cannot aid you by other meansss?"

Ariatta began pulling the silky garment from her body in an erotic fashion, to tempt him. Her charms were uncovered and like none other seen by man. The permanent markings etched on her arms, legs, and torso were a reminder of who he was dealing with.

"Your wife isss long dead, you hunger for the touch of another. I can feel it in your esssence...ssstay the night, priesssst."

The candles' glow danced on her skin from all sides; she touched her breasts and hissed again, "Ssstay."

The priest stood like a rock, not to be seduced from his sworn mission.

"In desperation only I come to you, witch. I should not even be here in the presence of your foulness." The priest's words were cold, but the might of the Nile raged in his chest. He reached into his bag and produced a gold coin, one of his last. He looked at the face of Caesar, then flipped it over to her, landing on the straw mat at her feet. Ariatta grabbed the ornament and hid it away, in a little ornate box.

"Cccenturiesss from now, the Vampirusss arrivesss in a world not yet imagined by sssuch asss yoursssself."

"What is this place called?"

The witch smiled and answered. "It isss called...*Ah-mer-eye-kaaah.*"

CHAPTER 4

Many miles through the desert wreaked havoc on the priest's sandals and tired feet. He found food where he could, but there were no heavenly beings bringing manna along the way as Moses enjoyed during the long Exodus from Egypt. He felt solitude on his shoulders like the weight of a Roman crucifix. Sweat burned into his pupils yet he remained vigilant. If he were to die, he would take leave of this world laboring to find his children. It would be a good death. Noble. He tried not to think about their fate at the hands of the evil incarnate, that thief in the night. No, he would not die. He would find them and die saving them, if that was his future.

He walked up to a long dead traveler, his skeletal remains laying in the sand. The priest took pity on him and knelt to deliver last rites for the poor soul. This concluded, he rustled through the man's belongings, found a good knife and a few other useful trinkets. A few feet away lay the dead man's walking stick, a fine sturdy one that he had then inherited. He did not bury him, not having the strength, proper tools, or anything to wrap him in for tribute.

"Forgive me." he spoke to the man, "May you fly with the angels to God's Kingdom, into his waiting arms."

He stood, almost waiting for a reply, then turned and continued on. He was going to find the Nazarene, for he was the only one who could be of any help to him then. The rumors were that he and his followers were camped outside of Callirrhoe, along the Dead Sea. So this is where he would go as well. He hoped he could make it.

Reaching the fishing city of Callirrhoe, he inquired of the somewhat radical teacher that he sought. Many shied away and would not speak to him. Others were rude, and he sat under a shade tree to rest his weary bones. He could see the water's bank, and the boats coming and going. One man tossed him a denari, thinking him a homeless beggar. He supposed that perhaps that was how he appeared, and thanked the man, but he kept walking as if he did not hear it.

The priest walked to the sea's edge, knelt and splashed the water onto his face and rubbed a little on the back of his neck. It was cool and welcomed. A young boy appeared unannounced beside him, watching him with wide intense eyes. He must have been all of seven.

"Hello." the priest said to the youth.

"Hello." the boy answered.

"Is your father a fisherman?" the priest said, attempting to create some kind of conversation.

"No." the boy answered, very matter of fact.

"Tell me of your father then." he tried again.

"*My* father cleans the fish." the boy said in a proud manner, "he cleans them better that any other."

"That's wonderful to hear. Is he teaching you this trade, so that one day you may clean the fish even better than he?'

"Sometimes." the boy said, "Just not today."

"Oh, I see. Be careful, though, the scriptures warn of the sin of vanity. I do not doubt your father's skill, but it may be overzealous to boast of it."

"Are you a priest?"

"Sometimes." he replied with a slight smirk.

"You are!" exclaimed the boy.

The boy knelt beside the priest and whispered in his ear, "The one you seek is just beyond the city, to the west. Among the groves. He awaits your arrival."

And with that, the boy ran off, towards the boats and the men hauling in their nets. The priest knelt there a few moments longer, watching the boy run out of sight. He knew he had just been blessed with a divine message from The Lord, the words of an angel delivered from the lips of a boy. There was something to the yarns of the Nazarene after all. Inside he knew it all along, but it was still so moving to experience that miracle, and to know a calming in his chest for the first time in weeks.

"Thank you." he said to no one in particular. He rose and began his own Exodus across the city of Callirrhoe. West. Within an hour he reached the outskirts, and beheld the magnificent groves. Fruit was in abundance that time of year, and he picked a most ravishing looking pomegranate for his own.

The sun was setting and he continued. The farther he walked through the bushes and trees, the lighter his steps became, and even more a gentle peace filtered into his body.

Reaching a wide clearing, he observed several men starting a campfire across the way, and for the first time felt as if he may be intruding. Was this he? And what would he do for a wandering nomad in trying times? He recalled the words of the witch. What would he even ask of this man; where would he find the audacity to even speak of his troubles? Considering his troubles were not a mortal's usual troubles, he may have good reason to be there. It was good enough for him. And so he took the next step towards the man, and his impending destiny.

The priest was not sure what to even expect. Angels frolicking, playing instruments and singing in an unbridled fervor of praise. No, just a modest, unobtrusive fire with a few robed men huddled around it. He counted eight. One foot in front of the other at a methodical pace he was determined to join that solemn party. The man in the middle was first to recognize his approach, and did not seem alarmed, as if he knew of the priest's presence all along. A thin man with striking features, piercing eyes, and a calm over him, making the priest feel at ease and welcome before he even spoke.

"Join us, brother." he said as the other men turned their heads to look.

The priest sat down next to him, and his heart told him that that was the man he had come to see.

"Tell me of your burden." he inquired, although the priest knew this question was indeed a polite formality.

"I know who you are, rabbi." the priest said, "Look into my eyes and know what burdens me."

"Your pain is great," the Nazarene continued, "Do you know the scriptures?"

"Yes, rabbi."

"Vengeance is mine, sayeth the Lord God of Abraham."

The priest knew these sacred words like the back of his hand.

"The man I seek is no longer a man. The Lord may have his vengeance. I only wish to save them. If I cannot I fear I shall live out my days with a tormented soul, as I am already in the bowels of Hell."

That was a mouthful, thought the priest, noticing the others paying great attention to the new developments. One behind the Nazarene with a hood still covering his head, turned to look but then turned away. Jesus, as he was formerly known by many, moved forward and touched the priest's face with an ever so gentle caress, and kissed his cheek. A second kiss to the forehead and he held the priest there as he looked skyward and murmured a few phrases towards the darkening night's clouds.

"Go in peace, my child." the last words from that prophet that the priest would hear. The men watched with serious intent,

23

waiting for the next move from either. The priest rose and began to depart, but stopped to offer thanks to his host.

"Thank you, Lord." he uttered with respect and graciousness, as he turned back towards the tree line, reflecting on what had just happened. Jesus turned his head towards the hooded figure just behind him, on his right.

"Ariel."

The cloaked figure looked up and removed the covering to reveal her beautiful flowing blonde hair.

"Walk with him. He follows the stench of iniquity. He will need you."

"Yes, master." her short answer, and the angel Ariel arose and followed the stranger away from the camp as they all looked on.

"Paul," Jesus said to his disciple, cutting the tension in the air, "Tell us again of the fishing in Galilee."

CHAPTER 5

Ariel and the priest walked together for what seemed an eternity, through the deserts, forests, and all manner of terrain, making their way far from Palestine or any recognizable land. Their rapport was jovial, and they grew to depend and rely on each other, weaving the foundation of a lifelong friendship. If not for their camaraderie, he would question his resolve, but her presence kept his mind clear, and free of distraction. She was a gift from the Creator, to travel by his side for as long as it would take. To offer wisdom and information during his relentless undertaking. It seemed she was but a teenage girl, no older than Penninah, but this was no ordinary young woman. Her flowing golden hair and full lips gave her the appearance of an innocent child, but she would wield power and unending knowledge straight from the will of the Master himself. It was she that reassured him when all he could hear was the abounding laughter of the Vampirus.

They walked through many harvests and seasons, through times of war, witnessed the flags and armor's colors change, and the world changed around them. Sometimes getting involved when it was necessary, as the priest could not ignore injustices as he fought to avenge his own. On the edge of the battlefield she would wait for him to emerge, with shield and sword, fighting for the glory of Heaven and the impoverished suffering victims. Different countries, nations, and causes rose and fell around them as they journeyed to not only their destination's locale, but its time as well.

She had explained to him long before what sacrifice he would have to make to appease his pure heart's longing. The Shepherd of Men had indeed bestowed a limited immortality upon his years, to live until his daughters were safe, only then to find his resting end. It evened the playing field, allowing the priest to follow his own personal odyssey to the place his daughters had been taken, in the distant future. The Vampirus had arrived there centuries earlier, but the priest would be there as well, never undaunted. There were days that he would weaken, as his body grew stronger throughout the decades, his emotions would prevail and he would weep. Ariel was forever there to comfort him.

They were to board a sailing vessel, and the priest would need her guiding hand once more.

"This…is madness." he proclaimed with a gasp as he collapsed.

"We will rest here. You must rest. The ship will depart at dawn."

"How long…has it been?" the priest implored, dragging on his breaths, "I fear I shall never see them again. I am fading."

"You have come too far. Rest, man of God. You have much to do."

"How long?" he insisted.

"To your daughters and the wretched one it has been but an instant. To you, 1802 years, and we have farther yet to go. Rest."

"My sweet Ariel. You have been by my side for eons. My eternal companion. For this I must thank you with all the energy I have left."

"No need. Rest now."

The priest lay down and Ariel rubbed his forehead as he drifted to sleep.

She crept with a quiet saunter, to a nearby Oak where she knelt to pray.

"Father. The glory be all to you, on the earth as it is in Heaven. Strengthen him. And strengthen me to carry him forward."

Ariel was then startled by a sound, and the company of another angel.

"You have done well." spoke the beautiful Nicholaus, crouching on a large rock a few steps from her.

"Nicholaus!" she responded, with a controlled glee as to not awaken the slumbering priest, but also for it had been so long since conversing directly to another of her kind.

"God adores you, Ariel." he said, "as do all of us. We miss you."

"I am here." she said.

"God sends his blessings to you, His faithful servant. Persevere. I myself pray that soon you will return to us."

Ariel glanced back at the priest. And said, "He is a good man. I have seen him evolve into a hardened leader of men, as many kings have come and gone."

"Indeed." Nicholaus answered, "God's grace is with you both, in the countless steps you take. Peace be with you, in your hearts and minds. You are almost there."

Nicholaus reached out to touch her face, kissed her on the lips, then moved away, spreading his magnificent wings and bidding her farewell.

"Have you told him?" he offered, in parting.

"Not everything, not yet. It would be too...overwhelming."

"So be it. Goodbye, Ariel."

"Goodbye, Nicholaus."

Ariel returned to the priest's side as he slept. The ship was to set sail with the morning's light, the ship to the new world, America.

CHAPTER 6

The dusty street was deserted save for a few curious faces peering from dirty windows. It was as close as those townspeople wanted to be, or dared as the elderly sheriff stood in the thoroughfare alone and bellowed the feared name everyone had come to abhor.

"Richard Blood!"

Only silence followed, only a slight breeze blowing across his body, the silver star pinned to his chest glistening in the sunlight.

"Richard Blood!" he called a second time, "It's time."

Beads of sweat formed on his forehead under his wide brimmed cowboy hat. He was as frightened as anyone else, but he had mastered the art of not showing it. The gunfighter emerged from the saloon, and took a slow methodical descent on the wooden steps to the street. He faced the lawman with a confident swagger and a mischievous smirk.

"Damn if it ain't time, Bill." he said, "I've been waiting on you to grow a spine."

"This ends today." the sheriff replied with a quick cadence.

"Nothing ends, "the man known as Richard Blood said, spitting onto the ground, "This is MY town...and you know it."

"Not anymore, Blood."

"Well then. I've never seen a man so eager to die."

"You've killed your last good man, Blood. You've destroyed everything this town used to be. You and that Wilson fella. It thrived once, until your thirst for murder choked the life out of it. This is where it stops."

The sheriff couldn't believe that he strung all those strong words together as he struggled to hold his composure. Blood was an imposing figure at 6' 5", cold as ice and one of the best with a gun in all the western territories.

"O.K., Bill." Blood answered with a sarcastic edge in his voice, "Righteous to the end. The good sheriff."

He laughed and continued, "You broken down old bastard."

"I'm serious, Blood." the sheriff said, with not a shred of humor.

"I'm serious, too." Blood replied, all candor erased from his tone.

A few moments of silence that felt like an eternity passed before Richard Blood drew his weapon from his side, as the sheriff did, and the burning sound of gunfire erupted from one end of the street to the other. Blood looked down, then back up again at the sheriff with a hateful scowl.

"You son of a bitch. I'll get you." were the last words of the notorious outlaw as he fell to his knees with a thud, and then face down in the dirt. The sheriff stood, frozen in disbelief. A few people made their way outside and approached the body with great caution, themselves in a state of shock combined with a joyful relief.

"You got' im, sheriff!" shouted an enchanted small boy.

Sheriff Bill took off his hat and wiped his brow, moved, with his emotions spent.

"I guess I did, son...I guess I did."

A lone clapping was heard and heads turned to see the strange new man in town, sitting in a chair on the porch of the saloon. Two young girls were with the mysterious stranger, flanking him on either side. He seemed entertained by the entire afternoon's ordeal.

"Bravo, sheriff...bravo!" he exclaimed as he got up and ushered his female companions into the building. The sheriff looked perplexed at this, but no matter, as he turned once more to the fallen Richard Blood, who remained face down in the street. He almost expected Blood to rise and spit at him, as the stories of his treacherous deeds preceded him everywhere he went, making him like a fictional character, legendary in his cruelty. At last, it was finally over. Little did Sheriff Bill know that a dark evil had enveloped his world even then, but he would learn of it soon enough.

CHAPTER 7

The orphaned girl followed the strange threesome to their rented abode on the outskirts of town. She stayed some distance back of course, so as not to be noticed. She felt a weird connection to the younger girl, about her own age, who seemed restless and unhappy, almost bound to the other two by a sort of desperation. An odd arrangement no doubt was their norm, and she was curious, drawn to them. Imagining that maybe she could do something to help, although she didn't know what that could be. She was always curious, living hand to mouth since her parents had died of the smallpox back in Arizona. She had lived a hard life since, surviving in any fashion she could, making her way across the cold prairies and lonely desert, arriving in that sleepy, dry and drained little city known as Damascus, California. She was a witness to the viciousness in the streets and the frightened innocent people, robbed and often murdered by Richard Blood, Winslow Wilson, and their horrid band of thieves and miscreants.

She existed in the shadows for some time, on occasion assisting the blacksmith until he was gunned down by Wilson over a dispute about horseshoes. She longed for a companion, someone to trust, someone to relate to, cry with. To make the world a little more bearable. She had turned sixteen that summer, she thought, or perhaps seventeen, but no matter anyway. She fancied other girls her age, praying for a sister figure; but her foolish, unanswered prayers turned to a different type of desire. She would not speak of this, if indeed there were to be anyone to speak of it to, or if there was anyone who cared in the first place. Everyone had their own guarded existence, unwilling to seek out new friendships, especially something too forbidden to even mention.

There was activity within the small chalet, and she crept to the window to spy inside. He was a long haired frightful man, although his chiseled looks were misleading. He was indeed handsome but with a wicked core. She could tell.

"Do you like your new dress, my dear?" he asked, "My dear Sapphira."

"Yes, my lord", the older girl answered, "it is the prettiest dress I have ever seen."

Sapphira admired herself as the monster watched with an intent stare.

"How long will we be here?" she spoke again.

"Four moons if my calculations are correct, and they *are*. We have great and glorious purpose here."

Sapphira took it all in as she smiled at her reflection in the stand up oval mirror. "It is a different world you have brought me to. A much better one at that."

"You, Sapphira, also have glorious purpose here in this different world as you call it."

"Do I? What is it, my love?" Sapphira babbled, falling into the vampire's arms.

"In time all will be revealed. But believe my words, child. You are essential to this world becoming even more magnificent."

Peninnah sat on the floor, quiet as always, yet disgusted at the turn of events. She didn't know where she was, or why, but she was not ignorant to the fact that something was wrong and they were in danger. The emotions welled in her, but only produced a single tear in the corner of her eye, to wipe away before her smitten sister had a chance to mock her for it. She was growing to hate Sapphira. She could only think of father, and the anguish he must have been going through. His heart had to be shattered.

They used her as a servant, her own sister barking orders alongside the insults that had only begun to break her heart before they arrived in that place.

"Water, Penninah...we need water." Sapphira interrupted her train of thought as she often did.

"To the well with the bucket, monkey." she commanded from the older man's knee.

"So authoritative," he added, peering into Sapphira's eyes, "you were meant to be a queen, not the peasant daughter of a lowly priest, representing a dying religion, a religion of fools." Their lips came together with a fiery passion.

"You are like no other man on earth." Sapphira gushed over him, as their faces grew near again.

"Because I am more than a man, and soon, I shall be a *god*." Their mouths enveloped each other as the beautiful dress began to fall from Sapphira's shoulders.

"The bucket, Penninah!" she yelled.

Penninah grabbed the wooden pail and started out the door.

"And...come back." reminded the vampire in a threatening tone.

Penninah closed the door behind her and hung her head in despair. Where else could she go? She was lost in another world she knew nothing about. Alone. One small step towards the well, and another put her on her way.

The orphan girl watched from the bushes as Penninah made her way down the path. She followed, being as silent as possible. Maybe she could speak to the girl and learn more. Or if anything, gain a friend. Night had fallen and the sky was clear and filled with a million stars. Merely looking towards the heavens on an evening like that, allowing your imagination to guide you, was sometimes enough to escape reality.

Penninah was barefoot still, and in her old tunic dress as her captor had not bothered to acquire any new clothes for her as he had for Sapphira. Not even a new pair of sandals. Some pebbles on the ground caused her to wince as she stepped over them. She was glad the moon was so bright or she may not have even been able to find the well. And if she did not return with haste, then unpleasantries awaited. Her entire existence had become an unpleasantry, really. She stopped at the well and sat down for a moment, long enough to have a little cry.

"Hello?" a voice came from behind her. She spun around, startled.

"Don't be afraid," the orphan girl said with a soft inflection, "I just want to talk."

Penninah looked to the left and right, not sure of what to do.

"I won't hurt you..I'm just looking for a friend, and maybe you could use one, too."

No one in this place had spoken to Penninah before outside of her sister and the despicable man who brought them there. Of course, Penninah could not reply, only offered her trembling hand. The girl reached out and with a gentle touch, took Penninah's hand in hers.

"I'm Bettie. I heard them call you Penninah. Is that your name?"

Penninah nodded but did not speak.

"Sounds like something out of the Bible. Is that where your parents got your name from?"

Penninah did not understand, shrugged, but still did not speak.

"You don't have to be afraid." the girl repeated.

Penninah hung her head and looked back up again, then pointed to the bucket. Bettie began to notice that she was perhaps stricken with the silent curse she had heard about.

"Are those people hurting you?"

Penninah turned, reaching for the bucket and moved towards retrieving the water. Bettie watched as she did. Grasping the full bucket in both hands, Penninah turned and the two girls came face to face once more.

"I can meet you here whenever you want." Bettie said.

Penninah passed her by, going back to the house.

"Penninah..." Bettie called, "that's a real pretty name."

Penninah smiled a bit, not a big smile, but enough to curl up the sides of her mouth. Then back to business. Bettie stood at the well to observe Penninah walking down the path. She could tell that something was wrong with that scenario, and decided right then and there to help that sweet mute girl if she could.

CHAPTER 8

"A stage is a'comin', sheriff!" a voice cried out, and Bill looked up from his whiskey to listen for a second announcement, for those words sounded foreign at that point.

"Sheriff! A stage!" the voices rang from outside the saloon, as if it were Christmas morning. Curiosity overtook him, for there were very few stagecoaches that passed through that territory anymore. Every couple of months maybe, with some supplies, that or the driver was lost and needed directions. He placed the cork back into the bottle as he downed a last shot of the harsh liquid that burned its way down his gullet and ignited his stomach lining. Perhaps they had brought more alcohol, he thought. The one item that was more popular than any those days, with no wonder as to why. He rose and peered out of the swinging doors before stepping out onto the dry-rotting wooden porch of the saloon. Indeed a dust cloud from afar, indeed a stage. Some townspeople gathered, the few that remained, as it was an exciting occurrence by any measure.

He glanced at the spot in the street where only the day before lay the dead body of his town's persecuting tyrant, the outlaw Richard Blood. He felt cold just then, as if he has upset the balance of nature...as if Blood would appear from around any corner to take his revenge. A long sigh as he continued down the steps, careful to avoid the loose board in the bottom, and set his boots on the dirty thoroughfare. Blood's remains were resting in peace on a table in his very office, awaiting a burial which needed to be performed sooner than later. If only there was a Christian preacher anywhere near. The last one gunned down by Blood himself months ago. Bill could not recall the reason why, as it were all a blur at that moment. What reasons did that animal have to do any of the horrific deeds he perpetrated there in Damascus, and everywhere else. A once thriving mining town now teetering on the brink of becoming an extinct wasteland.

The saloon's only employees were Ned the bartender, a quiet man who was too good at Poker for his own good, so good that nobody wanted to play him anymore, and Mandalay, who served triple duty as waitress, singer, and the dying town's last whore. They followed Bill outside and Mandalay drew near, resting a soft hand on his shoulder.

"Will they have whiskey?" she asked, with an anticipation.

"I don't know." was Bill's reply. Bill had no idea who or what was on that stage, but they would all find out together. There had been quite enough drama that week to last a year. He prayed for whiskey.

The horses slowed as they reached the city limits, and sauntered into Damascus' main street, tired and in dire need of rest and water. The driver waved, jubilant to see signs of civilization, and jumped down from his seat.

"Afternoon." he said to the eager group.

"Afternoon." Bill returned the pleasantry, "what you got for us there?"

"Two travelers, man and a young girl. A preacher man."

Bill thought to himself that god was good, and also hoped there was some whiskey packed away somewhere on that stage.

Their stock was running low, and the town was in desperate need of that liquid libation escape.

"My name's McCreed, 'Ace' McCreed they call me, since school. I'm pretty good at cards I suppose. I sure hope y'all got a deck or two in there somewhere."

"Son," Bill started, "if you've got a preacher and some rye on that stage, you can stay for free and play cards to your heart's content. Just don't try beating ol' Ned there."

"I sure thank you kindly, sheriff, and for the advice."

"I'm Bill, Bill Drake."

"Bill." the driver nodded and shook his hand. McCreed then turned, not intending to be rude, but there were passengers. He opened the door of the coach and Bill took his first look at an angel, although he didn't know that was what he was looking at. Ariel emerged from inside and was assisted down by McCreed. A nice enough kid, happy at least that the latest leg of his journey was over. She was a thin blonde girl, easy on the eyes, and the preacher's ward, or daughter no doubt.

The priest stepped out onto the street. He scanned the people's faces one by one, nodding his chin in non-verbal yet polite greetings. His clothes had changed in drastic fashion from time to time throughout those years, now to the uniform of the land. A long black coat hung on him with a black & white clergyman's collar around his neck. His long brown hair tied in a tail behind him, and his long rabbi's beard now trimmed to a neat goatee.

"Afternoon." Bill repeated to the couple.

"Afternoon." the priest returned, "This is sunny Damascus, California I take it."

"Yes sir, it is, padre. What's left of it."

"It will do."

"It'll have to, if you're staying. Are you...staying?" Bill could not withhold the inquiry.

"Yes." the priest replied, short and to the point.

"Good," answered Bill, "welcome. We've got a burial today that's got your name written all over it. Glad you're here."

"I thank you, sheriff. I sure would not mind a drink first before going straight to work." A smile appeared on the priest's lips, followed by brisk laughter from the sheriff.

"Of course, my friend, of course."

The priest looked at Ariel and she looked back. Without saying a word he knew that they had arrived at their destination, after centuries. He knew that his daughters were there, and that the ordeal would soon be over, by the grace of benevolent God. After all that time, he was ready.

The dirt was waiting to be shoveled by the two grim-faced gravediggers. Every one of those small towns had their own 'boot hill' where the dead lay in their final resting places, often crude and marked with vague inscriptions upon the head stones. The priest, Ariel, Sheriff Bill, and several townsfolk gathered for this monumental occasion...the haphazard funeral of bad man Richard Blood. Bill could see in some of their eyes that Blood didn't deserve even that much human decency, the cold murdering bastard that he was. Yet they were relieved past words to bury the scoundrel. It was a joyous and somber time rolled into one. The pine box was lowered and waited to be covered. The closure they all prayed for.

"Padre." was Bill's cue, and the priest took the event to its conclusion.

"I did not know this man," he began, "although many of you felt his cruel hand on your loved ones, friends, and home. Perhaps I am fortunate not to be swayed by memories of this criminal and his foul agenda. Perhaps the entire known world is a better place devoid of his presence. No matter, as we must try with all of our might to do as our Lord Jesus Christ has commanded us. To forgive is a difficult task in cases such as this, but we must find it in our fearing hearts to do so."

"Richard Blood." he continued as tears flowed from a few on-lookers, not for Blood himself but for victims on the receiving end of his abominable ways.

"Richard Blood, aptly named, has shed much blood and taken many lives that the Lord deemed precious. In the eyes of the Lord, even the life of one such as he was precious, having been created from His own hand. Manipulated by Satan, but to be judged only by God. We can only pray that there was a miniscule white spot on this man's otherwise black soul. This can be difficult to imagine by mortal man, but believe me when I tell you, there are some things that mortal men are not meant to understand, for the Lord works in mysterious ways, and to him do we deliver Richard Blood either into His waiting arms, or to eternal damnation. It is not for us to choose, but a much higher power that we must all strive towards. Whatever tortured the mind of this lawless outlaw, we pray this day that he rests in peace, until such time comes when he must answer to his maker."

Bill stood amazed but remained silent, as did the people, stunned that anyone could find a kind word to say about that hideous, remorseless vermin. In the end, it was what men of the cloth were for, the find the words of comfort when all others were unable. It was indeed good to have a reverend back in their hellhole of a town. The tiny church may come to life once more, instead of an abandoned hull of lonely meditation. The priest had inspired them to move beyond their sorrow and believe that there was more to life than fear and hopelessness.

"Gentlemen." he prodded towards the diggers, as they took up their shovels and began their work. It was not a deep grave, but deep enough. The sheriff rested a hand on the priest's shoulder.

"You know, its nice to have you, padre. That was more than Blood deserved."

"Thank you."

"If you ask me," Bill continued, "a wooden box is too good for his likes; he should have been wrapped in a blanket and dropped in the hole."

"Come on now, Bill. Do you *really* mean that?"

"Well..." Bill answered, "I guess not. He was a human being after all, like you said. A terrible one, but human all the same. There's folks who would swear he was a monster, a demon in fact."

"Are demons killed by bullets, Bill?"

"No...I suppose not."

CHAPTER 9

Mandalay brought a bottle to the table and two glasses for Damascus' new priest and Sheriff Bill. Ariel sat as quiet as a mouse as she often did, watching the room and everything transpiring around them. A light reassuring hand on the priest's shoulder blade, ever present since the day they met so long ago.

"So, you got a proper name behind that title?" Bill asked.

"Nasser," the priest answered, "Nasser Absalom."

An odd name, thought Bill, and the crucifix necklace he wore did not match it, but he dismissed the thought almost as soon as it came to him.

The priest noticed the pause and added, "It is Jewish."

"Well, ain't nothin' wrong with that." Bill replied.

"Converted," said the priest, touching the cross around his neck, "I have seen things most Jews have not. But anyway, have there been any more strangers in town in the recent weeks, Bill? Anyone who seems...out of place?"

"Well..." Bill recollected, "There is a weird group that showed up not too long ago. Didn't come on a stage, neither. I did think that was weird."

"What do they look like?'

"A man...long haired fella like yourself. Dark hair, but taller. Got two girls with him. They rented a little place on the far end of town. Don't know where they came from or how they got here, now that I stop and think about it."

The priest glanced over to Ariel but did not speak. She could see the burning in his soul through his eyes, the pain and anger, the longing, all in one sorrowful look.

"In time." she said to him without an utterance of her own. They were there; they had made it. Soon all would be made right. It would just be a matter of patience and timing.

"You know these folks?" Bill said, interrupting their moment of reflection.

"I do." answered the priest, emptying his glass and reaching to pour another. His fingers were trembling on the bottle with anticipation and nervous tension. It had been so long and they were so close. Ariel took the bottle, and poured the drink for him. She was so attentive and loyal, his faithful companion to the end.

"You're welcome to the hotel. Ain't nobody in it," Bill chuckled, "'cept for that McCreed boy. Town's about dead, I'm afraid. It'll take a while for the news of Blood's demise to reach the rest of the world, and people start comin' back. Still some hard times ahead."

"Yes," the priest agreed, "yes there are."

A few minutes later, the priest strode down the dusty thoroughfare, looking nothing short of menacing as Ariel attempted to suggest some sensible action to him.

"It's not the time...not now." she implored.

"Two thousand years I have walked this earth and sailed her seas to save them. They are here, and now I am here as well. I can wait no longer or I shall go mad."

"Wait." Ariel urged further, yet the priest would not hear any reason. His blood boiled and she knew this may not end well. He stopped for a brief minute at the deserted blacksmith's shop and inside went through the abandoned tools. He pulled out a large pickaxe and wielded it, feeling the strength of it in his hands.

"This will do. Straight through the heart." were the only sentiments. Ariel sighed and realized this was happening and there wasn't much she could do to stop it or calm him. It would have to transpire for better or for worse. She had power to stop it of course, but followed specific instructions not to interfere. The priest was given this vehicle and the means, but he would have to make decisions on his own to drive his campaign along to a desirable conclusion. Ariel could only follow and pray that after all that time, rash actions then would not be a critical error.

The priest must have appeared insane to anyone watching, but he moved like a tortured soul on a mission, and was exactly that. Ariel also knew there was no danger of the vampirus retreating into another dimension, for he needed to be there, in that time, under those circumstances, for his hellish plan to come to fruition. Whatever was about to happen was going to happen regardless of her pleading. It was a living example of the love for his daughters, and the valor that he clung onto to get them that far. The priest was a strong, proud man, and at that moment, furious. His dedicated footsteps on the streets of Damascus were testament to that.

⊰┼┼⊱

"I do not think that I can wait for our lovemaking, Bel." said Sapphira to the seated beast.

"You have no choice, child," he answered, "our wedding night shall be more glorious than it has ever been within your simple dreams or imagination."

The vampire stopped speaking then and raised his nose in the air.

"What is it, my love?" Sapphira asked.

"Silence." was the reply fired back, his expression altered from frivolity to extreme seriousness in an instant.

"What is this...?" he muttered to himself, "I smell...a priest. Well, I will...be...damned."

Sapphira and Penninah were even more shocked than the vampire itself when they heard their father's voice ring out from the street.

"Belkuthe the Stained! You treacherous dog who is not long for this world nor any other! It is I who have tirelessly hunted you, and it is I who will deliver you on your knees to the throne of Lucifer in the heart of the ninth plane of torment! Face me!"

"Face me!" he repeated, louder with added conviction, as if any more could be contained within the heart of a mortal man. The front door of the small villa flew open, and Penninah ran out of it, towards her father. The priest's heart sank when she was whisked away, up into the air and sucked back into the house by an unforeseeable force. A look of horror enveloped her sweet face as she was flung through the air with the violent outburst. He took one step forward, and the vampire appeared in the doorway, to look upon that priest for a second time.

"You have acquired much knowledge in these centuries, priest."

"You know what I am here for. Surrender my children."

Sapphira stepped from around the vampire to once again scold her father with her vile words of teenage ignorance.

"Do not be a fool, father, and assume I would desire a savior from my dark plight. It is not as dark as you may think!"

"Whether or not you desire it is not of my concern, Sapphira. And this thing's intentions are darker than the deepest, blackest pit of Hades. You know nothing of what you speak nor the consequences of your actions. Step away from him!"

"No, priest, I will not," Sapphira blurted back, "I love him and he is my beloved!"

"I grow weary of this meaningless banter." the vampire stated with a cold demeanor as he shoved Sapphira by her throat back into the room. The priest raised the axe above his head and dove at the monster, only to be frozen when an icy hand from Hell moved faster than the human eye, clutching the weapon under the blade. Before the priest's very eyes, locked in closer to the undead creature than he had ever been, its fingers crushed the axe's wooden handle in half, leaving the rusted metal portion to fall to the ground by their feet.

The priest had learned extensive hand to hand combat techniques over those eons, engaging in wars and rebellions when it appeared the need was there. He had the experience of battling bigger, stronger men, but none with the supernatural gift of that day's deadly opponent. Before he could blink or even come close to processing those immediate events, a palm with the might of a locomotive struck his sternum, sending him off the ground and through the air, landing in an abrupt heap in the dirt at Ariel's feet.

Struggling to rise, he knew there was no strategy to overtake that fiend. His angelic companion had been correct about rushing in, and while valiant, it was foolhardy and unwise. Back to a vertical base, he brushed the dust from his black attire and mirrored a stare with the one known as The Stained.

"Now will you listen to reason?" Ariel asked.

"Yes." was his defeated reply.

The priest knew this was not the end, but it took every ounce of self restraint in his humbled bones to turn and take that first step back towards town. He yearned to rush in again, to give all he had in the effort, to see his own blood spilled and lose his life if need be. Indeed he had the heart of a warrior, but the brain of a fool realizing that he must rely on Ariel's sound advice if he were to ever succeed in rescuing Penninah and Sapphira from the clutches of that inhuman entity. He heard the door slam behind him, imagining his youngest child crying at the window as he retreated. He was a coward, he thought, for not looking back. It shredded his very soul to pieces to take a second step, and another.

"One battle's outcome does not decide a war." Ariel reminded him, "His just penance will arrive."

She could tell that brought little comfort, and took his arm to lead him further down the deserted dusty thoroughfare, as the first drops of rain found their way to his waiting cheeks, proceeded only by his own tears. She had witnessed countless acts of heroism from that man throughout their long and grueling exodus, but at that moment, regardless of how the priest felt about himself, Ariel regarded him as one of the bravest men to ever live.

CHAPTER 10

The priest sat by the window, from the second story room, watching the rain. There was no activity on the street that evening, just California dirt turning into California mud. No people, no life. He could see a candle light shining from Sheriff Bill's office. A once profitable mining town teeming with life and visitors from all over, gasping its last breaths, almost as dead as he felt inside. The kind of failure that wells up deep in the pit of the stomach before advancing right down to the tips of the fingers and toes, making one want to take a straight razor to one's own throat and just call it a day. It was not a large room there in the Damascus hotel, just one bed and a window. No matter about the bed, for Ariel and her celestial body required no sleep. She was indeed an angel, and as Heavenly as one could get, the priest assured himself. She was the only one he had ever met. Besides Jesus himself. He recalled how this 'Holy Bible' had been translated from the early Greek, Arabic, Aramaic, and Hebrew texts, watered down and edited into what those modern day simple folks had to cling to in times of strife. He remembered stories of the crucifixion, and the master rising again. Those people there in that time, he proposed to himself, were so tied to their faith. He had been blessed to sit with The

Christ himself around that meager campfire, so long ago. So very long ago. Ariel herself was not the mighty angel Ariel spoken of in the Christian tome, but named after. A good thing.

He turned to see her, sitting cross legged on the center of the bed, peaceful in her meditation. He did not expect her eyes to open and look back at him, as if she had been reading his thoughts the entire time.

"You have suffered much." she offered in a low, quiet voice.

"What do we do now, boss?" he asked of her, half joking but somehow deathly serious as well.

"Tell me about your wife." was her instruction.

The priest was silent.

"Please." she added, "You need to concentrate on more joyful times for now."

"I couldn't save her either." was his cold retort, "I lost her, too."

"That is not helpful."

"It is the best I have right now." the priest said, hanging his head at that line of questioning, "I...I do not know if I even can any more."

"Talk to me, good priest. Tell me a story."

It was apparent that Ariel was serious and was not about to let it go. The priest conceded and searched his memories for a pleasant diversion.

"There are so many."

"Tell me a story." Ariel repeated. The priest glanced back at the window to see that nothing had changed. What little daylight that remained had been consumed by the ominous storm clouds. The puddles were transforming into small river canals in the street. There was nothing left of that evening outside of sleep or telling stories. And sleep was out of the question.

"There was a time, during Passover, that Penninah had dragged home the ugliest, filthiest stray cat." the priest began, "I attempted to shuffle the animal out of the house, and Penninah as well. She was a girl of six and just as filthy as the feline monster. Scratched about her arms, and her hair matted with dirt. I pleaded with her, pushing her out of the front door before Abigail would come in the back and witness that travesty. It was too late, of course, and we all felt her wrath!"

The priest had forgotten himself and a smile was on his face for a fleeting moment. It retreated as fast as it had arrived. "She was my everything. My world. My rock. A love so fine. Then she was gone, and I was lost forever. I did my best raising the girls, but the problems with Sapphira began shortly after. It breaks my heart. It all breaks my heart. What I would do for just ten more minutes with her. Five to just hold her, and five for her to…tell me what to do."

The priest's face fell into his hands and he was silent. He did not cry, for there are only so many tears to fall in one lifetime, and he had reached his limit earlier that day.

"There is a reason I sat with the Master that night." Ariel spoke, "He awaited your arrival. I was chosen by Him."

The priest did not look up but remained in the same position as Ariel continued, "He chose the one who could aid you the most, and I have enjoyed this time with you, regardless of the circumstances."

"Why could you aid me the most?" the priest asked, "Out of all the angels of Heaven?" His curiosity prevailed through his sorrow.

"Nasser…" came his own name from Ariel's lips, but her voice was different. The priest raised his weary head from his hands to see his world, his rock, his everything, sitting where Ariel had been.

"It is I, Nasser. It has always been I."

The priest stared in disbelief, even after all the mystical and magical things he had witnessed. He was speechless.

"You have ten minutes, priest. Had better use them wisely." she grinned and extended her arms to him. It felt as though his body was not his own, and he floated to her. Embracing the love of his life once more, the mother of his lost children, his wife whom he shared one flesh and years of happiness. He mumbled some incoherent words, but there were no words at that frozen moment in time, and he held her tight. He kissed her and cradled her body into his own.

"The Lord has found great favor with you, my husband. A place for you waits in eternal paradise, as soon as your earthly tasks are complete. Know this and have peace in your soul this night, good priest."

"Abigail...what do we do now?"

"The vampirus has reason for being in this place, and his plot will come to fruition in two nights. The sun, moon, and the spirits are aligned in such a way but every few millenniums. Your mission will either end in glorious victory or a torturous defeat, *here.*"

"I will save them, Abigail."

"I know you will."

He gazed into her big brown eyes, and they gave him the strength to carry on, as they always did.

"We have to visit some friends now." were her last words before their lips met for the first time in two thousand years.

CHAPTER 11

The rain fell harder then, and Winslow 'Whiskey' Wilson strode through the muck with a purpose, his boots filthy as they often were, and his clothes and hat soaked. He had been sitting in a saloon in Ghost Story, Wyoming when a giant of a man parted the swinging doors. A cold, callous man who proceeded to rob the establishment and every one of its patrons. Wilson had once heard of an outlaw cursed with an odd 'giantism' disorder. He had a larger head than a normal man, thick bushy eyebrows and an enormous forehead. Huge hands with specially crafted pistols just for him, as his fingers could not activate the trigger on a regular weapon. There were stories, rumors, and tall tales of Richard Blood, and he wondered, until that night, whether or not the beast actually existed. He had reportedly killed too many men, women, and children to count, cleaned out whole families, whole towns. A savage with no conscience to speak of, and on that day he stood before Winslow Wilson. Wilson sat at the bar collected, never flinched, sipping his bourbon like there was no calamity at all, while everyone else cowered in fear.

"You, Whiskey!" the booming voice bellowed, as it also branded Wilson with his nickname from that day forth, "What do you think you're doin'??"

"Drinkin'." Wilson answered, "Buy you one, friend?"

"You thinkin' of dyin' this evenin', Whiskey?"

"We all gotta go sometime, big man. At least have a drink with a fellow outlaw before you send him to the afterlife. Might find out you like him."

Blood rarely met men who weren't shaking in their boots at the mention of his very name, much less his horrific appearance. Something about that cowboy intrigued him, he had balls, and they shared the first drink of thousands to come. He kept the name 'Whiskey' to that day, and had rode with Blood ever since. As gang members came and went, Whiskey and Blood were best of friends, terrorizing the western frontier together. Damascus being the most recent. Blood was obsessed with that one, taking the mining town apart brick by brick. Whiskey had tried to convince Blood to move on several times, but he would hear nothing of it. A rivalry of sorts with the elder sheriff Bill Drake had kept Blood there for sheer amusement. That is until he became careless, wanting that last showdown with Bill to put the icing on the cake and sink a knife deep into the heart of his town.

But it didn't go down that way. Whiskey had been out hunting when Blood went down there on his own and got himself killed. So then there was Wilson, tromping through the slosh with a shovel over his shoulder and a length of rope to tie around the body after he dug it up. It sickened him to think of those townspeople gloating over Blood's lifeless corpse. He was not going to give those bastards the satisfaction for another second. He would take Blood back to camp, and give him a decent burial fit for the notorious outlaw that he was.

Figured he should; he imagined dying himself one day and having to explain to Blood in Hell, looking down the barrel of one of those giant-sized smoke wagons. As if there were a deeper part of Hell you could be sent to upon being murdered while in Hell. He would get those guns back as well, but breaking into the sheriff's office and retrieving them would be a job for another night. They would more than likely put them in some museum somewhere, probably some fancy place in San Francisco. Fuck that, thought Wilson, never happen. Not while he still lived. The 'Blood and Whiskey' Gang was aptly named, for two liquids of the same name that were spilled on a daily basis like clockwork.

There was little life to speak of when he arrived at the cemetery, and the storm had likened to a driving monsoon. A downpour fitting of what he was about to do. He had stolen and pillaged, raped and murdered, and while not being particularly proud of it all, knew that grave robbing was a brand new low. He did not wish to make a habit of that practice. But that was his loyal associate, his brother, and the only true friend that he ever had. The extensive rainfall had created large ponds, with decaying tombstones and markers sinking into the mire. Richard Blood has no such marker, just a long stick planted in the ground. Wilson wondered if he took no action, would there ever be any more than a goddamned rotten stick stuck in the dirt for the most famous outlaw in the West. Here lies Richard Blood, and here's a goddamned stick. His shovel found its way into the grimy water and into the soggy earth below it. Not a deep grave, and it did not take very long to hit the casket. It took every bit of strength in his body and more to heave the heavy box from the flooded hole, and he fell backwards into the mud. Laying there on his back, looking up at the thick drops cascading down onto his face, he contemplated for a few seconds the nobility of his mission, and leaving Blood where he was. Maybe he would procure a larger marker, and some flowers. Would Blood leave him there if the roles were reversed? The answer of course, was no, and Wilson struggled to pull himself up. A sharp pain in his spine revealed the damage from the rock he landed across in the fall.

"Goddamn." he cursed as he searched for a foothold.

"Yes, precisely," a foreign voice came out of the darkness, "Goddamn."

The stranger was a tall silhouette against the moonlight, a black figure who extended a helping hand.

"Who the hell are you?" said Wilson.

"A friend. Please Mr. Wilson, take my hand."

It seemed legitimate to Wilson, in the state he was in, having decided he had bitten off more than he could chew in this recovery debacle. He reached for the outstretched offering and to his surprise, was whisked upright and back on his feet in a single second. Wilson was not one to become unnerved in any given situation; it was one of the qualities that Blood valued in him those last years, but at that minute he was a bit moved.

"Who are you, mister?" he asked again, but his voice trailed when he had his first look into the coldest eyes he had ever seen.

"Call me Bel. Mister Bel, better yet. It is an abbreviation for my true name that should not be uttered by mortals at any time. It was spoken in its entirety earlier this evening and I was not amused by it."

"Fine then, Bel it is."

"Mister Bel." the vampire repeated.

"Fine, *Mister* Bel. I got no quarrel with a man's preferences. Now what do you want? I'm kinda covered up busy right now, son."

"I wish to procure the services of the earthly terror known as the 'Blood and Whiskey' Gang."

The two stood and stared at each other for a moment, without a word, as the unrelenting cold drops pelted them both.

Wilson thought his visitor was crazy, and said, "That's a little on the impossible side right about now, *Mister* Bel. Our men scattered after the news of the gunfight, and there's the matter of Blood being stone cold deceased. So as far as the gang right now, you're lookin' at him."

A treacherous grin came across the stranger's features, and he said, "Mortal death does not confront my intentions, *Mister* Wilson."

"What..." was Wilson's only word before Bel waved his hand through the air, causing the coffin's lid to fly off by itself, landing several yards away with a thud and a splash. Wilson was suspended in animation, not trusting his own sight. There was the pale, cadavered face of Richard Blood, at rest and soulless in his slumber. A half chewed thin brown cigar still clenched between his yellowed teeth.

"He merely sleeps in Shoel. There will be no need to replant him as you intended, although I applaud your sense of honor."

"What...what are you doing?" stammered Wilson as Bel reached into the coffin that was filling up with water, and placed his fingers upon Blood's chest. Unintelligible words under Bel's breath left his mouth, as if some Satanic ritual were being performed, and Wilson thought to himself that that was the strangest thing he had ever seen. Maybe he should shoot the ghoul and go about his business. Maybe he should run. Maybe he should go and find that saloon girl in St. Louis that he felt like he may have been falling in love with. Buy a ranch and raise some children. Leave it all behind, that dangerous life. He would have to grow a beard to change his appearance since his face was plastered on wanted posters from Louisiana to the Pacific Ocean. This last temptation of Winslow Wilson lasted only a brief few seconds, until he saw Richard Blood's bloodshot eyes look up from his watery grave. His blood ran cold, and he choked on his own saliva as Blood sat up in the box. The stub of a cigar that the townspeople had left between his lips shifted to the other side of his mouth, and he looked at the vampire as if he understood what had happened.

"Light." his gruff voice demanded. The mysterious Mister Bel's laughter filled the night sky as he lit a match from his fingers and reignited Blood's smoke. After a long inhale, Blood reached up and took it from his mouth.

"What took you so long, Whiskey?"

CHAPTER 12

A beam of the day's first sunlight fell upon the priest's face, stirring him from his slumber. He opened his eyes but did not move. He was on his side and a slender female arm was draped around his waist. The wonderful dream of making love to his wife once more was not a dream, but a reality. The events of his life were becoming more and more fantastical. He turned over, slow and easy as to not wake Abigail, but upon having her again in his scope, it was not Abigail spooned close to him in that little bed. It was his angel, Ariel. She had transformed back into her current incarnation, a beautiful blonde girl with stunning features that he knew so well. She was so peaceful, and he realized that was the first time in all those years that he had witnessed her sleeping. She had changed during the night and still held him to her as the morning crept about the room. Revitalized and then with a renewed purpose, he kissed her soft lips once more, knowing that one day he would be in the arms of his beloved Abigail once more, after departing the earthly coil. He rose, in ginger movements as not to disturb. He stepped naked to his clothes, where he had disrobed earlier the previous evening. He slid on his trousers and heard her shifting in the covers behind him.

"You are awake." she said, wiping her face.

"Yes. Good morning."

"I know you have a question. I feel it."

"You know all, Ariel."

"But you do not. Ask."

The priest took a deep breath and posed what was on his mind. "Are you still *her?*"

The angel sat up in the bed, also nude from the night's tenderness. She lowered her chin and brought it up again, as if finding the right explanation, one that even that extraordinary mortal could comprehend.

"Yes, she dwells within me. But also no, for I am Ariel. It is... complicated, Nasser. I may only convert to my former existence but once. Your precious Abigail sees through my eyes, and feels through my fingertips. She awaits you, in Heaven."

The priest struggled to reply. His heart elated and broken at the same time.

"Thank you." he said.

"Bless your heart and soul, sweet priest. She is so proud of you."

There was no reply for that which the priest could imagine. He looked at the girl and turned away, reaching for his shirt, thrown over a chair.

"The friends you spoke of." he said after a pause, bringing the whole charade to a conclusion and back to the business at hand.

"Indians." she said.

"Indians?"

"Or bloodthirsty savages, whichever you prefer, staying true to the local tongue."

"Alright, I trust you."

"It is necessary, believe. We need them, and they are expecting us."

⇥⊹⊹⇤

Penninah huddled on the floor as she often did, taking in the activity of the house and waiting until she was given an order, or until one of them felt like berating her. Her cruel and misled sister sat on the evil man's knee as if she were queen of all she surveyed. As if that terrible man were to make her an actual one. She was puzzled at the entire ordeal, but was settling in to her captive existence. Knowing that father was there, somewhere in that dreadful place, brought her a measure of peace, but seeing him fail to rescue them disheartened her to a degree. She knew he would not give up. She felt it, and believed that she would see him again.

Now there were two more men with them. Crude, obnoxious and vile, cursing and laughing with that 'Mister Bel' and Sapphira as if old comrades. She sat alone in a corner until one of them needed another drink or to light a foul smelling cigar. The large man frightened her, and she feared even approaching him, for his goliath hands could take her life at a moment's fancy. The other one, the one called 'Whiskey' kept watching her and it made her uncomfortable, as if he had diabolical intentions. Being sent to the well was her only temporary reprieve, and she longed with eager abandon for the command to dump the chamber pails or fetch more water. She thought of the kind girl she met, and wondered what she was doing and where she was. Wondered if she was watching even then from a secret hiding place. Bettie. She needed a friend in the worst way. She wanted to see father and she wanted to go home.

"Penninah, my child." the words from the vampire shook her out of her daydream, "Mister Wilson needs more whiskey."

"Get off of your lazy behind, Monkey!" the words from Sapphira bit even harder. Penninah grunted and rose from her plot on the floor. She took the bottle, which contained about a glassful left in it, from the table and poured the remnants into the man's waiting cup.

"She's certainly a pretty one." said Wilson, slurring his vowels. It made her hand shake a bit as she tilted the container. Then her nightmare worsened as she felt his dirty hand reach around to grasp her hindquarters.

"Nice little ass, too." Blood chimed in, entertained by the conduct of his partner in crime. The laughter rose again. She pulled away and scowled at the drunken outlaw, but as soon as she did, she was grabbed tighter and hauled into his arms. Fingers with black dirt under the nails encased her cheeks and in an instant she was locked into a forced kiss, the alcohol on his already putrid breath taking her to a personal hell, and she wished she were dead. His disgusting tongue snaked into her mouth and as it did, the poor girl let go of her faculties and urinated on herself and the wooden planks of the dusty floor.

The laughter was deafening and she fell backwards. The tears poured from her sad and horrified eyes, that otherwise were so bright and shining with love.

"Look what you have done now, Monkey!" scolded the heartless Sapphira, "You are beyond embarrassing! Clean it up!"

Penninah crawled for a cloth and began to wipe her own urine as the audience chided her. Her teardrops fell into the mess as she worked. It was then she felt her tunic frock being lifted behind her, exposing her bare buttocks for everyone to see. It was Wilson.

"You're correct, Mister Blood. That's a perfect little virgin ass."

"Just the way you like 'em." Blood joked.

Penninah felt violated to the highest degree; her shame was endless, praying to God for it to end, so she could go back to her peaceful corner and blend into the surroundings. His hands were upon her then, his plundering digits inside her, digging into her anus. She lost her breath when the first one went in, terrified that she would suffocate there on her knees, staring at her own puddle before her. She could not scream, only mustered pathetic chirping noises and grunts, making the episode that much more hilarious to the villainous onlookers.

"Fuck her!" rang out, and stung her ears as it came from the mouth of her sibling, Sapphira. No, she begged in silence, please no.

Another finger moved to her most private place, her 'bird' as her mother used to call it.

"Make sure to wash your bird, Penninah!" she would call at bath time. She saw her mother's face then, her father's face. Her muscles tensed and her teeth clenched hard, almost to a breaking point.

"She's dry!" was the next comment from Wilson, shouting for all to hear, "Could use a little salve!" The ensuing laughter, to Penninah, drowned out every sound in the world. What had she done to deserve that torment, she asked God, why was it happening?

"Enough of that." said Bel, "We are in need of more ale. Penninah. Collect yourself, child, and go to the saloon."

If she ever enjoyed hearing the sound of that living atrocity's voice, it was the time. She regained her composure the best she could, wiped the remaining stain from the floor, and with the creature's blessing, hurried out the front door.

"Why do you despise your sister so?" inquired Bel to Sapphira, not expecting an answer.

Penninah walked the thoroughfare, her bare feet caked in the drying mud. Humiliated and disgraced beyond description. She felt sick as if she would vomit right there in the street. She held her belly and continued to the saloon on the far end of town. Without warning, Bettie appeared from an alley between buildings. She hurried over and could see the condition Penninah was in, shaking and petrified.

"Did they hurt you?' she asked, and the genuine concern was welcomed. Penninah allowed herself to be taken into Bettie's bosom, and held.

"I'm so sorry, Penninah. I'm so, so sorry."

Penninah could only allow her puffy, despondent eyes to tell the story.

"Where are you going?" Bettie asked, and the mute girl pointed towards the saloon.

"I'll go with you."

The two girls walked together, hand in hand up the weather beaten wooden planks leading to the porch of the establishment. Penninah glanced back, as if to see if her father there. Where was he? She thought. Her sole hope was that he would come for her, that he would know what to do, like he always did. In the darkened barroom, the soothing voice of lady Mandalay was refreshing after what she had been through.

"What are you ladies doing?"

"She was walking." answered Bettie, "They sent her for something. She can't talk so I'm assuming they want more to drink."

Penninah pointed to the bottles behind the counter.

"Whiskey, eh? Who are these people you're with, sweetheart? Is that your daddy?"

Penninah blinked several times and shook her head 'no'. She turned away, letting the lady know that she was not in the mood for conversation.

"Alright, honey." said Mandalay, taking the hint. There was something wrong with the picture, but she could not imagine how wrong. She handed a couple of fresh bottles to Penninah.

"I'll put it on their tab. Do you want me to say something to Sheriff Bill?"

Penninah shook her head again.

"I'll walk her back." Bettie attempted to reassure her. They left the saloon and upon reaching the bottom of the steps, Bettie pulled Penninah in the alley between the saloon and the bank.

"We can run away," she said, "together. I'll take care of you, Penninah. We can get out of here. They'll never find us. *Please.*"

Penninah shook her head a third time.

"I don't have anybody, just like you. I'm alone. I'm scared, too. We could lean on each other. We could live together, travel together."

Bettie was talking too much and she knew it. Too much for Penninah to digest it all at once, but she did not know how much time she had to make the impression, or when she would even get to talk to her again.

"Think about it. I'll wait for you, by the well. When they send you for water, we can run."

Penninah was lost in thought. She saw grief in Bettie's face to match her own, and she wanted with all her heart to escape with her, right then at that moment. To run as fast and as far as their legs would carry them, holding hands and feeling safe again. She hugged Bettie farewell, a bottle of bourbon in each hand, and gave her a slight smile. Twenty minutes earlier she thought she would never smile again. She turned and made her way back to the other end of Damascus, the mud splashing from her steps and drying in splotches all over her legs. Bettie watched her until she was out of sight, thinking maybe it was a stupid plan. She had been running her whole life, and maybe, just maybe she needed to run a little further, with that lovely girl by her side. For the first time, she may have had something to run to, instead of away from.

CHAPTER 13

The priest rode the spotted appaloosa up and along the rocky trail. A fine beast, strong and willing. Ariel was behind him, her arms around his waist and her head resting between his shoulder blades. It gave him a restored confidence on their way to meet the mighty Native American shaman, the last of his great tribe. He knew he could not do it alone, and welcomed whatever assistance was offered and available. Ariel told him those people were anticipating him. He would not disappoint. Observing from a far ridge, Black Jackal indeed was ready to serve his Great Spirit and fulfill his given duty to help that holy man in any way he could. He stood and called for his wife.

"Tameka!" he sounded, "Holy man is here. Another rides with him. Prepare food, and the tobacco. I will build the fire. This very night will be a great ceremony, and celebration."

Another few miles and the priest arrived at the Indian's campsite. A large teepee was constructed, and a small bonfire was beginning to glow as the sun went down, and dusk was covering the landscape. The smells of an animal roasting in a pit was intoxicating in its aroma. In the middle of the clearing stood an imposing figure, Chief Black Jackal in full face paint and tribal regalia.

"Whoa, boy." said the priest to the horse. He got off and then aided Ariel down. The proud Indian took one look at Ariel and fell to his knees. Tameka approached and Black Jackal grabbed her by the cloth of her dress and pulled her down with him. The priest was stunned, but Ariel put them all at ease.

"Rise, warrior. I am not Great Spirit, but the embodiment of his word and message. We come in brotherhood and peace. Rise."

The priest was amazed that the Indian recognized Ariel's divine presence at a glance. Ariel turned to him and said, "He is shaman to his people, the communicator with God. He can feel His power in me."

The Indian rose and said, "I am Black Jackal, last of my tribe. This is Tameka, my wife. Welcome to our home. Great Spirit has told us of your arrival."

"I am Nasser, Nasser Absalom. I thank you."

"You are the holy man who rides from a distance. I have seen your face in my visions. The abomination is here as well. I have felt the disturbance in nature for nine moons. The animals, they can sense it as well. Nothing is as it was."

The priest nodded 'yes', and outstretched his hand. Black Jackal hesitated for a moment, but then took the priest's hand.

"White man's greeting," he said, "even though you are from another tribe than the white man. Another nation, far from this place."

"Farther than you know, my friend." said the priest, "Farther than even I knew or could fathom. I am glad to be here now."

"We will destroy this great evil." said Black Jackal, "But first, we eat."

Ariel smiled and touched the priest's arm with a gentle grip. A touch the priest never took for granted. Without her, he knew he would have withered away by then, wandering the earth like a madman, lost and broken. He would not have found the resolve to make it that far. Perhaps he did not give himself enough credit, as Ariel was fond of saying.

⚔⚔

Ariel did not eat, of course, instead locating a large stone to perch upon, to observe the feast from an elevation. It was a magnificent deer that was prepared, and they were all filled with the fire-cooked meat, the most glorious meal the priest could remember. Afterwords, Tameka went into the teepee, and reemerged with a colorful and decorated cloth bag, bringing it to Black Jackal as they sat around the flaming centerpiece of the pit. The red and orange colors danced upon the Indian's face as he unwrapped a long instrument, the ceremonial peace pipe.

"We smoke." he said, "The smoke from the pipe sends praises and prayers up to Great Spirit. We ask for his might and wisdom to battle the evil one among us. The one who walks upon two legs, but is not a man nor beast."

The men passed the ornate and feathered pipe between them, as Tameka held onto her husband.

"He is neither man nor beast, nor god nor demon. He is Vampirus." Ariel interjected after remaining silent throughout the dinner, and a bit on the serious side as the priest had not seen her before. Black Jackal placed the pipe on the cloth it was encased in.

"Tell us." he said to Ariel, "Messenger made from the glory of Great Spirit. Tell us all."

"The Stained One," she began, "was the lover of Queen Jezebel of Isreal, the daughter of King Ethbaal and wife to King Ahab. It was she who incited her husband to abandon the worship of Yahweh in favor of the evil deity Ba'al the Destroyer. She persecuted the followers of God until the good prophet Elijah slaughtered

66

her minions and all disciples of Ba'al. All save one, her secret inamorato, who after the cleansing was made into Vampirus, as she was by the guidance of Ba'al himself, through the hand of an ancient being known as Ab'ba. Her death was swift after attaining the immortality, executed by members of her own court, thrown from a tower, her bleeding remains eaten alive by dogs as she screamed. Listen closely, priest, for this is truth that I have not yet revealed to you."

The priest and Black Jackal sat in awe of the words delivered from Ariel, who then seemed more an angel than ever before.

"Belkuthe the Stained professed his obedience to Ba'al, and begged of a way to reunite with his beloved queen. The demon responded, charging him with the task, in exchange for his servitude and loyalty, and with the promised pledge that upon his victory, he and Jezebel would sit by his throne into the eternity of time itself, and rule over portions of the very earth created by God. Filling the planet and surrounding dimensions with blackness and death in his cursed name."

"Will Great Spirit allow this?' was the question from Black Jackal. The priest had no comment as he was shaken to his foundation.

"Ba'al answers only to the serpent Lucifer, and this rebellion will be greater than the last. There will be war in Heaven, on earth, below, and within the very folds of space. That living blasphemy in Damascus, just mere miles from this peaceful place, will lead a crusade against the whole of humanity and angels alike, as a general of destruction."

"Ariel..." was all the priest could force out.

"The events of today go far deeper than saving your daughters." Ariel continued her fiery monologue, "You will be diverting a catastrophe of Biblical proportions."

The priest crawled on his hands and knees towards her in desperate need of more, and cried, "Ariel! What part do my daughters play in all of this? What does he want with them?"

"Dear Nasser, husband of Abigail, priest of Jehovah God. This is where your life has intersected with this chaos. A sacrifice must be made. When the suns and moons of the universe have aligned, when all is favorable to The Destroyer, a virgin daughter of a priest from the time of the physical Christ must be severed in six parts and disembodied before Ba'al in a ring of hellfire. Jezebel will return and the world will be cast into darkness. He waits upon his general to lead his forces against all that is decent and right. And *all of this* happens with tomorrow's full moon. That is why we are here now, in this place, in this time. The stage is set for doom to rain down upon us all."

The priest wept with this proclamation, "Sapphira...my god... she's the one."

"Yes. He did not intend to take your Penninah, but now he may be using her as a secondary device."

Black Jackal returned the peace pipe to its enveloping material and handed it back to Tameka.

"Bring me war pipe."

<hr/>

Miles away, back in the town of Damascus, Penninah sat on the wooden floor of the small chalet filled with depraved venomous snakes. The whiskey flowed as well as the heinous activity. She sat with her chin lowered to her raised knees, wishing she were far away from that place. The sun had set and the temperature had dropped to a cooler feeling on her skin.

"What's wrong with her, anyway?" the question arose from the mouth of the outlaw, the one who had touched her.

"She's mute, wordless." Sapphira answered, "And dumb."

"Was there an accident? Somebody cut her tongue out or somethin'?"

Penninah tensed her muscles at the thought. Please, please, leave the dumb mute alone, she begged in silence.

"She never spoke again after our mother went missing. Father's favorite little rodent." Sapphira joked from her constant throne she had created from the vampire's knee. Penninah thought she looked like a life size doll, all made up with her pretty dress. She looked down at her soiled sleeping gown from another world. Her bare dirty toes compared to Sapphira's shiny shoes with the tiny buttons in a row, rising up past her ankles. Those clothes were so odd to her, and paired with her emotional misery, she deduced that she may as well have died and been sentenced to an eternal woe.

"We could do with some fresh water, my love." Sapphira suggested to Bel, "Could we let sister out into the night for a few minutes? She's beginning to smell."

"Of course, my only. Send her on a glorious mission to the well. An exotic vacation from this debauchery would do her some good."

His sarcastic tone was not amusing to Penninah, as she rose to her feet and reached for the bucket. She cracked the door enough for her to slip through, but as she was half the way out, the wicked voice called for her once more.

"Penninah."

She froze to await the rest.

"Do not delay."

She did not look back, and closed the door behind her. She then leaned on the frame and inhaled the pleasing scent of freedom. Even if it was just for a fleeting few minutes. She remembered Bettie's words earlier in the day and dreamed of how wonderful it would be if only she had the nerve. She wanted to be stronger, like father. Like mother. But the well awaited, and off she went. She stepped over the tiny stones that hurt her feet as usual, then onto the cool grass of the field. The moon was big and bright, she thought, and knew that the following night it would be full, and even bigger. In the pale blue mist she saw a figure at the well and her heart raced in anticipation that it may be Bettie.

Another hundred yards and she saw that it was indeed her only friend in that dismal destination she had found herself in. She had a burlap sack beside her on the ground. Penninah walked right up to Bettie and the ardor overtook her. She fell right into the orphan girl's arms. Her emotions poured out of her pores, clinging onto Bettie's body. She did not have to speak; that fervent display dictated the tale of her suffering. When she did release her grasp, the two girls were face to face, breathing each others air and staring deep into each others eyes.

"Are you ready?" Bettie asked.

Penninah turned her face away, unsure of what to express. She was scared, and Bettie knew it.

"It's OK. It really is. I've got some things packed, some food and what clothes I have. I'm sure they'll fit you, too."

It all sounded so magical to Penninah, as her life had been reduced to constant distress.

"I've been waiting here for you." Bettie said, "I'd have waited all night. I don't have anybody. I know it sounds stupid but you're my only friend, Penninah. And I think I'm *your* only friend. Those people treat you so bad, I know. Come on. I...need you."

Now it was Bettie's turn to cry as she began to break down. Penninah longed to call out to her, to confess how much she wanted to run with her, run to another town, another place far away, where her sister and those terrible men that held her captive could never follow or find them. Somewhere in all that outpouring of sadness, their eyes met again, and their lips as well, and the two wayward girls held each other with all the urgent passion they could muster from within. Desire born from the unpleasantness in their respective lives, at that juncture the despair and desperation overtook them. Bettie was right; they needed each other, and it was time, Penninah thought, to take matters into her own hands, to do what must be done. They kissed again and again. Penninah had never experienced that before, being such a help to her father the good priest, dedicating herself to making life easier for him after losing mother. She was alone then, and had found a kind loving angel of her own.

Bettie picked up the sack, took her hand and whispered, "Let's go."

The enticement had passed and Penninah was all in for the adventure. It was the most liberating instant of her existence. They darted to the left, and ran together towards town, behind the buildings in the shadows. Before Penninah knew it they had reached the bullet-riddled 'Welcome to Damascus' sign at the other end.

Penninah paused to catch her breath, but Bettie was adamant.

"We have to keep going, before they miss you. By morning we can be near Lawson City. We can bum a ride on a stage there and get to Ehrenford. There's a train station in Ehrenford."

A quiet whistling sound came from Penninah as she took Bettie's hand and they escaped into the unknown. She stumbled once but her partner in flight caught her. Their bodies were close once more, and Penninah did not ever want to let Bettie go. A sharp pain had started in her side, and her legs were already tiring, but she vowed to flee as far as they would take her before they failed her.

Without warning, and without a sound, Bettie was ripped from her side. Penninah fell that time and hit her head.

"Penninah!" Bettie shrieked in terror as Mister Bel's sharp teeth entered her neck and began to drain her of her precious lifeblood. Her feet dangled above the ground as she was held aloft and besieged by the dark embodiment of malicious sin. Her skin fell to a pale rendering of what it was and her struggling stopped. It was done in the blink of an eye. Penninah could only watch in helpless abandon as Bettie's neck was broken with a sickening crack, and she was dropped in a heap on the dirt below. Penninah mouthed the word 'no', but no sound came, only a thin drool spilling from her wide open orifice as the horror unfolded before her, knowing that she was going to be next. The crickets and owls had ceased to sing, and in silence the poor girl could only heave in heavy breaths. One curdling outburst was all she could project. *Aaaaargh. Arrr. Aaa.* She threw out what she could towards the murdering vampire standing over Bettie's dead body, her face still twisted in fear and her cadaver eyes wide open, staring into the night sky, but seeing nothing.

"What a naughty girl you are." he said with an unfeeling voice, with not a shred of remorse, "Do you not know how valuable you are to me? How...*crucial* your presence is to my mammoth ambitions? Even I failed to behold your worth at the start of our odyssey together, dear child. You, priest's daughter, have the distinct honor of being your foolish sibling's alternate. You cannot...*leave.*"

His unsympathetic face offered a smile then. A dreadful smile.

"You must be exhausted, little silent one. Come."

His hand came down and touched her forehead, and that was the last thing Penninah remembered.

CHAPTER 14

The priest awoke to a brilliant, beautiful dawn. The sun over the east, risen to a perch just at the tips of the majestic California redwoods. Vibrant colors throughout the morning sky filled with songs of the cheerful birds, flying here and there. Like all was right in the world, but he knew all was not right and there was a job to be done before he would close his eyes again. He lay on his back, shirtless, by the smoldering remains of the fire, where they had danced the night before, sending praises to the Creator in the Indian's own unique way. He, Black Jackal, and Tameka had become entranced and glorified The Great Spirit with their celebration of life and tribal culture. He remembered falling exhausted in the very spot he retired to hours before. Lifting his head, he saw Ariel, still atop the boulder, in a trance of her own, praying and meditating. Her smiles during the previous night's festivities made him feel confident and secure that there was a chance to succeed against the actions of the maniacal force that had turned his entire existence into a nightmarish episode of pain and despair.

He rose and glanced about. The chief and his lovely squaw were wrapped in an embrace, asleep. The fire and passion in Tameka's eyes as she pranced around those flames was not something he would soon forget. They were dedicated to the cause, and he felt fortunate to have such assistance in that dark time. A great blessing. Their bodies twisting and contorting, spinning and jumping. It was a sight to behold. But it was time to arise, and get to the ugly business at hand. After those centuries on the road, one more day without his family would drive him mad. It had to end, and he made a silent promise to himself that it would. All the days he spent traveling had led him to that day. The wars he had fought in along the way, the things he had learned, the countless languages he could speak as a result. The blood he had spilled. The ravenous hordes of Mongols and monsters he had faced and cut down on battlefields across the world in all its conflicts. Tibet, China, England.

"Ah-mer-eye-kah," he muttered to himself. Recalling the words of the witch so long ago. He could still see her mocking face, telling him to go home and give up. It was not in his nature with so much at stake. The lengths a parent will go to, to save his children. The boundaries had been tested to their absolute breaking point. Failure was not an option, not after it all. Some nights he could feel the immortality in his veins, burning with a fervor of purpose. He stood and collected his clothes that had been cast aside, walking towards Ariel and standing before her without a disturbance of her tranquil dream state. Her eyes opened anyway, and looked upon him. A sense of pride that they had made it that far, with a mix of a sense of dread, that they had made it that far. It was time.

'Whiskey' Wilson opened his heavy eyes as the sun peeked through a crack in the curtains and brought a faint beam of light into the house. He rubbed them and felt the sting of a sharp hangover, something he had gotten used to over the years. Alcohol was his companion in life, and he accepted the pitfalls that his colleague brought with it.

"Coffee?", the rugged voice of Richard Blood called out to him, even though he was speaking in a low tone. His throat's deep vibrations were incapable of subtlety.

"Coffee may be too strong of a word," he continued, standing over the wood stove, "at this point its mostly old grounds and chicory."

"The name's *Whiskey* Wilson, not *Coffee* Wilson, Blood." Wilson answered, still in a hazy stupor.

"Big day today, friend." said Blood, "Going into town to get my guns, and pay a visit to our old familiar, Sheriff Bill."

"Where's Bel?"

"He left out before the dawn. Something about preparing the spot for tonight's entertainment or whatever, right after he brought the little mute runaway girl back and dumped her in the corner."

Wilson glanced over to see Penninah, sleeping in a peaceful heap. The soles of her once soft pink feet were then blackened with soot and dirt. Her hair tangled and disheveled, but her angelic innocent face preservered, still just as flawless. He wanted her.

"Bel brought her back a few hours ago."

"The other girl?"

"Asleep in the other room. Its early yet." said Blood, settling into a rocking chair with his cup, sipping the dark concoction, "Never cared much for chicory, but coffee's coffee...a necessary evil."

"I suppose."

"Wake up, Wilson, goddamnit! Or go back to sleep!"

"Naw, its a big day, like you say. That Bel, what a character, huh?"

"He controls dark forces. He's why I'm even here. After my personal business is concluded, I serve him. Make no mistake. I encourage you, my old friend, to get on the fuckin' bandwagon. Its in our best interests."

"Sure, Blood, I am. Just scares the livin' bejeezus out of my ass, that's all. Like somethin' we ought not be messin' around with."

"I haven't got the luxury of a choice." Blood said, more serious then, "He owns my soul. You can pack up and ride back to Kansas City or St. Louis if you're too spooked."

"I'm in. Don't fret over me."

Blood sipped from the cup that appeared as a toy in his large fingers. The two outlaws sat in silence for the following few minutes. Wilson thought of the banks and stages they had robbed, the gold in the strongboxes they had killed for, the whores they had shared along the way in every cow town in the Midwest. The lawmen that had fallen in the streets to their bullets, to their unbridled greed and lust for life. He remembered all that history but his musings were interrupted when his eyes again found Penninah's body. She was ripe and tender as a full peach in season. He could recall how fresh and smooth her skin felt under his invading fingers the night before. All in jest in front of the others, but in a minute or two Blood would be on his way, and she could be his. He could almost smell her charms from across the room, even though this was his imagination on a run through his tortured brain, squirming like a captured mosquito hawk with its tail tied to a fence. He could not live another hour without touching her, without deflowering that young beauty. He dared not consider the other, for that was Bel's woman, and there was no enjoyment in the idea of crossing that beast.

⟞⊹ ⊹⟝

The Indian was an exceptional tracker, hunter, warrior, provider. He prided himself on being a leader and doing what was right for his family and tribe. He had been given the gift of communication with The Great Spirit, living every day filled with honor, and a reverence for life. He used his skills then on the most important duty of all, stalking the abomination that walked upon two legs, to the site of its greatest and most wicked treachery. His charge was to follow the vampire and discover where the terrible sacrifice was to take place. The priest had gone into town on his own endeavor, shadowing the gunfighter Richard Blood. They had to end that madness in short order, that very day.

Black Jackal remained a distance behind Bel, watching and trailing him across rocky terrain. In an unexpected instance, Bel's voice rang out through the air.

"I know you are there, shaman."

Bel turned on his heel to face the direction of his pursuer. Black Jackal stepped unafraid from the brush to face him. A stern look but no words.

"I know all that surrounds me. Instead of hiding all this time, we could have been indulging in a bit of light conversation to ease our journey together."

The chief stood like a rock, unmoved after Bel's flippant remarks.

"I see, the strong silent type." Bel continued, "Nothing in your mind but your glorious mission to overthrow the madman bent on bringing endless peril to humanity. I have news for you, savage. The paint on your face likens you to a comedic buffoon, and by this time tomorrow your great and powerful Indian spirit in the sky will be on his knees, groveling."

At that Black Jackal pulled a tomahawk from his side and hurled it towards Bel, in one swift effortless motion. It found its mark, planted in the center of Bel's chest with a hollow cracking of his breast bone. Bel, taken unaware and in a rare show of awe, took a step backwards.

"I will have your heart." was his reply, his right arm outstretched as he unleashed a barrage of dark magic from his crooked fingers. Black Jackal plucked a worn hawk's feather from his hair and waved it once through the air in front of his demonic foe. The vampire's power tore into two streams, striking and breaking two giant trees in half on either side of them. The splitting of the sequoias could have been heard all the way back in town, as well as their thunderous landings that shook the very earth beneath their shoes. The dust settled on the scene, as the fierce Indian stood before his startled opponent like a stone statue, expressionless. Bel stood opposite, the weapon still in his chest, a rich burgundy coursing from the wound.

"I will...have your *heart*, Indian. Before the sun sets upon this day. You will see it ripped from you. Your weeping shall be..."

"Enough." said Black Jackal, "The good and righteous man will prevail over you. Spirit has shown me. It shall be so."

Bel pulled the blade from his body and dropped it in the dirt at his feet, turned and began walking as before. Black Jackal looked to the sky and closed his eyes, feeling a cool breeze wash over his face. To him it was the reassuring touch of his ancestors, and enough to carry him through to the end, until he one day joined them among the heavens and the stars. He continued to hound the villain to the site of the impending ritual. A ritual that had to be stopped by any means. He was unafraid.

Richard Blood kicked the door to the sheriff's office open and walked inside, ducking his head as to not bump it on the frame. His guns were hung over Bill's desk on two nails like some sort of trophy, and that only fueled his rage. He took each one down, loaded them, and placed them in the weathered leather holsters at his sides. Turning to leave, he saw his face glaring back at him on a wanted poster. Not a bad portrait, he thought. He took it down as well, folded it and stuck it in his back pocket as a souvenir. Headed to the door as that phase of his plan was concluded, a voice rang out through the small building.

"Hey, who's there?"

Blood turned and took a few steps towards the two small jail cells in the back. A prisoner was alone in one, holding onto the bars and straining to see around the corner.

"Blood!" he shouted, with an immediate recognizing of the oversized outlaw, "It's me, Henry Richardson! Bill's had me in here for four days."

"I don't know you." Blood answered in his cold and callous fashion.

"Henry Richardson." the man repeated, "I...I took care of your horses in Wichita while you were there. You and that Whiskey fella told me I did a fine job. You gave me a bottle of rye. It made me real proud helpin' you, Mr. Blood. I was hopin' you could let me outta here."

"Richardson, you say?"

"Yessir, Mr. Blood. I'd do anything, whatever you need. I'd be powerful obliged."

"Don't need any help today."

"I'm...I'm sure there's somethin' I could do, Mr. Blood. Please don't leave me in here. Bill's got a man comin' from Ehrenford to take me. He'll be here tomorrow."

"Don't need any help today."

"But Mr. Blood, I swear to Jesus I'd be a good man to have around, I swear. You'll see."

"Where's Bill now?"

"He's over at the saloon, Mr. Blood."

"Good. I'm fixin' to take care of some unfinished business. I'll get the keys off Bill and come back for you. Fair enough?"

"Yes! Thank you, Mr. Blood, you won't regret it."

"I'd better not."

Blood turned and walked back out of there, Richardson's voice trailing behind him in a barrage of thank you's and I swear's. Blood strode the thoroughfare like a man with a new lease on life.

His long legs carried him to the steps of the saloon faster than a normal man's would have.

Mandalay watched Ned playing cards with McCreed, and filled Bill's glass again, keeping an ever watchful eye on who needed a beer or another bottle of liquor at their table. Her lot in life it seemed was to be stuck in that mining town on its last leg, without a crutch. Any past she had was a foggy memory that may or may not have ever happened. She leaned on the bar and daydreamed as she often did, wondering what exciting events were transpiring in other parts of the world. She thought of her father, a chef back in Boston, when she was but a girl of fourteen. His dream was to open his own restaurant, and when the opportunity came to real-ize that aspiration, he took his family on a wagon across country, to the 'new world' as he called it. In Topeka, Kansas, he was so op-timistic over his venture. He rented a building right next door to a hotel, and it appeared that they were on their way.

It went well until the day a grizzled gunslinger called 'Crossroads' Corbin took a seat at one of the attractive tables she had prepared herself, with a fresh tablecloth and flowers. The story that preced-ed him went that meeting him in any fashion put your very life at risk, at a 'crossroad'. He was not a tall man by any means, about an average 5' 8" with a long faded red beard, almost orange colored in the sunlight. His eyes were deep set and gray; she would never forget those cold eyes as he complained that his dinner was 'too fancy looking' and demanded to see the cook. When her father came out of the kitchen to greet him, Corbin pulled his gun and shot him down right on the spot, right in front of her. He stormed out as she held her dying father, mumbling some last words to her through a mouth filled with blood, his white apron spattered with crimson as well. Corbin was caught by the marshal hours later, and scheduled to hang a week later after a quick trial, but it gave her and the widowed mother little satisfaction, only sorrow and fear of the future. Especially after the news of Corbin escaping the jail in just three days time, aided by a ruthless gang of wild ruffians.

Her mother sold the business after that, and succumbed to a heart attack only six months later, while working in the post office for extra money. Mandalay knew it was actually from a broken heart, as her mother depended on her father to be her solid rock in those trying times. She was lost without him. In the years to come, Mandalay bartended in different establishments, and at her lowest worked as a saloon girl and prostitute. The young ones made the most money, after all. To that day she carried a scar on her left breast from the cowboy who cut her with a bowie knife, while inside her. He climaxed seconds later, thankfully, and rolled over to find his half filled bottle of whatever rotgut booze he was drinking on the bed stand.

She left Topeka soon after that, vowing to travel as far from those wretched drunks, rapists, and butchers as she could. She ended up there, in the gasping Damascus. The faces of the passers through became blurred over time, and all looked the same, as identical twins coming and going in a constant cycle. She would die there, she thought.

Mandalay's private musings would end there, as all in the bar froze at the sound of Richard Blood's unexpected dreadful voice. He cleared his throat with a cough, and spit, before he roared, "Bill!"

Mandalay appeared at the swinging doors and a look of pure shock overtook her features. She was gone again as quick as she had came, replaced by Sheriff Bill. He stepped out onto the saloon's front porch, the old boards creaking under his boots, as not another sound could be heard for miles on that dead street, save the slight flow of the wind. Bill's eyes were not sure if they were looking at a nightmare, and reached up to rub them as if he were asleep and did not know it.

"*Blood...?*"

"Surprised, Bill?"

"But, but, Blood, you..."

"Can't find the words, old man? I don't blame you. You should have seen ol' Whiskey's face. I thought he was gonna shit himself right there. But no matter; I've come for you, Bill."

Bill descended the steps and onto the street to face that apparition, in disbelief.

"One lucky afternoon and think you put Richard Blood in the hole for good? The baddest man in the whole goddamned U.S. of A? The sun was in my eyes, Bill. Seems it wasn't a fair fight and a rematch is in due order."

"You..." Bill stammered, "You're under arrest, do you hear? I don't know what's goin' on, but..."

"*Come on, Bill.*" Blood said with a smart retort, "You know better'n that. I've come to shoot you down. Send you to the same purgatory you sent me to. Now draw, Bill. I ain't got time to waste."

Bill reached one hand towards his gun and the other pointed a finger at Blood. "I saw you die."

"That you did. But I ain't gonna give you the whole rundown, Bill. I'm just here to conclude our business and send you straight to Hell."

The two men stared holes through each other, as Bill became aware of his trembling digits, but not out of fear alone. He was no longer a young man, and not the same gallant lawman that he was years ago. Retirement was a subject he often entertained, but did not know how to let go of the badge, afraid of what his life would become after he was was no longer needed. Sitting in a lonely rocking chair on a porch somewhere seemed an empty fate without his dear wife, who had passed before him some time back. A bout with consumption sent death to darken their door, and all he had left was that silver star on his jacket and that dying little town.

"You either draw, or sing Red River Valley, Bill, but I'm gonna kill you anyway." Blood's hateful words interrupted the memories.

Bill could see his wife's graceful features and her smooth alabaster skin, almost as if she were there, waiting for him to join her.

"I love you, Coraline." he whispered to her.

Bill grabbed the handle of his revolver as Mandalay let out a piercing scream. With resounding booms, Bill fired a shot straight into Blood's heart, and another into his belly. Smoke drifted from the new holes in his shirt, but Blood stood there and raised an eyebrow at the sheriff, unaffected. There were no words to describe Bill's stunned consternation.

"My turn." Blood said, as bullets from both barrels unloaded into Bill's chest, lifting the good sheriff off his feet with the force of the barrage. Bill landed on the hard dirt in a crumpled heap.

"No, no, no!" yelped Mandalay, running over to him with tears flowing, "Why? Why? You bastard! Blood...you're a no good bastard!"

"That was never in dispute."

Blood's frigid reply and the fact that he was then pointing a huge gun at her turned her blood to ice in her veins. Blood approached, and placed the barrel up against her temple as she sobbed.

"Back away, girl. I'm takin' Bill with me."

McCreed jumped to the ground from the top step with a rifle in hand, but Blood shot him through the neck before he could react. Another scream from Mandalay as she crawled to the bottom step of the saloon, beside the stage driver's limp body, horrified and shaking, as Blood stood over Bill's corpse reveling in his terrible deeds.

"I told you I'd get you, Bill." he said as a slight smirk emerged across his hardened face. Blood holstered his guns and reached down to lift his victim, hoisting him over his broad shoulder. He turned to see the priest, standing in the middle of the street, facing him in the opposite direction.

"Well now, the good priest I've heard so much about."

It had been a long ride back from the Indian's camp and he regretted not getting there in time to save his friend.

"Put him down." ordered the priest.

Blood laughed in a defiant manner, and bolstered a hearty "Or *what?*"

"The terror you've spread over this land has run its course, Blood. Now put him down."

"Fine." Blood answered, "I got no quarrel with dragging two dead folks back to Bel."

Blood dropped Bill's mangled, bloody form to the ground once more, and began firing at will, his giant guns bellowing not unlike two miniature cannons. The priest did the same, lead erupting into each other's flesh. Frightened onlookers peered from random windows, and saw both men fall to their knees as their firearms emptied themselves across the thoroughfare. The faces with their noses pressed against fogged glass panes, wait-ed in suspense to witness what would happen next in that grisly scene. The world stood still as the four bodies lay in the street, until Blood rustled and rolled over. He sat up and surveyed the stretch of road as the dust cleared. The priest rose as well. Both men stammered to get to their previous stance and face one an-other again.

"What in the *fuckin' fuck*." was Blood's reaction.

"It takes..." the priest informed Blood as he caught his breath, "...an immortal to kill an undead."

"This town's turnin' into a regular freak show." said Blood as he took his first step towards the priest. They locked in combat, grap-pling hand to hand then, as guns were declared useless. Blood, still being the larger, stronger fighter, lifted the priest and flung him into the blacksmith's doorway, sending him crashing into the wood and metal, as assorted tools fell all about him. He moved so fast for a big man, and he was on top of the priest with no de-lay. Fists, elbows, and knees fell upon the two in a turbulent fury.

Blood fell back into the street but saw Mandalay, standing there with Bill's gun in her quivering hand.

"Stop...you stop right there, Richard Blood." she said, with all the nerve she could command, her voice a shuddering mess.

"Well," Blood started, wiping some of the red liquid gore from his chin, "look who's got some gumption all of a sudden."

He rose and walked to her, as she panicked and fired three shots into him, with her eyes closed as tight as they could be, her teeth grinding and her heart beating like a freight train. She didn't see him, only tasted his nauseous breath on her face, and felt his overgrown hands wrapping themselves around her slim throat, twisting and breaking it in one swift, violent measure. Mandalay fell dead as Blood joked, "Now who'll get our drinks?"

He turned and the steel of a pick axe entered his forehead with the force and will of a cyclone reducing a farmhouse to splinters. Bewildered, Blood did not fall, instead staggered forward in a stupor. The priest readied the second axe, a chopping one for trees, and that colossal man looked to the priest enough like a tree at that moment. The first swing separated Blood's right leg from his torso in a macabre and brutal way. The enormous outlaw collapsed as the priest raised the blade to the sky to bring it plunging down again, severing Blood's head from his shoulders.

The priest stood over Blood's dismembered remains, breathing hard and moving his sweated long hair from his face. He squinted into the morning sun to the saloon, seeing Ned the bartender standing there dumbfounded and spent.

"Ned. Jedge. Some help here. Help me get them out of the street."

Blood was dead, and could not be brought back again, by anyone. Some people found the fortitude to come out of the buildings and gather, among them Ariel, who walked up to the priest and ran her hands over his blood stained vest and shirt, riddled with bullet holes.

"I hate killing." he confessed to his ever present companion.

"I know, Nasser. But in this case you have killed what was already dead. The lives you saved..."

"Too late for Bill. And Mandalay, and McCreed there." he cut her off and surveyed his fallen friends. Kneeling over Bill, he delivered some last rites. Ariel watched as he did the same for the poor girl, and the stage coach driver. He closed Mandalay's eyes, as they had been when she was firing at Blood with a rabid tenacity, but then peaceful and somber.

"She tried to stop him herself. To save everyone. To save *me*. So brave. She deserves better. How long does this go on?" he asked the angel.

"Not much longer," she assured him, "not much longer at all."

CHAPTER 15

Whiskey peeked out of the door to see if he could spy Blood on the road. He heard some gunfire from town and knew he would be returning soon with his endeavor completed. No sign of his overgrown compadre meant he still had some time. He crept into the doorway where Sapphira slept and hesitated there. She was a vision to behold. As much as he would love taking a liberty with her, it was the younger sister that he was fascinated with. Penninah slept with a comfortable peace over her unspoiled teenage features. A girl of twelve, possibly thirteen, that had burned a desire into his quintessence. What a perfect wife she would make, he fantasized to himself. Cleaning the house, washing his clothes, cooking, and all without a single utterance of protest from her mouth. No back talk, no sass or disrespectful lip for him to suffer through. It was difficult in those days to marry one so young, but he knew men who had. There were states that were enacting laws to prevent it, but there in what some called 'the wild west', it was legal. Local lawmen and territorial marshals had so much more to concentrate on than who was marrying who. An inconsequential oversight, at least for then, until the world he knew embraced its eventual civilization.

But for that fateful morning, she could be all his for the taking. The possibilities mounted in his brain. To Hell with Bel, and whatever insane plans he had concocted. Bel scared him to death, just being in that devil's presence. Yes, he could take Penninah, take one of the horses and ride south, perhaps into Mexico, and live out his days with his tiny mute missus. He could leave all the revelry behind, the pilfering and mindless death could be a distant reminiscence. He could work a farm, or raise cattle. Livestock, anything, and after the sun set beyond the trees, his lovely Penninah would be his to ravage, every night for the rest of his days. She would learn to love him, for she would have no choice, and he would never let her go. Fantasia such as that had often impeded his usual rebellious lifestyle, and caused him to drink so much more than he should in an effort to squash such unrealistic plans.

But there it was, a rare opportunity waiting to be acted upon. A turning point in his crude existence. Hell yes, he thought, fuck Bel, and Blood, and how anyone perceived him. He peered out the door a second time, watching for his partner's approach. Still no Blood. Perhaps he was sitting in the saloon drinking to celebrate Sheriff Bill's demise, or having a go with that pretty barmaid. No matter. He knelt over Penninah, ran his fingers through her scattered locks. He bent his neck further to touch his nose to her cheek, to inhale her scent and breathe the very oxygen that she was breathing, sweeter then that it had been in her lungs.

He had to have her. He had to taste her if it was the last thing that he ever did on that earth. Lifting her demure dressing gown, he moved his palm over the lustrous skin of her thigh. The caress was explosive, and a rush of adrenaline cloaked him down to his toes within his boots. He felt inebriated all over again, light headed and woozy, just from that initial intimate gesture. Both of his probing hands were on her then, and Penninah awoke to see that dirty deplorable man over her, touching her. Her instinct was to lash out, which she did and struck him over and over about the head and shoulders while her voice failed her as it had for so long.

"Mmm...mmmm...mmm." was all she could enunciate, with her vocal chords bursting at their seams. Whiskey fought to hold her down, fumbling through a flimsy explanation in an attempt to calm the girl, until his own rudimentary reflexes overtook him, bringing a fist down to her temple, knocking her out cold. Her skull banged onto the wooden floorboard and she lay motionless and still. Whiskey, aghast and thinking he had killed her, held her in his arms and apologized.

"I'm so sorry." he whispered to her flaccid figure. Emotions welled in his chest cavity, feeling her sternum area for a heartbeat, and her throat for some sign of a pulse. The slight thump-thump-thump under his fingers reassured him that all was not lost. It would be easier that way, he speculated, and later she would be so much more receptive once they were away and on their own. He reached over to the breakfast table where a dish of butter was residing next to the remnants of the loaf of bread from the previous evening's festivities. He dipped his fingers deep into the butter and lathered it between Penninah's legs to make his penetration less intrusive. His unwashed appendage was freed and pushed its way inside her virginal nether regions. Holding her down by her developing breasts, Whiskey thrust like a starving mongrel, invading her body and destroying her protected innocence. He could no longer reason with his mind blanked and heart racing. He lifted her legs by the ankles and held her soft insole by his reddened and sweating mask of ecstasy. Her foot resting on his cheekbone was a supple as the rest of her, a treasure you could not find in a grown woman. He imagined her in that hypnotic moment as a fairy tale character, and not a human at all. A mythical creature of lore. A flying pixie he had captured in a jar to admire. He worshiped her.

His physical onslaught came to a frenzied pace as he prepared to unleash his seed into her. Just seconds before, Penninah's eyes once again opened to behold her fate. Her arms felt like sandbags and they would not move, her loins afire with stinging anguish. Her body rocked back and forth as the terrible man hurt her, and she acceded to the notion that her life was over.

That strange land, her father, her wicked sister, the evil beast, those two heinous bad men, poor Bettie her love, murdered before her. The darkness of the world surrounded her. Hopelessness. Best to die right there and then, and go home to mother. To be free of it all. The man raping her smelled of liquor and dank stale urine. His teeth clenched so tight she thought they may shatter into pieces. Sweat from his furled brow dripped on her exposed stomach and collected in a little pool inside her belly button. The veins in his neck pulsed and protruded as if they would erupt. He wasn't a human being, but a remorseless barbaric ogre, and there was nothing she could do.

Take me, O Lord, she prayed, *I am ready to come home. Bless my father and may he save Sapphira somehow. May all be made right again, may all our suffering come to an end, Amen.*

Then, without warning, the man was pulled from her and sent sailing through the air, smashing into the wall on the far side of the room.

"What...have...you...*DONE*?" The menacing voice of Mister Bel echoed throughout the house. Sapphira appeared nude from the bedroom doorway, clutching a blanket.

"Bel, what is happening?" she asked.

The vampire did not answer her, just stood towering over little shivering Penninah, her genitals bleeding and telling the story in all the detail anyone needed to know. Wilson used the back of a chair to pull himself up. He opened his mouth to speak but no words could take shape before he was hurled through the window, glass fracturing and pieces landing everywhere. Outside, he landed in a clump in the dirt, rolling to a conclusive stop. Bel's face became a twisted veil of wrath, a look neither girl has seen before and never wished to see again. He stepped out of the door to the fallen outlaw.

"Bel! Look, I can explain. I wasn't gonna...do it to *your* woman..."

"Fool!" Bel began, "You senseless ignorant fool! You have ruined her! She is of no use to me now!"

"Bel, Bel, I'm...I'm sorry, Mister Bel. I didn't know..." Wilson sputtered in unlearned vain.

"And now, Mister Wilson, neither are you."

Bel raised his hand, his fingers cringing with maniacal urgency. Wilson was swept up, held up by an invisible force, his heart that moments before had been filled with lust then overflowed with sheer terror. Bel advanced on his hapless hostage, severing both of Wilson's arms from their sockets in a vicious display. Sapphira vomited in the doorway, throwing up the syrupy digested remains of the previous evening's meal and ale. Penninah lay on the cold floor where she had been, listening to Wilson's shrill shreiks and imploring Bel's forgiveness as he begged for mercy. She rested in a sense of satisfaction and calm, giving ear to the remainder of his grim ordeal. All four extremities were ripped away like the arms and legs of a doll being pulled off by a child.

Sapphira cowered in the doorway, agape at the brutality and vengeance of her devoted fiancée. Wilson's entrails were unraveled as blood poured from his opened torso, gashed in an insidious manner, and entwined around his throat as Bel strangled the last signs of life out of what used to be Winslow 'Whiskey' Wilson. The head and chassis fell to the ground as a jumbled hunk of meat, guts and bowels. Bel then stood reserved, his eyes closed in transcendent thought as his rage passed.

"My love." he said, turning to Sapphira, "Wash yourself. For tonight you become my bride."

A giddy Sapphira hurried back to the bedroom, pausing long enough to throw a last jab at her woeful younger sister.

"How was your first time, Monkey?" she giggled. "I cannot believe that you beat me to it. Back home they would make you marry him, or *stone you*."

Disappearing from sight, she reemerged from the room to add one more insult. "Whore."

Penninah felt so sorry for her. It was agonizing to know more than her gullible sibling who thought herself so smart, and not be able to warn her of the doom they faced. Bel reentered the house, covered in Wilson's insides like he had just slaughtered a pig with a hatchet.

Glaring at her, he said, "Time for you to go, child."

Bel took her by her forearms and tossed her like a bag of garbage out of the wide open door. She landed upon the crimson soaked carcass of Wilson, his eyes bulged and tongue hanging out. It was then her turn to regurgitate, expelling the contents of her stomach onto his deceased stump.

"Go back to your father, the priest. I am certain he will be delighted to see you." Bel suggested, "You are free. *Go*."

And then she was alone as the door slammed shut behind her. She lifted herself from Wilson's gruesome cadaver, her clothes now drenched with his raw refuse, that continued to ooze from him like an indecent bubbling fountain. She could not help but step into the gathering maroon colored pool to get away, her feet coated in the outlaw's red filth as she made ginger steps down the road.

CHAPTER 16

The priest sat on the steps leading to the saloon, beside Ariel, watching the bodies of Sheriff Bill and the others carried away by volunteers.

"Preacher? Brother Nasser?" a man and his wife approached and spoke.

"Yes."

"We...we all loved Sheriff Bill, he was family to us...and...we know this town's been through a lot lately. Without him, we're all gonna feel more than a little lost."

His wife continued, "We don't understand all that's happening, but seeing Richard Blood walk up this street after he was laid to rest, well, we know that its the Devil's work."

"You are right about that." the priest answered, his head hung low and never making eye contact with the concerned couple.

"My name's Collins. Arthur Collins, and this is my wife Cathleen. We were overjoyed that a new pastor had come to town, to lead church services again. But after today, me and some of the townsfolk have been talkin'. And we'd like to ask you, sir, if you'd be interested in becoming the new sheriff of Damascus."

The priest raised his head to look upon those two grieving souls. Moved, he paused before making an answer. Collins offered the badge from Bill's vest, and said, "I think he would have approved."

The priest's eyes fixed on the piece of silver forged into the shape of a star, with a glint of sunlight reflecting off of the edges. He turned to Ariel and then back to Collins and his wife.

"I do apologize, but I cannot." he replied to their sincerest inquiry, "You may not understand the circumstances, but I intend to die this very night, after I have rescued my daughters from that despicable wraith, whatever he may be or whoever he may serve. I will take my children from him, and look into their sparkling eyes once more before I lay my head to rest, after an eternity of..."

His words faded to an unintelligible hush as he saw the figure of the young girl staggering down the thoroughfare, one pitiful meager step at a time. The Collins' and Ariel turned their heads as well to the direction of the priest's attention, and moved back as he rose and bounded from his perch, running at a full sprint. In the mere heartbeat it took to reach her, his eyes filled with tears as he whisked Penninah up into his arms and held her close to his chest like a newborn babe, kissing her face and thanking the Lord. He dropped to his knees, still holding her, as he had dreamed of doing for the past two thousand years.

"Thank you, Lord, thank you..." his words drifted to the higher power that guided him, that had shown his divine benevolence.

═╋═╋═

Sapphira walked out of the bedroom in the elegant white gown that Bel had procured for her. She was stunning, and happier than she had ever been. She whirled and laughed as Bel was her sole audience. Oblivious to his true intent for her, her joy would soon turn to dire trepidation.

"I cannot wait to be your immortal beloved." her words almost sounding like a song.

"You already are, my dear." he answered with a composed temperament.

"Will you make me like you? To live forever? Right after? Tonight?"

"Whatever you desire."

"Do it while you make love to me! Let us revel in each other for all times."

"Whatever you desire."

She melted into his arms and exclaimed, "Oh, Bel. You have saved me from a life of drudgery and weakness. I shall always be your strong and grateful mate, traveling the world and ruling all we survey."

"Come now, love." Bel said, "Everything is prepared. We must ride."

"I will ride anywhere with you. Anywhere and everywhere."

"So you shall." The venomous vampire continued to play that beautiful youth for the ultimate imbecile. To have her go with him, hand in hand, to her own harrowing execution, he likened to child's play. Her own rebellious nature would be her undoing, and his ruthless cunning would free his true mistress from the depths of Shoel's abyss.

"We must ride."

The two left the modest abode, and Bel saddled the steed that would carry them to the culmination of a fiendish plot conjured so long ago. A distant gurgling sound caught Sapphira's ear, and she was taken aback at the annihilated bag of skin laying in the street, taking its terminal breaths.

"He lives still." she pointed out, to even Bel's surprise.

"Impossible."

A hungry blackbird stood upon Wilson, pecking away at the crevasse in his midsection.

"That is a revolting sound." she said, "So sad for him to suffer. All he did was ravage Penninah."

"Oh, child," Bel corrected her but without elaborating, "he did so much more than that."

"Before we go, can you end it, Bel?" Sapphira requested in a rare show of sympathy, "Leaving him like that; it is inhuman."

Bel's lip curled into a grin hidden from view as she continued, "Please, Bel. The memory of him will interfere with my delight, and I do not wish anything to damage the greatest night of my life."

Bel was reluctant to act, until he foresaw his grand plan being delayed, and walked over to Wilson. The bird took flight at his approach, but to the vampire that was a significant sign. Enough of a sign to levy a pardon on that pathetic waste of muscle and bone.

"You impress me, dog." he said, "Warming yourself by the last glowing embers of dying coals. Realizing your demise is imminent, yet you are still defiant. I can respect that."

Wilson could not reply of course, just lay and stare up at that atrocity of a being, humbled, and begging in silence. Bel's arms ascended as he uttered a long forgotten Aramaic spell as Wilson's crippled limbs began to spasm and move, inching their way back to his demolished shell. Tendons and arteries reached out to their former partners, joining and becoming one once more.

Sapphira covered her mouth as she gasped a second time, as she did when she witnessed Wilson's initial destruction earlier. She was astonished as his intestines recoiled and were sealed back from where they came.

"Rise, Wilson." Bel commanded, and the outlaw who was at a far boundary from his former self, rose to one knee and then to a vertical base, his outer hide the color or porcelain, and his whiskers as white as fresh fallen snow.

"Look at me." Bel said, "I have found a constructive usage for you, Wilson. You have my bride-to-be to thank, and the winged scavenger that fed upon you, for the lonesome blackbird is a spirit animal, representing the presence and the grandeur of Ba'al himself. He has spoken and you have been judged worthy by the Master. It is not for I to question."

"*Why...*" Wilson choked as attempted to speak.

Bel whistled to the treetops and the fowl returned, perching on Wilson's head.

"Winslow Wilson, contemptible failure, as God once marked Cain, I leave the mark of Ba'al the Destroyer, and charge you to walk the earth for all eternity, heeding my call whenever I may beckon."

Bel pressed his thumb and index finger to Wilson's brow, burning a symbol of evil into his pale complexion. As black blood vessels convulsed underneath and came to the surface, visible underneath the translucent milky flesh, his appearance transformed into an awful mask of deformity.

"*Thank you...Mister Bel...*" offered Wilson in a demoralized haze.

"Thank you...? replied Bel, seeking a more definitive title.

"*Thank you...Master.*" Wilson abridged, saying anything then not to be torn apart a second time.

"Master. That will do." Bel approved, "Now, follow. You can be my...best man."

Bel feigned a look to Sapphira for an endorsement of that, and she flashed a brilliant smile back at him.

"Welcome back to the land of the living, Wilson," Bel added, "but cross me again..."

"*Don't worry about it.*"

"Sapphira was...always the difficult one." the priest said, as he stood over the bed where his darling Penninah lay sleeping, "Since she was very young."

"She is still very young." Ariel added.

"Yes, that is what I am afraid of. Ariel...what if she will not come with me? What if she refuses me?"

"When she learns of her fate, and realizes her mistakes, she will cry out for you. Be at ease."

The priest raised the bottle of spirits to his lips as he had been doing throughout the afternoon. Ariel never spoke a word of it, for she knew what a momentous eventide he would be facing. She hated seeing him under such duress.

"The Collins woman. She is going to stay with Penninah. She is coming?"

"Yes, Nasser."

"Good." he replied, going over every detail in his conscious mind. A knock at the door intercepted the next swallow of liquor. Ariel opened the door to see Black Jackal and Tameka.

"Are you ready?" the priest asked him, in the stead of a commonplace greeting.

"Ready." the Indian replied, then noticed the bottle.

"Firewater. Is this wise?"

"My nerves are more alive than they have ever been, I need to calm them."

"Hmmm." said the Indian, "Black Jackal's nerves are also alive. Maybe Black Jackal needs firewater."

The priest found his first smile of the dismal day as he passed the infernal hooch to his new friend, who turned it up in a show of solidarity.

"My husband..." whispered Tameka, blushing and pretending to be shocked but unable to conceal the slight grin on her face.

"Your daughter's slumber in this place is blessing of Great Spirit. Holy man's job is half over. Look on the bright side." announced Black Jackal.

"So, you were not only medicine man, but also the tribe therapist."

"Something like that." he answered in a deadpan tone as he took another drink.

"*My husband...*" Tameka repeated.

"You know, if we are successful and Sapphira is freed," the priest said, much more serious then, "it will be the end of me. I shall give up my ghost knowing that they are safe. It will happen the instant she is secured."

"And if we fail?" Tameka chimed in, although the looks on everyone's faces at her question made her regret speaking, and she decided right then not to speak a second time.

"I do not wish to consider what will become of me." the priest said.

"We must consider consequence of failure." Black Jackal interjected, "You will know that your other daughter has been freed either way. She will dance on the wind and ride the breeze to the side of Great Spirit. Let it bring you peace knowing that her mother will embrace her again."

"Actually, no." Ariel said, turning to gaze out of the window.

"What do you mean?"

Ariel sighed and continued, "Once she has been sacrificed as an offering to Ba'al, or any other demon lord in the major arcana, her very soul will belong to him and he alone. She will be a slave to Ba'al on his plane of the netherworld. So I cannot begin to insist that failure is *not* an option."

That silenced the room in an effective manner, bringing much disconcerting reflection. Black Jackal passed the bottle back to the priest, who emptied it into his gullet, every last remaining drop.

CHAPTER 17

Sapphira clutched Bel around the waist as tight as she could. They rode together on the dusky black palomino, through the wilderness towards the site where all she knew would come crashing down to oblivion. She was ignorant of it of course, still believing she was in the midst of her blissful wedding day, about to be joined with the most amazing man who ever lived, and uncover freedom from a lackluster life of boredom and mediocrity. She could not wait to experience the embodiment of his love planted within her, as she had dreamed every night since they first met, unaware of her hidden plight. It did not matter that the Damascus he had taken her to was a strange land, and not the Damascus she knew, or even that the ordeal had broken her father's heart, or that her sister had been introduced to traumatic nightmares. That warming glow of happiness consumed her from head to toe, and she was going to be the companion of that beautiful, powerful god-like crusader, journeying to the ends of every exotic undiscovered land that the universe and all its dimensions had to offer.

"Are you content, my love?" his exalted voice barged into her dreamscape.

"Oh, yes." she cooed, "so content."

Wilson followed a hundred yards behind them on foot. Sapphira shifted in the saddle to see him walking, then turned back to Bel.

"What of father?" she asked.

"What of him?"

"Will he...try to stop us? He is here for a reason."

Bel did not give a response at once.

"Bel?"

"Your father," he began, "is an inconvenience. But do not bother yourself with trivialities. Nothing or no one will hinder our date with destiny."

Sapphira, satisfied with that, nestled her cheek into Bel's strong shoulder.

After another half mile of riding, he spoke again, "I have an inclination that young sister may be of some usefulness after all. Perhaps we should retrieve her once more."

"But how?" Sapphira inquired.

Bel pulled back on the reins, halting the horse. They waited a few moments until Wilson caught up with them. He pulled a cigar and matches from his coat pocket, lit it, puffing to get it going.

"You have need of me?" he asked.

"Yes, Wilson, my friend. Go back to that rotting hole of a village and collect the young one. Make haste, for time is of the essence. Go."

Wilson nodded and pivoted on his heel, towards the way they had come.

"Why did you spare him?" Sapphira asked.

"It was the Curse of the Blackbird." Bel answered, "I had no choice. We do not question The Destroyer, for just as The Creator conceals his motivations, so does Ba'al."

Sapphira glanced back again to view Wilson walking away, but he was not there. She squinted her eyes to make him out in the distance, but there was no sign of the resurrected outlaw.

"Where did he...?" she questioned before Bel halted her train of thought.

"I told him to make haste, did I not?" Bel said, and snapped the reins to once again move his dark colt.

⥰⥳

Henry Richardson sat in the sixfoot bysixfootcell, awaiting a sign of life from anyone. It was well past supper time, but no one had arrived with any food. He thought to himself that it was indeed the worst jail he had ever been in.

Getting up and gripping the iron bars, he called out, "Hello..."

He glanced across to the outstretched body of Richard Blood on Bill's long table, or the pieces of Blood that were there, covered in a bloody sheet. Men had brought it hours earlier, but ignored his request for sustenance. He was in shock, quite frankly, that anyone could have carved up the infamous outlaw that way. It was unfathomable to him.

"What a way to go." he said out loud to no one in particular except Blood himself, "Damn, Blood, I guess this town finally got sick of your bullshit."

His grievance was aimed more towards the fact that Blood would not be springing him from stir, as was the original agreement, at least not in his current state of being dead. He rested his forehead against the bars and closed his eyes. He would pray if not for the theory that God no longer cared to listen to his incessant ramblings. It was pointless, he considered, as his life spiraled downwards to its eventual tragic end, which was not too far away if and when he was transported to Ehrenford for his trial and swift execution. But if no one brought him any dinner, he may starve to death before that dickless judge there had a chance to finish him off. Nash had once sentenced him to sixty days for refusing to pay for a drink, even though that watered down piss in the Carousel saloon was not worth paying for. He swore he would never set foot in Ehrenford again, but just then it seemed he would be forced to. That is, until the ebony feathered bird landed on the window sill across the room.

"Shoo, bird." he called out, to no avail, "You're probably here to work on Blood, at least one of us will eat tonight." He spoke to the bird with all the sarcasm he could produce in his sour circumstance. He turned his back to the bars and leaned on the opposite wall, letting out a heavy sigh.

"Where are you, Bill?" he asked the confining bricks.

"Bill's dead."

The unexpected reply sent shivers down the length of his spine. He spun to see a damaged looking Whiskey Wilson standing at his cell door.

"Goddamnit, Whiskey, you scared me to fuckin' death! What in the hell happened to you?"

"It's a long story, Henry."

"Where in the hell'd you come from?"

"Window was open."

"But...it was a crow at the window."

"Blackbird. Not the same."

"Since when?"

"Blackbirds live mainly in the western parts of the country whereas crows are all over, and have different beaks and tails. They're a little smaller, and they don't make as much fuss."

"What the fuck, Whiskey? Who cares?"

"Anyway, look, things have changed." Wilson explained. "This is gonna sound like I'm fuckin' with you, but I assure you I'm not. I'm now the servant of a powerful vampire, and I'm helping him in his mission."

"Vampire? What have they done to you, Whiskey? You know what? Fuck it, just get me out of here."

"It's not as simple as all that, friend. I can help you, and then you help me. That's the way it works."

"Well sure, Whiskey, you crazy ass son of a bitch. I don't know what you're talkin' about, but get me out of here and fuck it, I'll help out the old vampire, too."

"I need to trust you." Wilson continued, "trust that you will be obedient and loyal. I need my own...apprentice, if you will."

"Your own...*what?* Whiskey, you ain't makin' a lick a' sense." said Richardson, "But if you're talkin' about takin' over the gang now that Blood's gone, hell, I'm in."

The candid conversation ended there with an abrupt admonishment. Wilson pointed a finger and Henry Richardson was thrown backwards into the wall, and fell hard onto the metal bunk. His windpipe constricted, and he reached for his own throat in a frantic scramble. He could not speak but only pleaded in silence as drool leaked down his chin.

"You will serve me, Henry, and by proxy, the Vampire. Swear it." said Wilson to the petrified inmate.

"I swear, I swear." Richardson driveled out as the pressure lessened. He dropped to his knees on the cell floor, coughing.

"It's a brand new world, Henry. Or it will be soon. You wanna be on the right side, I promise you."

Wilson broke the lock on the cell door with his bare hand, the iron demolished under his new found strength. Richardson crawled out and used the bars to hoist himself back up to his shaking feet.

"Whiskey, I...don't...understand..." he said, but Wilson cut him off before he could spit out the rest.

"Blackbird," Wilson corrected, "call me Blackbird."

"Whatever you say."

"Now, come on. We've got a job to do."

Richardson nodded, confused but processing the new developments. At least, he imagined, he wouldn't be going to Ehrenford anymore, and that cock sucking Judge Nash could wait. Whiskey took a few steps and paused at the remains of his former companion, Richard Blood.

"I will avenge you, brother." he whispered to the hunks of meat, "I *will* avenge you."

Cathleen Collins sat by the bedside while Penninah slept. The poor child, she thought, no girl should have to go through what she had, especially at that tender age. She thought of her loving husband Arthur, who try as he might, had never been able to impregnate her so they may have their own. There was a time that she held it against him, a year or so into their marriage, but later she felt guilty over it, and perhaps had been unfair. The blame could lay with her own body's physical limitations, but living out there in that California frontier gave them inadequate and often non-existent medical care. She had urged him to move closer to a big city, like Ehrenford perhaps, where there was a train and modern facilities. The outlaws had devastated that mining town that once thrived on its own, threatening to become a larger municipality.

Damascus had the potential to be so much more, a landmark, until that 'Blood and Whiskey' gang arrived, behaving like hoodlums and the bloodthirsty vagrant damned. Arthur had refused to leave, as so many others had, being a hero in the great War of Northern Aggression, thinking he could make a difference somehow. She would never forget the rainy wet afternoon that he confronted Blood in the thoroughfare, attempting to be such a dauntless soldier, standing up for what was right. Blood laughed him down, and instead of drawing a pistol, slapped Arthur, and then he and his men drug him through the fresh mud that had collected in the street. They left him there, humiliated, and returned to drinking in the saloon. Arthur was never the same after that. It was as though every ounce of valor within him dissipated with the wind. All in all, he was her man and she loved him so.

He kept his medals in a pine cigar box under the bed, and after that day would never look at them again. Always rambling that he did not deserve them. A part of her spouse had died that day in the puddles of sludge and mire. He had battled the Union blackguard in Virginia like a valiant champion alongside his brothers in arms, but there were no more stories or tales of victories as he saw himself as nothing more than a beaten castaway.

She caught herself beginning to well with tears, but dried them as she decided that enough had been shed, and she accepted her fate. She felt Penninah's head for fever, and was thankful there was none. The priest and the others had rode out of town to confront that Mister Bel and end whatever evil deed he was up to. She did not understand it all but knew it was important and of great significance. If she had a child in danger, she would do anything to save them as well. It was just what you did, without hesitation. But she would never know what that was like.

As she pondered her meager existence, she heard the sounds of heavy boots ascending the staircase and approaching the door. She stood and clasped the small knife that she kept on her, wishing then that it was a little bigger. A polite knock went unanswered as she stayed fast with the blade out and ready. The doorknob rattled, and then pushed open to reveal the white haired ugly man, and she recognized him as Blood's right hand as every one of their wretched faces had been burned into her memory forever. Disheveled, but it was him.

"Excuse me, ma'am," he said to her in a non-threatening manner, "but I have need of the sick girl you appear to be guarding."

"Get out!" she grumbled back at him.

"I assume you have sworn to protect her with your life." Wilson replied, still applying a rather respectful tone.

"I have," Cathleen shot back, "and I will."

"A pity, Mrs. Collins. I had hoped this could be accomplished by civilized means."

"No, no, no!" Cathleen yelled and drove the knife into Wilson's abdomen, with all the grit and mettle she had. He did not fall as she expected, or make any action of note, so she stabbed him again. She could not hold back the flowing tears then as she continued to lash out with the shiv, again and again.

She struck as many times as her muscles would allow, until she was spent of action. She fell at Wilson's boots, crying out loud as her mind whirled. A bit of blood ran from the wounds, what should have been blood, instead a thick, black, tar-like substance coated her tiny weapon.

"Why? Why? What are you?" she wailed as Wilson stepped past her to bend over the sleeping child and take her into his arms.

"No! Don't take her! What use could you have for her?"

Wilson did not speak to Cathleen again. With Penninah in his possession, he walked past her as if she were no longer there, exiting the room with the same lack of indignation with which he arrived. The desperate woman crawled on all fours, weeping, as Wilson started down the stairs, to the lobby of the hotel.

"No! *Please!*" she lamented as she tumbled down after him, down, down, head over feet, her frail bones wrenching and rupturing along the way. She landed with a forceful last smack in a crumpled heap at the foot of the stairs.

"Father, why..." began her last words, "why have you forsaken me?"

The last tear Cathleen Collins would ever shed ran its course across her face with a cold drip, behind her ear, and was then lost from view.

Wilson walked out of the front door of the hotel with Penninah, and met Richardson there.

"Any trouble?" Richardson asked.

"None to speak of." Wilson answered, "Now, I'm taking her to Bel. You stay here, and if anything goes south, wait for me or my signal. Then torch the town."

"The whole town?"

"Whole town," Wilson repeated, "whole goddamned thing."

CHAPTER 18

B lack Jackal looked up to the sky and pointed out the swirling storm clouds gathering at a certain point a few miles ahead, over a thick grove of trees.

"There."

"I see." the priest said.

"That is where we are going." the Indian informed them.

"It is frightening." Tameka stated from behind her husband. The four travelers on two horses journeyed closer to the place of reckoning that the priest and Ariel had come so far to see.

"I do not feel well." Tameka said, loosening her grasp on Black Jackal's torso.

"What is wrong?" The Indian asked, stopping the horse.

"I...I...just..." were her closing words before slipping off the horse and falling. They were all off of their mounts in a second, tending to her. A line of crimson escaped from her lips.

"Tameka! Tameka!" Black Jackal called, realizing the seriousness. They laid her on the ground with a rolled blanket under her head to comfort her.

"Ariel, what is it?" the priest asked. Ariel came close and looked deep into Tameka's dim umber eyes, deeper than mortals could look.

"It is not physical," she said, "but the work of maleficent forces. Something is attempting to take her."

Black Jackal looked left and right, but stood helpless to that perilous news. Feeling helpless was not a sensation that the proud warrior was used to. He fell to his wife's side.

"Tameka...speak to me."

"Husband, my precious chief." she could articulate only loud enough for them to hear, "You must continue. Spirit commanded us to go. But I cannot. You must."

"No! I will not leave you."

"You *must*," she insisted, "I do not know why Spirit has done this, but you must continue with the holy man. I will wait for you."

Black Jackal drew her to him and held her as the priest and Ariel convened in private.

"Ariel, what is happening to her?"

"I do not know."

"She was fine a few moments ago."

Ariel shook her head as not to be redundant in her statement.

"We cannot leave her out here," the priest implored, "but we also cannot delay. Sapphira..."

"I know. I will stay with her. Go and save your daughter."

"But Ariel...Abigail...I need you."

"God is with you, Nasser. He is all you need."

The priest knew she was right. Having her beside him all those decades was not only a comfort, but a well of strength to draw from. To face the final battle alone was something he had not considered, nor desired in any configuration.

"Go." she said.

The priest and the Indian remounted the horses, with much agitation.

"Black Jackal will kill the conniving devil!" the Indian promised the priest, "For you, for your children, for Spirit, and now, *forME*! He does not belong in this world."

The priest reached over to take the Indian's hand in a show of never ending alliance.

"We will do it together, my friend."

Ariel watched the two men ride away on their stallions. She knew the priest's undying resolve, and his restless heart. She also knew that she could not interfere. From the beginning she had been a source of information when needed, a companion, and a constant shoulder to rely on in his times of hopelessness. She was confident at that zero hour that he could handle whatever he may find in the demon's lair. He was in fact, armed with the secret weapon she had *suggested* he acquire in a pass through Mesopotamia so long ago, even if he did not understand then. He trusted her wisdom with a steadfast belief in whatever she had recommended he do, without question.

She knew he would walk through the lake of fire itself to liberate the two girls from their captor. She wished him well, to herself in silence, then brought her attention back to Tameka, who was then standing and facing her with a sickening smile on her bloodied mouth. Stunned, Ariel struggled with words.

"Tameka, what are you doing?"

"Sssweet angel, ssslave to Jehovah," the Indian woman began, "even you cannot ssstop the dark retribution, not even you."

Before Ariel could react, thick roots burst from the ground under her feet and encased themselves around her legs to her waist, trapping her in place. She grimaced as they tightened, close to crushing her where she stood.

"You are not Tameka!" she exclaimed, realizing that the wife of Black Jackal had been possessed by another entity, a hostile one.

"Tameka isss gone and I remain...the Ssstained ssshall not fail, no, he ssshall be victoriousss."

"Who are you?' Ariel questioned through clenched teeth.

"The virgin mussst die, and Ba'al ssshall reign. I am hisss ssser-vant, insssuring a holocaussst of which man nor god will ever wit-nesss again."

"Your name, dark one!" Ariel insisted.

"Would you not like to know." the inhuman voice spat at her, before stepping past her, and continuing along the trail after the Indian and the priest. She turned at a point about twenty yards away, and pointed an ominous finger towards Ariel and her predicament.

"Virgin isss not the only one who diesss thisss day." she said as the unforgiving wooden arms pressed harder into Ariel's com-pacted bones.

"Nasser..." she gasped in desperation as the fleeting ability to breath was leaving her, "Nasser..."

⇒⊰⊱⇐

Nasser rode along with Black Jackal without speaking. For a few moments he eluded the events of the day to speculate why God never spoke to anyone anymore as He had in the past, in the days of his birth, back in the old world. Men in that current reality lived without the luxury of His divine voice, and were forced to exist in a faith based environment. So many unbelievers and souls that were lost, drifting through their years unconscious to Him. He himself had the thrill of being in the presence of The Savior, who went on to fulfill His destiny as The Christ. His Hebrew brothers reject-ed that notion, to that very day, still waiting on their prophesied Messiah to appear. The world was left to its own devices, to accept or dismiss The Scriptures, available only in a thick bound edition known as The Holy Bible, that resided on dusty shelves. Selected lines were taken out of context and misunderstood. Followers seemed too lethargic to interpret the coded parables, instead tak-ing them word for word and missing the true meanings. There were even several chapters that had been omitted by the monks charged with the translations. A shame, he thought, but he had no control over that. A shame there was no more overlaying proof, in plain view for eyes to behold. The wonders of the world itself were not enough to convince or provide solace.

But then there was that Indian, sanctified with visions and messages from his Great Spirit. He wielded drops of The Lord's power in his own fingertips. How amazing for that mortal to be touched by God that way. But even then, the Indian's own tribe would not listen to him. He remained vigilant, that noble fighter.

The sky drew darker as they came closer to the spot where he had been led since that disturbing night so long ago. The longing for death was an unnatural desire, but to that priest, it meant that his children were safe. He would face the reaper with a contentment over him, his toils near their end.

Sapphira's nude body lay sprawled on the cold ground. A clearing in the midst of a lush forest would be the great finish to the vampire's plan, glorious to him in his great convergence, leading to a triumph over the tyrant Creator and His winged vassal servants. So arrogant and condescending they were, Bel thought as he worked. They would all know the brilliance of Ba'al, and grovel before the governor of the underworld and uncrowned overlord of all, the true minister of insurrection, Lucifer Himself. He imagined that the angel of perfect rebellion smiled upon him that night.

He took great care illustrating the Arabic symbols across Sapphira's body, from head to toe over her unspoiled flesh. The words and prophesy of Satan, soon to be the rightful ruler of all. Hebrew, Greek, and Egyptian hieroglyphs among markings of long dead languages forgotten but to the dark headmaster and His minions. He would be in high favor, opening the floodgates for the soldiers of Hell to emerge and spell doom to the old guard. The tired and boorish monotony of their stranglehold would soon be undone.

Every stroke of his hand, painting with the blood from a sacrificed goat, given to Ba'al earlier, was precise until little of Sapphira's skin remained to be seen. She was unaware and bound spread eagle to hammered stakes, in the center of an immense pentagram etched on the ground, highlighted by blazing fire pits on the five outer points. As Bel labored, he anticipated seeing his soulmate once again, conjured back to physical life by the grace of the supreme deceiving archfiend. Jezebel's lust for life and debauchery had no equal.

He was but a boy in the kingdom of Northern Isreal, ruled by King Ahab. His parents long gone from a venomous plague, he grew homeless in his nearby village until selected to work as a stablehand, feeding and caring for the royal horses. It was then, as a young man in his early twenties, that he met the once Phoenician princess who became queen. She would come to the stables by nightfall, where he also slept, and they would make love for hours, sometimes even until the dawn. She enlightened him in the ways of Ba'al, whom she had convinced her hapless husband to decree as the true god of the land. How could he have refused her anything? Her radiant eminence and unparalleled elegance could seduce any man to her bidding. Even a king, and what a fool Ahab was.

Bel knew he was not the only one, as an insatiable fury kindled in her loins demanding its own worship, from the king, his mightiest soldiers, dignitaries from foreign lands, and anyone she desired. But it was the young Bel whom she adored, and their romance brewed with a fervor. She introduced him to the Black Arts and witchcraft, and he would never forget the night of the bright orange harvest moon, when she appeared with another in the stable.

A dark skinned, long haired man of whom seemed about thirty years in age, yet the hellish yellow glint in his eyes suggested he was far beyond that number, far beyond mortal coil.

"This is Ab'ba." her words branded into his memory with the flaming iron of the Devil. He was the most handsome man he had ever stood before, the burning eyes, the jawline chiseled from immortal marble. His long robe was black satin, as dark as the infernal abyss, light and flowing around him, as if it too were alive and not just mere clothing.

"Ab'ba has traveled far, to join us, my love. To join us for all time as one."

Bel could not refute her, as no being could. He did not fully understand then what was about to transpire, and how his life was about to be altered forever, but the thirst for his beloved paramour could not be quenched. He would submit to anything, otherworldly or not. Ab'ba approached them both as they joined hands together. Jezebel squeezed his palm so hard it was painful, but Bel was soon to experience the real discomfort. Ab'ba was vampirus, and Jezebel had summoned him there to take them both that very night.

Ab'ba, the striking creature that made him what he was, sealing his fate and bonding him to Jezebel for then and ever more. He felt the pinching of sharp fangs sinking into his open neck as Ab'ba embraced him in his cloaked arms. A single minute in time that was like hours, even days, as he hung suspended in a euphoria. His free arm found its way around Ab'ba's back, never wishing to release him as waves of delight cascaded through his head.

Before he could comprehend, he was horizontal in the hay, staring at the wooden beams of the stable's ceiling, in a haze. He turned his head to observe Ab'ba repeating the act to Jezebel, sucking her life's essence and then allowing her to fall to the straw covered floor beside him.

"It is done." said Ab'ba, "Peace be with you both."

And with those simple phrases, he walked out of the stable and disappeared into the night. Bel never saw him again, the one who made him, remade him as a child of The Destroyer, ruler of the

Eighth of the Nine Circles. Ba'al, who the imprudent fools of the day considered no more than a mere Canaanite idol.

Jezebel rolled on top of his prone body and sank her new razor incisors into him, startling him. He exposed his own and latched onto her perfect throat, and they lay there feeding from each other in a state of blissful depravity that humans would never know.

In the days after her death, Bel wandered, vowing to find a way to avenge the four hundred and fifty murdered prophets, and to rejoin his lover. To see Elijah humbled and defeated. He would curse the name of Yahweh's faithful instrument for years after witnessing the coward's evasion by vanishing into the whirlwind. Consumed with a desire for revenge, he discovered a course of action that would not only accomplish that, but bring down the hierarchy of Heaven itself. As he finished the last inscription on Sapphira's nakedness, he felt a peace come over him, knowing that all would be resolved.

Bel looked skyward to see the flying blackbird approaching from the west. It carried in its claws a child's doll, and upon lighting on the ground before Bel, just beyond the outer edge of the ritual site, the bird and its toy were transformed back into their human forms of Wilson and Penninah.

"Very good." complimented Bel, "You are learning so much. As for her, behind me. Keep her there in the case of difficulty, if I require her."

Wilson nodded and again lifted Penninah's body, that time only a few yards, to place her at the foot of a large shrubbery bush, near the outer rim of the clearing.

"Gettin' dark." Wilson stated the obvious.

"As intended." Bel replied, "Be ready. The time grows nigh."

Wilson sat close to Penninah and his fingers made a light pass across her cheek. The acolyte frowned, knowing his new flesh was not the same as it was, and there were aspects of life that he would be forced to leave in his past. But he could dream. He noticed that

Bel had fallen into somewhat of a weird trance, rocking back and forth on his knees and chanting odd gibberish as he did so. So it had begun, and he had a front row seat to it all. Glancing back down to the girl's sweet face, he thought that if she were his, he would never relent to keep her from harm. The priest would not either, and Wilson, in all honesty, did not blame him.

CHAPTER 19

The wind picked up, in swirling gusts, like a Kansas twister setting in. Wilson noticed that figures now sat by each fire pot, dark freakish hellions that resembled shadows or specters more than bodies. They brooded there, also waiting, for the event to begin. A little scarier than before, he thought, a little more serious. Then he heard the high pitched scream from deep within Sapphira's lungs. Her eyes were stretched open like china white saucers, and the shrieks were unsettling as fear enveloped her. He could not help her, nor did he consider it. He knew his place in that order, and helpless Sapphira was discovering hers.

She howled in fright, seeing Bel beside her, his eyes vacant and his incantations summoning all manner of spiteful irreverence. The cold bursts of the gale force streams washed over her nudity; she was bound and imprisoned there in that unholiest of positions, and her mind overloaded in misery. For the first time she realized what a fool she had been, and her end was near. A natural impulse to yell out for her father was suppressed by the realization of her betrayal of him, that then not even her loving father would save her, nor did she deserve saving. She had, in the literal and figurative senses, dug her own grave. Her greed, disobedience, and disloyalty had sealed her fate. There was no time to repent, and God would send her to Hell to burn for her selfishness.

She continued to scream until her vocal chords failed her at the end of each extended outburst. Alone, naked, damned. Exposed before all. The whipping winds brought with them grains of sand that stung in her burning eye sockets. Her brain jumped in disarray. The worsening weather and her loud cries awoke Penninah who was taken aback at the entire grotesque scene. She crawled towards the pentagram's center but not farther than Wilson would allow, keeping the mute girl within his reach. At that moment, both of the priest's daughters watched as Bel, still rambling in an incoherent frenzy, raised a hand held shining blade above his head, the steel reflecting the full moon's brilliance.

Sapphira's eyes locked onto Penninah's, and in a last act of humbling confession, shouted with all her remaining strength, "Penninah! I'm sorry! I'm *so sorry!*"

Penninah's eyes flooded and she reached out to her sister, then fell to the earth, digging her forehead into the soil, not desiring to witness what would come next. Her hair danced in the wind as she lay there, wishing all of it was a nightmare that they would awake from, and be back in father's arms, safe in their small village outside of Jerusalem. Face down she remained, her hope collapsed as her body had, sobbing.

The sharpened arrow made a whistling sound, splitting the blowing squall before landing in its intended target, right between the vampire's glazed over white eyes. The protrusion from his head brought him from his hypnotic state like a bullet, and his eyes burned from pale to a smoldering red. That goddamned Indian, he realized, was the only being to shake his resolve after all that time, and had found him once again. He tried to rise, but disoriented he fell backwards with a thump on the ground.

"Kill them!" he wailed, "Destroy them as would The Destroyer himself! They must perish and wither!"

The wraiths spread their black wings and took flight to attack Black Jackal and the priest, who had emerged from beyond an orchard of oaks, several hundred yards away. The devils flew like flailing kites in a thunderstorm, the five of them of one mind. Bel lay on his back with a closed fist around the arrow, working it loose as he continued to curse aloud.

Wilson sat in a patient funk, watching the carnage unfold and awaiting instruction.

"Well, ain't this some shit." he mused under his breath.

The spirits swirled around the heroes, slashing with filed claws, knocking them into the dirt. Nasser fought with a furious intention, beating them away with a tall wooden walking stick he had brought with him. It injured them with its contact, as the first two slammed into the ground and rolled to a halt. It was the secret weapon Ariel had made him take from an ancient shrine in Mesopotamia, the staff of Moses, the one that parted the Red Sea in the great Exodus. Its touch routed the unsuspecting beasts into defeat, trouncing them to the earth or into the wide trunks of the trees. The shrill whining stung his ears, but was well worth it to vanquish those loathsome things. Black Jackal stood aside and watched in astonishment as the priest took them down with his enchanted weapon.

He held it out, pointed at the center of the circle, towards Bel, and shouted, "I am coming for *you*!

The rain poured then, and turned into driving hail as the priest took the first steps to the downed vampire. Black Jackal was by his side, still impressed with the display of ferocity. It would be a great victory, the Indian thought, the greatest victory. The victory of a lifetime.

Bel pulled the lance from his pierced skull and tossed it aside. He raised his hands once more, and a yellowish fog rose from the ground around the pentagram. The priest ran but the wall of smoke solidified, and encompassed the vampire and Sapphira in a protective, impenetrable shield. He struck the surface of the barricade with the staff, the only fortification between he and his daughter, who had passed out from all the tumultuous hysteria.

"Sapphira!" he yelled to the wind as he continued the assault.

"We cannot pass!" Black Jackal shouted as well, for the raging monsoon around them had reached a pinnacle.

The priest then saw Penninah, and bolted around the enclosure to find Wilson waiting on him. He did not relent in his sprint, soaked to the bone he struck Wilson in the head with the staff, sending him into a tree with the force of a Roman battering ram.

"*Get up!*" the priest commanded of him, the rain spilling from his face, making him appear as a deranged madman.

Wilson, from the ground, choked out the words, "Kill me, padre. I am...an immoral slight on humanity..."

Black Jackal secured Penninah in his arms and carried her to whatever shelter he could find from the onslaught of the storm.

"What has he done to you?" the priest questioned Wilson, his stick at the ready.

"I don't know the extent of it, and I don't think I want to."

"Can you enter the sphere he has placed around himself?"

"No. Sorry. You're on your own. Good luck."

The priest stood in disbelief, even after all he had been through, as Wilson turned into a blackbird and took flight away from him. He stared, the water washing over him. To his left he saw Bel through the wall, raising his knife on high a second time, over the painted body of his captured daughter. The rush of sinking inadequacy matched the gale force of the storm. It had come to that moment, those seconds frozen in time, knowing that he was powerless, and had failed. He clutched the staff as tight as he could until his knuckles were strained and colorless. He fell to one knee and bowed his chin in reverence, for the mercy of Heaven was all that remained.

Bel turned to see the priest and granted himself a bit of arrogance, intending to drive home the fact that he had won.

"Your God's assistance in your futile effort are as sands in an hourglass! Jehovah himself will kneel to the Council of Hell and those who rightfully rule the earth! It is finished!

The priest did not look, just continued to pour out his longing to the ears of God, praying for some intervention before all was lost. When it came, it was as glorious as any miracle had ever been. The rains ceased in an instant and the winds were no more. Bel did not move from his crouched stance, confused, and then stammered in shocked bewilderment, "No...its not possible."

The behemoth of a man approached Bel from the far side of his magical rounded vault, walking right through its defense as if it were not there at all. The priest marveled at the magnificent twenty five foot wingspan and its feathered splendor upon his back. The long blonde locks fell about his shoulders like that of a Norse legend. It was the first time the priest saw the vampire tremble.

The flying devils they had fought scattered into the night sky at the sight of him.

"Do you know who I am, Belkuthe?" the angel asked.

Bel struggled to locate his own voice to answer.

"Yes."

"Then you must know that The Almighty would never allow a second war until the prophesied time. If Ba'al sought The Master's attention, he has it. To think of one such as he having dominion over the world."

Bel cursed aloud in crazed distemper, "Damn you! And damn Jehovah God! Ba'al will see Heaven's palaces in flames and..."

"*Enough.*" the angel said, "There is hope for you. Repent, evil one, that this disease afflicting you may be lifted and your humanity restored. I will not offer twice."

Bel dropped the blade to his right and slumped his shoulders.

Shivering, he appeared undone. The angel presented a hand to help him to his feet. The vampire raised his head, saw that gesture and for a brief moment, the young orphan boy working in the king's stables considered it. But then his eyes burned with perpetual hatred.

"Tell God..." he began before his last grand act of defiance, "Tell God that The Stained said to suckle the cock of Lucifer like the teet of Mary Magdalene! And to enjoy his last hour on the throne!"

With that, Bel fell over Sapphira's prone torso. In the same flash of blue blinding light that had haunted Nasser's mind for all those years, they vanished without a trace.

"No!" the priest exclaimed. The force keeping him out was gone as well, and he ran towards the center of the pentagram, throwing himself onto the dirt where Sapphira had just been tied.

"No, no! Where are they?"

The priest looked up at the grand stature of the angel standing tall before him, and asked, "Where?"

"Into the future. To...try again."

"How *far* into the future?" the priest shouted back at him.

"2017," was the answer, "in a city called Turner's Island, by the opposite ocean, on the other side of this continent.

"That is...that is..." the priest calculated.

"One hundred and twenty eight of your calendar years." the angel replied.

The priest rolled over and lay on his side on the ground, in the center of Bel's pentagram, at the angel's feet. Black Jackal's loyal hand touched him and helped him up. He took Penninah in his arms and held her tight as he began to cry.

"I do not know how much more of this I can take." he said to the angel.

"I am Michael. And this is God's gift to you this night, Rabbi Nasser Absalom."

He reached over and touched Penninah on the shoulder, then turned away and walked the way he came. With tears flowing on the priest's face, Penninah looked at him and spoke.

"I love you, father." she said and held him as tight as her hands and arms could hold him. Black Jackal was moved to kneel and thank Great Spirit for the blessing. The priest stared into his little girl's watering eyes through his own, speckling kisses all over her face.

"I love you, too, my child."

"Will we save Sapphira?" she asked.

"Yes." he answered, "Of course. If it takes all eternity, we will save sister."

The rustling of leaves from the forest made them turn, to see Tameka running towards them. The Indian smiled and arose to welcome her, but she ran past him as if he were not there. She took Penninah by the chin, produced a dagger and slit her throat from ear to ear. The blood poured as the rain had, and spat at them as she laughed and hissed, "It *will* take all eternity, priessst!"

She stabbed at the girl again and again before their dumbfounded sight as she screamed, "Ba'aaaal!" until Black Jackal grabbed her by the wrist, whipping her around to face him. She gnashed her teeth, struggled and kicked against the Indian's stronghold.

"What have you done? Where is Tameka? Where is Ariel? *SPEAK!*"

"They are raped in Hell while their mouthsss are filled with demonsss excrement! Glory to Ba'al! Death to you all! Glory to Sssatan!"

Black Jackal twisted her neck to a loud, nauseating snap. Her body dropped as the Indian fell with her, holding her close and weeping.

The priest held Penninah's body as the blood continued to coat his arms, face, and clothes. His heart was breaking into more pieces than could be counted. He remembered the voice of Ariatta the witch, knowing then that she had followed him, and attacked in Tameka's body. As Black Jackal cried out in his native tongue, and Penninah hung lifeless in his grasp, the horror overtook him and he realized that he had lost them both again. He had lost everything.

CHAPTER 20

Winslow Wilson, in his blackbird form, flew from his perch atop a tree and sailed back towards Damascus. He had to leave that place. He would fly far away. Free from the commands of the power mad vampire who had left him for dead and then brought him back again. He did not feel grateful to him or that Ba'al character. Nor to the man in the good book who had 'died for his sins' as the story went. The story his mother had told him as his drunken and belligerent father put him out into the world at thirteen. He would make his way a wandering lost soul, and deal with whatever consequences waited at the end of his life, wherever and whenever that would be. But it wouldn't be in Damascus, that was for certain. He would see it burn. Then to Ehrenford. Perhaps the air by the bay in San Francisco would bring him a little peace. He made it a point to find out.

⇒╬⇐

The priest and Black Jackal buried their loved ones there at the edge of that clearing. The horses were long gone, and they walked in silence down the rocky terrain that led them there. The overwhelming grief had run its course by then, and the priest began to feel angry. They saw plumes of black smoke barreling skyward over the treetops.

"What is that?" asked the priest.

"That is Damascus." said Black Jackal, "It is burning."

The priest looked on but with little emotion left.

"Damn."

They came upon a young boy sitting on the ground crying.

"Priest." the boy said.

"Who are you?"

"I am Nicholaus. A friend of Ariel's."

"Where is she?"

"She is gone." The boy said, his features filled with sorrow.

"Where?"

"She was taken. Her earthly form was extinguished, and her spirit was taken so that she may not return to Heaven."

"Where?' the priest asked again.

"To...the circles." the boy nearly choked as he spoke.

"In Hell?"

Nicholaus broke down all over again, "Yes. And I cannot save her. We as divine beings cannot venture there. She is the captive servant of Ba'al."

Ba'al. The priest thought he would become insane if he heard mention of that infernal name another time. He was weary of it all. But he also knew that as far as he had come, he still had so much farther to go. Especially then, after that news of his Ariel. He let out a heavy, prolonged sigh, and he knew what he had to do.

"I am coming, my love. I will find a way."

CHAPTER 21

The farther the priest walked, the more bitter he became. The events of the previous evening were solidified into his core for however many centuries he was to trod upon the earth. He had not slept. After parting ways with the saddest Indian there would ever be, he surveyed the smoldering remains of Damascus, California, burned during the night. The last residents had scattered, and any horses left had disappeared as well. The closest sign of life would be in Lawson City, his destination, where he and Ariel had boarded McCreed's stagecoach in the first place. He carried whatever remnants of belongings he had, which amounted to the clothes on his back, some assorted knives and weapons, and the enchanted staff of Moses. His hunger and thirst were no match for the sorrow in his heart, for the loss of his daughters, the loss of his steadfast companion, the loss of everything. His resentment grew, and he stood at a theoretical crossroad. If the evidence of God's existence were not so apparent through his life, he would find it easy to let it all go to the wind.

Why, the question repeated itself on an endless loop...why him? Why was he the one to face those insurmountable odds, and experience that terrible grief? Not to mention the grief of others around him, unsuspecting souls who were sucked into his fight, stepping unawares into that unforgiving vacuum. People who paid the ultimate price and sacrificed, only to help him in his failed mission, that just continued to deepen and worsen. He understood then why Ariel had kept things from him, why she waited for opportune moments to reveal the dangers ahead. He may have gone back to Jerusalem and hung himself.

Looking at the sky that afternoon, the smoke still wafting from Damascus, he imagined that it may not be too late to bow out. But then, what would be the point after coming so far? There were faces to meet, and tribulations yet to endure. He was alone, with no money, and little resolve. A glass of whiskey would taste good, he mused, or ten. Fade into the background until he was ready to take that next bold step towards his destiny. Mandalay, Sheriff Bill, Black Jackal, Tameka...they all deserved better than the cards they were dealt. *He* deserved better as a faithful follower of God. There was a time ages ago that he would not have dared propose such a flippant thought. He remembered the trials of Lot in the scriptures, and called to mind how he always thought it to be a bit unfair. he was indeed living the story, and examined the irony of it all. Then again, had he not tasked himself? he was the unfortunate victim of the vampirus, and he was the one who set out on the adventure. What choice did he have? Was it right to blame God, or that arrogant archangel from the night before? It hurt his head to keep that line of questioning alive. What did it all matter? He was where he was, and there was more to do. He was quite sure that the budding sourness within him would ease once he had arrived somewhere other than that empty trail. The flying dust would begin to choke him at every breeze, and burn his eyes.

A grove of trees ahead offered the first sign of life. He approached to find Arthur Collins, sitting on the ground, crying, with his revolver in his right hand.

"Arthur." the priest sought his attention.

"Preacher...", Arthur began, his tears flowing, his face reddened with emotion, "She's gone, dead. She, she fell. Her neck was broken."

"Who?"

"Cathleen. My wife. She's gone, preacher. She's gone. My whole life is gone!"

"We have all lost much. Get up, Arthur. Come with me to Lawson City. I could use a good man."

"I ain't no good man, preacher. I ain't no use to anyone."

"What are you going to do?" the priest asked, seeing the gun, "kill yourself? That is a coward's way out, but I cannot fault you for considering it on a dark day like this one."

"I ain't nothin' but a coward." Collins continued, "Ever since the war. I ain't even a man."

"Arthur..."

"No, preacher. There's no helpin' me. Could you just...pray with me? Please?"

"Before you shoot yourself?"

"Yeah...before I...well, you know."

The priest stared at the desperate cowboy, glanced around for a moment, then delivered his hard answer.

"No."

"*No?*" Collins questioned in amazement, "What kind of a preacher are you?"

"One that is in need of a drink. Now, get up from there, Arthur Collins, and come with me to Lawson City."

Arthur sat in disbelief, then in a slow, uncertain manner, rose to his feet.

"By the way," the priest said, "You are buying the first round."

End

Nasser the priest will return in
'To Hate or Be Hated'

LOVE ME
TWO TIMES

Part One

PROLOGUE

I don't know which question I ask myself more- how all this happened, or why? Searching my mind, or what is left of it, is more and more maddening as the days go by. My hands still shake a little in the morning. I always sit by a certain window; over the years everyone just kind of knows it's my spot. I am only allowed to sit by the window for a few hours a day and I always count the minutes until the time comes again. There are always watchful eyes upon me, though. The men by the door are always watching. I was told their names some time ago, but it didn't matter to me, and that information was shit-canned somewhere back in the farthest reaches of my mind, if it was retained at all. I wish I could forget everything else as easily. A daily horror show replayed over and again before my helpless eyes, no matter how hard I clench them shut, it is still there. My window is the only place I find solitude and peace. I want to sit here forever, and never leave my precious beautiful window. The only place I am free.

Do I sound pathetic? Pitiful? I haven't even started yet. I am the most pathetic pitiful person on the face of the earth. My god has abandoned me and my eternal soul is damned to hell, if there is such a place. I am the definition of lost. It is way too late for me to fall on my face and beg forgiveness and mercy. There is none for me. Only my cold white room and my medication. And oh yes, my beloved window.

Sometimes in the dead of the night I will awake screaming, or at least attempting to scream. My lungs heaving, but no sound escapes my lips. My sheets are soaked in my own sweat and urine, as I lay whimpering in the darkness. I have cursed until my breath is gone; the tears flowing freely down my face and neck. I was someone once, a long time ago. But now I am a shameful wreck of a human being. Even that description is being kind, I am indeed no more than an animal now, waiting to die. I can't even do that. Plastic forks and spoons, no laces in my shoes. And always someone watches. The warm wetness soaks into my pajama bottoms and then turns cold against my skin. It is cold in here. It's always been cold in here, since the day I 'arrived'. The memories flood back again to haunt me once more, as they will every hour of my life until my last breath. And I pray that my next breath will indeed be my last one.

All they saw was me, standing there with the hot gun in my hand. They didn't ask any questions; they just wrapped me up. They said I was insane, and goddamnit, they were fucking right. I was much insane by that point. I didn't even try to tell them what had happened; I knew no one would ever believe such an incredible tale. I should have just put the pistol to my temple and pulled the trigger. Why didn't I do it? Why? I suppose because I was insane. I should have blown my brains right the fuck out. I didn't. And now, I am a solitary shell of what I once was. This place seems like a personal hell, but it's nothing compared to what awaits me when that terminal breath arrives. I'm ready to take my chances. Sometimes I run into the walls, slam myself against the hard plaster. I throw my body into the walls again and again until I've made so much noise, they burst into my room and I feel them swarm around me. Then the sharp pain of the needle, jammed into a thigh or buttock. Its contents mix with my blood and I fall lifeless to the floor. I want to die.

"Why did you have to do that to me?" I yell at the ceiling with all the volume I can muster, "Why?"

And every now and then, one of the white-clad attendants will turn and gaze back at me. I see his perplexed eyes, and he considers, just for a second, that perhaps I'm not talking to them at all, but to someone else, someone who has driven me to this madness. I lie weeping on the floor, where they often leave me, whispering "why" and muttering to myself as I drift away into unconsciousness.....

CHAPTER 1
VICTORIA

A lot of people will say of their wives or significant others, "I'll never forget the moment we met." For me, the moment I first noticed Victoria across that crowded auditorium will live eternally in my tortured mind. Initially, a trusted friend I had grown up with, there on a chance surprise visit from out of town, grabbed my arm and pointed in her direction. Since high school he had known me all too well, in short, he knew what I liked. This time though, he had struck upon the proverbial goldmine. She was the most astonishing beautiful enchantress my eyes had ever feasted upon, and my god, did they gorge themselves. A few short years earlier I would have shied away, but my confidence soared that night, it was like the gods themselves had come down, lifted me, and carried me over, resting me gently in front of her.

The moment we met, to risk sounding more than a little cliché, seemed to last an eternity. Her large brown eyes and mine began the first conversation before our mouths had any chance. Long, thick, full hair, black as midnight, pulled up and out of her face.

Her Face. A princess, a queen, a goddess, god herself. Her body was as full as her raven locks, a perfect plus-size model encased in a long black dress. Her tanned heels slid into shiny black clogs, I would later learn that every inch of her was tanned an intoxicating golden brown. She smiled as if she had been expecting me. Her first "hello", the softness of her voice, the feminity, was sweet thick icing on the rich chocolate cake of this dream come true. Amazed, I did not stutter as I introduced myself.

"I'm Victoria." Her delicate voice was really kicking my ass, the disbelief swelled in my throat but I swallowed it and kept talking. I was working at the time as the spotlight operator of a popular Roy Orbison tribute theater in Turner's Island. I had been told the owner of the show would be coming this weekend, and bringing her daughter.

Victoria. I had been told tales of lucky individuals who had found their soulmates in this cruel, ugly world. I had dismissed them as just that, simple tales, until this glorious, frozen moment in time. Her luscious eyes glowed back at me as brightly as mine must have been towards hers. Our bright auras made love to each other right there and then, unashamedly and free.

We spoke a little more, but about what I could not possibly remember. We made a date for the following evening. That night I lay awake, staring at the walls. I wanted her more than anything I had ever wanted before, in thirty-two years on this earth, never had I experienced this type of unbridled desire.

Being a freelance illustrator, (which is what I really did for a living, when I wasn't operating spotlights, or some other odd job to fill the spaces between artistic adventures) I sat up that night composing her portrait from memory, which she was greatly impressed with when I presented it to her the next evening. Score one for artists! I have drawn or painted what seems like hundreds of pictures of her since that night.

The next few days would never be equaled again during my stay on this planet. Drinking and dancing the Shag to a picturesque ocean backdrop, passionately kissing for hours in darkened parking lots beside her shiny red sports car. Laying on the beach under the big full moon, listening to the waves making love to the sandy shore, as we did the same just a few steps away, thrashing in urgent ardor on a large colorful quilt.

She left with her mother, satisfied that the show was in good hands, but soon returned to me. An oceanfront condo in the north end was to be the setting for our summer adventures, and believe me, there were many. It was mid-August when she dyed her hair a fiery red, and ignited yet another flame inside my very soul.

I could never let her go. We were together constantly, our hands always touching each other's bodies in some way or fashion. She would greet me at the door with long, wet French kisses, squeezing and pulling at my nipples through my shirts. This always led straight to the bedroom, or often immediately to the floor for intercourse as I'd never known. Some nights we would pull the mattress off of the bed and out onto the balcony, lying nude in each other's arms under the starry sky of the Atlantic coast. In the mornings we would juice fresh fruit and vegetables, and throw bread to the gulls. It was a magical time and I savored every precious second like I would a perfectly grilled ribeye. Victoria had completed me, and I knew I would never need another woman as long as she lived. I was as elated as I could possibly be without bursting into flames where I stood.

CHAPTER 2
MEMORIES

E ven with my eyes tightly closed, I could see the red glare finding its way through my eyelids. The torturous hot August sun slowly baked us as we lay beneath it. I chuckled to myself, comparing us to sweating rotisserie chickens behind a steamy glass wall. I turned my head to the left and I saw her. Her eyes closed, her head tilted slightly upwards, resting on a rolled towel beneath. Her tanned skin glistened and sparkled. Her deep red mane tied into a bun, she was a golden goddess in every sense of the word.

I was about to speak, but hesitated, to look at her another moment. It seemed a crime to disturb her, but I feared she may have fallen asleep, and did not want her to be sorry later that she had done so. Her voice ruffled the sea breeze drifting over us before I had a chance to.

"You're watching me again, aren't you?"

I laughed out loud, and replied, "I haven't decided which is more beautiful, you or the ocean."

"Well of course *me*, silly!" she blurted back, laughing and rolling over onto her side to easily slide her tongue into my mouth for a moment or two. The unmistakable sweet fragrance of Coppertone filled my nostrils as her fingers found their way to my waiting nipples as they always did when we kissed.

Then she slapped me, straight across the face. Getting up and giggling madly, she ran towards the water with me on her heels.

"What are you going to do about *that?*" she shrieked, her feet splashing in the water as she ran. I caught her and held her close to me as we kissed again.

"I'll never leave you..." she whispered, our mouths just apart. She was as in love with me as I was with her, and that alone produced a euphoric feeling that all was right in the world. Let corruption run rampant in our police departments and government, let everybody in the world argue and kill each other over who's religion is right.

This girl would never leave me. How cool was that? My Victoria would never leave me, and I couldn't think of one reason that day why I would ever want her to.

Victoria and I were married just before Christmas of that same year. It was a small wedding; just close family, and my best friend Ronnie. We both decided there was no other place in the world better than our condo on the beach, so for the honeymoon, we simply went home. My bride was silent on the drive across town, down the boulevard past all the beachwear shops, restaurants and touristy attractions. She gently held onto my arm and rested her head on my shoulder as I drove. I could feel her sighing happily. The true joy and elation I was carrying could not have been charted. We kissed and fondled furiously in the elevator. The fourth floor could not come quickly enough and we spilled out into the hallway, our lips still locked to each other's as if for dear life. I produced the key from my pocket and we melted inside and then into each other for weeks afterward. We tasted and drank from each other, bathed together; we were inseparable. We ate from each other's plates and played like children, there was no end to our lovemaking. In the mornings I would chase her with a camera, naked around the condo, snapping endless photos of her voluptuous tanned body, shrieking with laughter, her large breasts bouncing and jumping. I never tired of her, or her of me. The desire was always there when we awoke, the intensity grew with every minute we were in each other's constant presence.

We lived in a wonderful part of the United States where it was warm almost all year round, and one particularly warm night in January we had been drinking wine and our usual round of horseplay became more involved. We found ourselves nude in the elevator after a series of drunken dares. The excitement rose and our blood flowed faster as Victoria pushed the button marked 'ground floor' and we began our descent. It was amusing to watch her then become a little frightened, holding on to me with all her might, almost crushing my ribs. The elevator opened into the parking garage and exposed us both to an elderly woman who lived above us. She dropped both her bags and gasped with astonishment. Victoria bolted out of the elevator laughing hysterically and headed straight towards the beach. I smiled sheepishly to the woman who was still speechless, trying unsuccessfully to cover my own nakedness with the only things I had brought with me, my pack of Kamel Reds and a black lighter. As I followed Victoria, I turned to see the woman shaking her head and stepping into the vacant box. I found my love lying in the sand, looking up at the night sky.

"Did you see that old lady?" she giggled, knowing full well there was no way I could have possibly missed her.

"Give me a cigarette." were her next words as I collapsed on the damp sand next to her. We relaxed naked on the sand for a few minutes, calming down and smoking.

"I've never felt like this before," she admitted, turning her head to look at me, "You are everything to me, and I never want you and I to be apart, ever."

I agreed and pledged my undying adoration for her as I had done at the wedding. She threw her cigarette away and pulled me up and to her. I was penetrating her before I knew it; it had become so natural. I was fully into her, or so I thought, and held myself there for a few moments, reveling in the scene of the two of us making love on the beach without a stitch of clothes or even a towel.

Then I gazed into her mesmerizing brown eyes. She was staring blankly up at me, like she was in a trance, and it took me by surprise. I felt her vaginal muscles grip me and pull me even deeper into her.

"Ever." She repeated softly, and again, speaking in a whisper, "ever…..promise me, we will always be together."

"I promise." I whispered back, feeling the surf washing over our feet.

"I'll never leave you." She said once more, as she shuttered and dug her fingers into my biceps. Her thighs quivered as she orgasmed, and I immediately joined her in her release. We must have been a sight, like two wild dogs in the darkness, grinding and howling with reckless abandon.

The next morning, we climbed into the shower together as usual, both of us wincing now, cursing the previous evening's adventure on the beach. It seemed that the whole beach had come home with us, if you know what I mean. Our thighs and assorted orifices were sore and chafed, and we swore we would never do it on the beach again without a blanket, no matter how drunk we became.

The days and weeks that followed were full of laughter and intense love. We worshipped each other; our bed was our temple and shrine to each other. One night, after a marathon session that left us exhausted and almost breathless, we managed to light a pair of Kamels and just lay there, silent, until they were both burned to the filters. Crushing them out, Victoria came near, placing her head on my chest.

"I love you…." Her whisper trailed into a hush, but I detected a slight, yet strange difference in her otherwise carefree voice.

"What's wrong?" I replied, trying not to sound too pressuring. She took a deep breath and began to tell me of her past; of details until now I had no idea. I had wondered what became of her father, but never pried. She or her mother had never brought it up in conversation.

"I adored my father." She began, "He died when I was very young."

She paused and I said nothing. Listening intently to her testimony, I absorbed her sorrow. She held me tighter as I stroked her hair. The brightness of the streetlights filtered through the bedroom window, and I could see her jet-black roots pushing out of her scalp. They were quite a contrast to the scarlet, and I decided right then that I really preferred her hair black. There have been moments like this, I remember her telling me some pertinent information, perhaps in a restaurant or some other public place, my mind wandering off into the color of her lips, or a stray hair hanging just left of an eye. Or her slightly upturned nose, giving her a snobbish, yet elegant look, even childlike at times. She was such a fairy-tale beauty, and I could not help but to be overwhelmed. I would silently scold myself and quickly return to what she was saying.

"He left the business to my mother, who overnight became a millionaire real estate broker. He was the one who did all the work and built it up, but she acts like...", her voice trailed once more, a hint of resentment showing its ugly head.

"She acts like..." I repeated, now seriously curious.

"She wouldn't even speak his name, like he never existed," she blurted out, "after my father died, she became a different person. She was so cruel and uncaring. She didn't have time for me or my brother."

A brother. I suddenly realized we had had such a wild romance that I overlooked such small details. I whispered to her, "Go on."

Her hands began to tremble as I heard her voice again.

"Danny became just like her..I couldn't even turn to him, I had no one."

Her fingers found the place they now called home, upon my chest and nipple. She slowly manipulated as every word revealed more to me. I felt a cold tear drop find its way to my abdomen. Her breathing became heavier.

"I rebelled in any way I could, I would run away. I would break things. I was only a child. I couldn't handle it…I was such a burden to her that she began to ignore me completely."

"Baby.." I muttered, holding her tighter. She was pinching my nipple now, and I felt that familiar twinge down below. I did my best to ignore it, she was far from finished, and I was hanging on every syllable. What she said next moved her to a full cry. The tears flowed down her face and onto me as it took everything she had to bring these miserable memories out into the light.

"She…couldn't be bothered…she made my brother punish me. He would beat me everyday. When he found out he could, and Mother didn't care, he beat me everyday."

She sobbed and pressed her face into my sternum.

"I was so scared…"she blubbered, almost incoherently then. I lifted her up to me and tried to wipe her face. Her cheeks were beet red and her lovely lips were contorted into an agonizing frown. I was horrified and appalled, imagining a terrified little girl on her way home from school each day. I wanted to kill this brother of hers. How long had she kept this bottled up inside?

"He would whip me…with a belt, everyday. Sometimes Mother would watch from her desk, emotionless, smoking her goddamned black clove cigarettes. I hated those fucking things."

She scrunched her nose just then, as if she could still smell them even then.

"When I was too loud, she made him drag me down into the basement, to finish me there. The whippings seemed to go on forever. Sometimes he would have this look on his face, his eyes glazed and shining, like he was possessed. I begged and screamed, but he didn't hear.

And I know Mother could hear me upstairs. I would run away, but they always brought me back, and then it would be worse. I was so afraid. One time he whipped me so long, that blood was running down the backs of my legs, and he only stopped because it was getting on him. He left me there on the basement floor, and I layed there for two days. I was thirteen."

I was speechless, and could only get out her name.

"Victoria…"

"I became like a zombie. I would come home and take my punishment," she continued, "Then one summer, on my fifteenth birthday, Danny took me down in the basement and made me wait there alone. He went upstairs and returned about ten minutes later, telling me he had a special surprise for me. I got worried when I heard footsteps coming down the steps, and panicked when I saw his three buddies from school, drunk. They had come to see him 'punish' his little sister. After all the abuse and hideous treatment I had endured, this was the most humiliating moment of my life. Even Mother would not have allowed this, but she was out and I had no chance of any reprieve. I was ordered to pull off my jeans and underwear, and bend over the back of an old loveseat that used to be upstairs until Mother redecorated one of those hundreds of times."

"The first crack of the belt came quickly and I gasped, a soundtrack of laughter now added to my daily routine. It hurt, as badly as always, I never got used to the pain, just the routine. That day was the worst though. He let them all have a thrill, giving them all turns turning my ass into hamburger meat. I cried until my vocal chords failed, dry-heaving silent shrieks, I was in hell.

When they finally stopped, I fell into a crumpled heap on the cold hardwood floor, and listened to them ascend back up the wooden steps, laughing and slapping each other on the back. I heard them talking outside, I listened to their cars starting, I listened to them leave. I heard the front door, and Danny come back into the house. I heard the basement door, and again the footsteps, descending now, and walking back over to me. I laid still, not moving a muscle, not acknowledging him in any way. I was shivering and sobbing, I heard a snap and then a zipper, and then my brother's voice ordering me gruffly to get up, and assume my position over the loveseat. When I didn't move, he yanked me by the arm, like a child, and placed me there himself. My knees buckled and I couldn't stand. I fell back to the floor. This infuriated him and he turned me over onto my back, facing him."

Victoria was just staring into space then, her voice became emotionless as she recanted the events of her sad, sickening fifteenth birthday party. I just lay there listening, in shocked disbelief, until she got it all out.

"I hadn't seen my brother's penis since we bathed together as children. It looked different then, was all I could think as my brain just kind of shut down. My mind was blank and empty. I saw his lips moving, but heard no sound. I saw the burning hate in his eyes, and the way his forehead lines scrunched together, tiny beads of sweat gathering there in the folds. He gritted his teeth and clenched his eyes shut as he was now just above me. I felt his stale beer breath on my face. I felt as though I was floating, in a coma. How did I get there? I remember thinking that I was dreaming, and it would all be over soon.

My brother tilted his head back and I saw his lips moving again, he looked as if he were in terrible pain. His sweat dripped off of his nose and forehead, splashing onto my cheeks and chin. I felt dizzy, in slow motion, like a bird who could not fly straight, I wobbled in the air. My head was really swimming then, I was totally disconnected to everything around me. I wondered why Danny hated me so much.

He suddenly rose, and I saw his penis again. It was red then, dripping red, and smaller than before, and then I didn't see him anymore. I stayed right there, staring up at all the nails and pipes running across the ceiling."

Victoria looked back at me, her tears had subsided and she looked more relieved than anything.

"I've never told anybody that." She said then, looking down. I was completely blown away, and honestly had no idea what to say or do next.

"Where is your brother now?" I stammered out, feeling stupid after I said it.

"I don't know," she said, "I never saw him again. After that I left, quit school and everything. Just left, and they couldn't find me. I just recently ran into Mother after all these years and attempted to reconcile, that's one of the reasons we were at the beach together. She has changed quite a bit."

"But you didn't talk about Danny?"

"Nope. I guess she knew that I didn't care, so she avoided it completely."

The memory of her lovely mother came back to me then. Dark tanned wrinkles, skin like leather. Smug. Rings on every finger. Gold shoes. My vision was interrupted when my Victoria came up close to my face and looked right into my eyes.

"You give me hope that there is more than just evil in the world. You make me feel alive, more alive than I've ever felt. I never want to lose you."

"You won't." I said, kissing her cheek. Then from her cheek to her lips, our mouths met again in a fierce embrace. She fell asleep in my arms and I lay there replaying everything I had just heard.

I was learning more about Victoria everyday.

I was awake. I had been asleep, but I did not know for how long. Everything was the same as before, it was still dark and the street light was still peeking into our window, illuminating just enough of the room for me to see my lovely wife, turned now on her side, away from me, slumbering peacefully. The thick white satin comforter had been kicked to the foot of the bed and the shadows of the blinds made perfect stripes across the soft full globes of her bottom. My palm instinctively went to them, and the memories of her horrific bedtime story came rushing back to me, I was dumbfounded that anyone could even imagine tearing the petals from such a stunning flower.

She did not awake, and I cautiously slid away and felt the plush carpet on my feet. In a moment I found myself on our balcony, the salty sea breeze filling my nostrils with its sweet addictive fragrance. It had made a prisoner of me the first time I smelled it, so many years ago, stepping onto the hot sand, tightly gripping the hand of my mother. The ocean seemed just as mighty and elegant now as it had then.

I was moved to walk. Creeping back into our bedroom to find my clothes, there she was. She had turned in the minutes I had been away, now on her back, her large breasts falling to her sides and her red hair painted in wild streaks across the pillows. The streams of light and shadows now fell upon her stomach and thighs.

I thought to myself that I could never tire of her. I clenched her right foot in my hand and bent down ever so gently to place a kiss on the tip of her big toe. I pulled on my jeans and was tying my shoes when her angelic voice whispered once again to me.

"Where are you going?" she mumbled, "Come back to bed."

I began to tell her I was bound for a short walk on the beach, but her consciousness had visited and left like the blink of an eye, and she did not hear me.

Stepping out of the elevator I saw no one. It was a few short blocks to civilization, and for some reason I decided to take the less scenic route of the sidewalk. I lit a Kamel and forged ahead, seeing an old man across the road, sitting on the front porch of his beach house. Our eyes met for an instant, and we were strangers again. He had giant palmettos planted around his property, and they were very full and green. I thought of Victoria. She loved the smaller seashore towns and villages as much as I did, and she had a special fascination for the huge palmettos with their leaves reaching the ground. We loved the tiny communities with their mom-and-pop grocery stores, with toys in every aisle, sand buckets and rubber alligators. They were becoming more and more of a rarity as the world kept buying up land and constructing high-rise condos. For an instant, I felt shamefully guilty, thinking of Victoria and I unabashedly living life to the fullest in our own condo, just a few blocks from there. I shook my head and decided it was best not to think of such things. I chuckled to myself and knew I was a hypocrite.

It was about that very moment that I saw the ominous sign for the first time. I stopped in my tracks and read,

> HEAVEN AND HELL
> Gentlemen's Lounge

I had not planned to go into a bar, but it was very late and I could not sleep after all. Something about the odd title pulled me to it, almost as if the door to the establishment was making its way towards me, instead of the other way around.

CHAPTER 3
HEAVEN AND HELL

I felt oddly compelled to reach out and take the large chromed handle and pull it towards me, and as I did so, I could hear the pounding, driving heavy metal music seeping from beyond the foyer. Slayer, I believe it was. It was soundproofed nicely, for just outside you could only hear the ocean waves and an occasional seagull's cry. Everything was red and black, and on the wall facing the door was a small window with a stunning Asian girl behind it. She glanced up at me, her face appeared as though it had been carved by a master sculptor, exotic and flawless. Her black hair was pulled back tight. I was about to speak when suddenly my eyes darted upwards, over the window, to a huge oil painting of Anton LeVey. It was eerie, and chilled me for a moment. It looked so real. He was staring straight down at me with that stern, unnerving face.

"Would you like to come in?" Her voice cut through the air and brought my attention back down to the window.

"Sure." I smiled, collecting myself. I paid the cover and she stamped my hand. She smiled back at me and said, " Have a good time."

I nodded and glanced back up at the portrait of LeVey. Creepy. I decided that I could definitely use a drink, and went through the door to my right. When I did, the music from the main room hit me head on like an out of control blue van running down Stephen King. The volume was piercing my eardrums, and caught me a bit off guard, as was everything about this place.

Oh, but the place.

It was the most incredible club I had ever set foot in. The deep red walls, the black trim, the mirrors, the chrome. The paintings, the statues. It was a hell of a lot to swallow. Every way I turned, images of the devil stared back at me. From paintings of Satan throughout history, to autographed photos of movie stars who had portrayed the devil in films. Chromed statues of demons and gargoyles everywhere. Someone had gone to great lengths and expense to put together this breathtaking collection….and then I saw the dancers.

I was floored. The girls onstage were completely nude, with small horns attached to their foreheads as if they were demons themselves. Their bodies were being splashed with different colored lights from above, and looking up I saw small black cauldron buckets, with real flames spouting and jumping from them. I was dumbfounded and in disbelief that this club even existed and I had never even heard of it.

It seemed to me that a nightclub such as this, seemingly glorifying Lucifer and his minions, dripping with evil overtones would have been the target of a dozen local busy-body church organizations by now, seeking to close them down. I had never seen an ad, or heard a word on any radio station. I wondered how long they had been in business.

A hand on my shoulder startled the bejeesus out of me and I felt as though I had jumped right out of my skin.

"Oh, I'm sorry." I heard as I realized it was the waitress. She was beautiful. Her long red hair was pulled up in front by two black berets shaped like bats. Cute.

"No, it's alright," I stammered back, "I had just gotten lost in this amazing place."

She had a huge smile that seemed to take up most of her face.

"It's awesome, isn't it?" she said, her voice raised a bit so I could hear her over the music, which was maddeningly loud.

"Can I get you something?"

I ordered a Captain and Coke, and she pointed to an empty table across the room. As she headed towards the bar, my eyes followed her bouncy behind that had a red thong pulled through the middle. She was adorable.

I made my way through the room, packed with male and female patrons, all seemingly having a wonderful time. I sat and watched a 'demoness' on stage moving methodically to a grinding Danzig song that I remembered from a cassette I used to have some years ago. Watching her move, my thoughts once again ran back to Victoria, sleeping in bed, back at the condo. I recalled how she had danced for me just the evening before, nude in our living room.

I wondered how she would look with horns.

That image was shattered by the returning red-haired waitress with the red thong, bringing me my Captain and Coke. Her smile seemed angelic against the sinister décor. I pondered the name, and wondered why this museum of darkness had not been titled simply 'Hell'. I suppose some would find it even more unsettling, but in truth it was no less than magnificent.

As the last chords of 'She Rides' faded into the first notes of the next louder-than-shit song, the girl moved from the stage into the chair next to me in what seemed one swift floating motion. I noticed first her eyeliner, slithering up to her temples.

"Goddamn it's hot." Was her greeting to me, "But I like it like that." She smiled and then closed her eyes for a moment, as if she were reflecting on the night's work. She got up again, wrapping her glistening body in a bright red satin robe that had small silver dragons embroidered on it. Then she sat again and turned her attention towards me.

"What are you smoking?" she inquired, a pleasantly deceitful way to ask for a cigarette.

"Kamel Reds." I answered immediately, almost proudly, and offered her the pack. It was uncanny how every move she made was so graceful and effortless.

"Thank you." She mouthed back to me. Obviously she had been in need of one for quite awhile tonight. I lit hers and then mine, and before speaking again, we both savored the first drag and exhaled into the air. She closed her eyes as the smoke, blue at that point from a colored beam overhead, left her lips as if in slow-motion. When her eyelids retracted, her pupils were focused on me.

"I'm Magdalene." She said. Odd dancer name. I don't know, I was just expecting 'Star' or 'Mercedes', or some other tired stage name.

She read my surprise before I could answer and said, "I know what you're thinking, but the owner thought it would be cool to give all the girls names from the Bible. I was lucky to get hired early, so I got a good one."

I agreed with the owner, whom I was then convinced was a brilliant man, that it was a very nice touch.

I was enjoying it. Taking all of it in, my mind wandered back to youthful 'tittie-bar' excursions, the coldness of most dancers who would immediately accost you with the standard "Would you like a dance?"

I always thought these girls could make a lot more money in the long run if they warmed up instead of treating you like some ignorant pig waiting to hand over all your cash. They always sounded like broken records, shamelessly going from table to table,

"Would you like a dance?"

"Would you like a dance?"

"Would you like a dance?"

When they did score a table dance, the ultimate insult was when they'd look around the room, stare at themselves in the mirrors, or even make light conversation with another passing dancer. What a slap in the face to the customer that just spent ten or fifteen dollars on this rude bitch. I suppose some guys don't care, but to me it was unfulfilling, a real letdown. That's most of the reason I quit going to the damned places.

But right then I was comfortable. Lounging at my table, smoking a cigarette with Magdalene. She had yet to even hint at soliciting a dance, she was just hanging out. And it was refreshing, I felt totally at ease. I was even getting used to the insane volume of the DJ.

"So, tourist or local?" Magdalene asked, crushing out her cigarette.

"Oh, I live here." I answered, wanting there to be no doubt. Being called a tourist was, around there, what Bugs Bunny occasionally referred to as 'fightin' woids'.

A small part of me was offended that she even had to ask.

"My wife and I have a condo just a few blocks away."

She seemed unaffected by the knowledge that I was married, or didn't care.

"Where are you from?" I quizzed her back.

"San Francisco." She said.

"You're a long way from home."

"Yeah, I miss it, but I love to travel. I love to see new places."

"So," she said, "your wife doesn't mind you going to strip clubs?"

Her change of subject took me by surprise. She did care.

"No," I assured her, "I hardly ever do anyway. I just couldn't sleep tonight, and had never been in here before."

She smiled and I heard a suppressed chortle.

"What?" I asked. She continued to giggle and I repeated, "*What?*"

"Couldn't sleep? What do you think this *is*, silly?"

I saw no meaning in her words, and wondered what she thought was so funny, until my head suddenly became heavy, and the room started spinning. I looked around in disbelief as the walls started breathing, like I was on some sort of crazed acid trip. It wasn't stopping, and now I was getting scared. My first thought was that somebody had put something in my drink.

"What's going on?" I had trouble speaking but managed to force the words out. Magdalene was laughing at me, and suddenly started gasping and bleeding from the mouth. I was dizzy, and nauseous, and tried to stand but fell to my knees instantly. What in the hell was happening to me?

The people all around us were laughing and talking as if nothing unusual was going on. I was frozen, horrified as Magdalene was choking now, reaching for her throat as the blood continued to flow, pouring now, spilling over her bare breasts. My head felt like a cement block, being forced to rest on the tabletop when I could no longer lift it. I couldn't tear my eyes away from Magdalene, as her mouth was opening wider and wider, becoming disfigured. Then something came protruding out of the now gaping hole in her face. Her eyes were clenched shut, her arms waving as the thing inched its way out. All I could hear now was the thundering music, returning to plague me but louder than before. Why couldn't the people around us see?

Terrified I watched as the protrusion now began to resemble a baby's head. I screamed in fear when I realized it was, a helpless witness to the bloody fetus pushing its way out of the stretched, destroyed dancer's head. With a splash it popped out onto the table as blood ran off the sides like rain off of an awning. I was still screaming as I dragged my head away with both hands and again tried to make it to my feet. I took a step, and then another, and really began to panic when my legs felt like they were made of concrete as well.

A man at the next table swiveled around and looked right at me. Finally someone had noticed! He was an older fellow, and I could have sworn I'd seen him somewhere before.

"You alright?" he asked, soft-spoken.

I stared back at him in wide-eyed amazement.

"You alright?" he asked again.

Stunned and breathless, I saw him reach out his hand and touch my shoulder. The torturous music stopped the second he did. I shook my head and realized I was outside, standing in the street, across from the old man's house with the palmettos.

"Ah watched you walk ovah, but then you jes' stopped." He said, "Ah watched you fo' a minute or two, but decided ah'd bettah do somethin' befo' you went an' got yo'self runned ovah."

I was shaking and still couldn't speak. I felt the cool ocean breeze once more, a burned out Kamel butt lodged between my fingers.

"You want me ta call somebody fo' you?" the old man's kind and soothing voice brought me back to earth.

"Um..no, I'll be O.K. I think. Just let me get home." I cautiously turned and took a step or two, then turned back.

"Thank you." I said to him.

"Oh, you welcome," he said, "Ah jes' didn't want ta see nobody get runned ovah, 'specially in fronta mah house." He laughed and waved as he returned to his porch.

Good God, I thought, as I continued down the sidewalk, my legs now moving freely. I pulled my smokes from my pocket and lit one with a sense of urgency unknown before. I kept glancing over my shoulder and finally made it to the parking garage. Stepping into the elevator, I wondered if I had gone mad. Momentarily fumbling with my keys, I stepped inside to see the place much like I had left it. I slipped off my shoes and in the bedroom found my Victoria, asleep on her side, clutching my pillow. I pulled off my jeans, slid in with her, and stared at the ceiling. I could feel my heart thumping now. It had been all along, but now in the silence, I could feel it beating out of my chest.

Victoria shifted, now up against me, she was like a living furnace, her body eminated so much heat. I turned to face her as well, and buried my face into her busoms. It was the only place in the world I wanted to be, the only place I felt safe.

CHAPTER 4
RUTH AND THE MARINA

I awoke the next morning amazed that I had had any sleep at all. The events of the night before were still very fresh in my mind, and I was still more than a little freaked out. Walking through the condo I sought out my wife, who was nowhere in sight. From the balcony I saw her, sitting in a lawn chair on the building's deck, reading a book. She had on her sunglasses and her big yellow floppy hat that she had found at the flea market for two dollars and was so proud of. I stood as a voyeur, drinking in her beauty, and suddenly the hideous vision I experienced, dreamed or whatever, was a million miles away. And no better place for it, as far as I was concerned.

I noticed an orange concoction left in the juicer and poured the last of it for myself. Victoria loved juicing apples with carrots, but this had a hint of something else, something sweeter. No doubt a spare strawberry or two she may have found in a refrigerator drawer. Not bad. My once ritual cup of morning black coffee had been replaced by this frothy health drink, (which was delicious, don't get me wrong.) and reserved for after the late night meal at the diner, with a cigarette of course. Coffee and cigarettes just always seemed to go together to me, like Sonny & Cher, or red beans & rice.

As I stood there pondering the relationship between Maxwell House and my Kamels, I spied a Post It note stuck to the fridge that read, 'You tossed and turned so much I couldn't stand it and went to the beach. But I forgive you.'

There were some little hearts, x's and o's and then it continued, 'That lady from the Italian place called and wants to see your portfolio after all. Good Luck! Love you, V.'

"Outstanding." I thought out loud, and headed to the shower.

Driving down Ocean Boulevard, I had all but dismissed what had transpired at the Heaven and Hell Gentlemen's Lounge as pure hallucination. Or much less tried to wrangle any kind of warped meaning out of it. It was still weird, but I made up my mind to put it behind me and concentrate on work.

I hadn't hit a lick (as my mother would say) since the wedding. They found some other shmuck with nothing but time on his hands to run the spotlight at the show, but the once grand spectacle it was fell to the wayside shortly after, when the guy playing Roy Orbison and the woman portraying Patsy Cline in the opening act fell in love and eloped without informing anyone. They just disappeared, and the entire production went down the toilet, spinning like a fresh turd on its way to watery oblivion. I suppose it would be tough to locate somebody on a moment's notice who looked and sang like the late great Roy Orbison.

My main source of income was painting murals, mostly in restaurants or children's rooms, and once in a while the occasional church baptistry or pool hall. I had gotten quite good at it, actually, and it provided a very comfortable living, when it was consistent. A dry-spell would send me straight to the nearest 'real' job available to make ends meet. (In that case, spotlight-operator) I have learned there is no greater motivation for lighting a fire under an unmotivated artist's ass than stuffing 8' x 3' sheets of styrofoam into a mechanical crusher for twelve hours at a time. Or maybe cleaning out junk from underneath eighty Tupperware-making machines every single night of the week. (I think you understand what I'm getting at.)

Generous wedding gifts had paid for the condo thus far, but it wouldn't last forever, and it was refreshing to get a lead on a new job. A few months back, before I had even met Victoria, I had received a call from an elegant Italian eatery called The Grotto, interested in having some scenes of Sicily done on walls around the dining area. Right up my alley, but then they unfortunately cancelled. I had dismissed the job as lost until that morning, and was on my way.

It was a little farther past the north end, in a small fishing village called Sebrings Port, I had passed it a couple of times, a little place safely nestled away from intruding tourists. There were no Burger Kings or Circle K's, or even hotels. Just a quaint place with a peaceful marina, its tiny downtown area seemingly nothing but used bookstores and antique treasuries.

I confidently walked into The Grotto with my black zip-up portfolio under my arm, filled with photos of past artsy projects. Roughly thirty minutes later, I walked out with a two thousand dollar mural job.

"Outstanding." I said to myself, as I had earlier upon hearing the news in the first place. I treated myself with a stroll down to the marina, and made my way out onto a long wooden dock. The wood was grayish-white, slightly warped and weatherworn, adding to the rustic feel of being in such a place. The sky was a perfect Carolina blue, with big fat puffy white clouds. The rich aroma of sea salt and fresh fish delighted my senses, and I couldn't begin to imagine living anywhere else but beside the ocean. Even if I did have to crush styrofoam for a living, it would be O.K., just as long as I could come down here everyday and revel in the majesty of the Atlantic. I decided I should have a boat down here one day. Me and my Victoria, sitting on the deck of our boat, sipping red rose' and watching the pelicans dive. Nice.

On that note, I turned and headed towards the car. On the way I stepped into a little shop with a sign, 'rare and used books'. I thought I would find something good and then get going to tell Victoria the news. There was still a few Stephen Kings I hadn't read yet and a very friendly woman named Ruth pointed me towards the horror section.

"In the back." She said smiling, "Let me know if you need any help now, young man." I smiled back and thanked her, and started towards the rear of the store. The outside was misleading in its size, the towers of paperbacks continued down an insanely long hallway around twists and turns that went into whole other rooms, marked 'mysteries' or 'westerns'.

I laughed inside thinking what if somebody were to write a book about a bunch of cowboys who were locked in a room together and one morning when they all got up, one of them had been murdered. It's up to Marshal Dillon to figure out 'whodunit'. What room would Ruth put that book in, mysteries or westerns? When I got to the last room after feeling like I'd walked a marathon, I decided my funny anecdote wasn't that funny after all, and began searching for Mr. King.

Victoria liked reading too, very much, but she had a thing about previously read books. She didn't want to read words that somebody else had already, as if the book was then dirty somehow, or wouldn't be as good. Everybody's got their quirks, I thought, as I scanned the shelves for my prize. I was reading the teaser on the back cover of *Gerald's Game* when something on the bottom shelf caught the corner of my eye. A thick black hardbound edition was mentally jerking my attention down to it. I paused for a moment, feeling awkward, then reached down and pulled the volume out. The gold letters embossed on the cover blew my shoes off.

HEAVEN AND HELL
By Anonymous

I stood staring, and almost put it back. I should have. But it was the old can't-turn-away-from-the-car-wreck mentality that stopped me. I read the title over and over, but came to realize it couldn't have anything to do with my odd blackout the night before. That was silly. I opened the book and read one simple phrase on the first page.

Welcome to Eternal Damnation

I flipped through the pages and they were all blank after the first, like a sketchbook.

"What in the world.." was my last rational thought before the book itself started screaming in my hands. A high-pitched banshee wail filled the room, and I imagined the entire building, as I took three stumbling steps backwards into a ceiling-high bookshelf, a sharp pain shot into my lower back. I flung the possessed book to the floor; it landed face down but continued its inhuman screeching. Paralyzed with fright, I clutched the shelves behind me for dear life and was a helpless captive audience as the goddamned thing started bleeding onto the hardwood floor of the bookstore. It gushed out like a faucet and seeped its way towards me, touching my shoes.

"Why is this happening to me?!" I yelled back at the book, rumbling and jumping now like a suffocating fish on the marina dock. My eyes must have looked like white tea saucers when I saw the book flip itself over, splattering blood across me and the rows of fiction. Crimson bubbles came up from its spine and then, once again, the protruding head.

I saw the infant's slimy skull pop free and the rest of its body followed, squirting out across the floor to my feet with a length of umbilical cord behind it, leading back to the open book, and its gurgling, gaping hole that must have led straight to Hades and the devil himself.

I felt like I was dead. I had to be. The dripping fetus slathered at my feet, gasping for its first breath and I stood there, shivering and silent.

The voice of Ruth split through that tension like a hot knife slicing through butter.

"Did you find everything you were looking for?"

I stood there, breathing heavy, unable to answer the sweet old shopkeeper.

"Oh, come on now, that book isn't *that* scary is it?" she said with a wry smile.

I tilted my head down to see *Gerald's Game* in my shaking hand.

"Oh, Christ." I shuttered.

There was no possessed book from Hell, no bloody baby writhing on the floor at my feet, no blood splattered across my jeans. I sucked in as much air as my lungs could hold, held it a moment, and let it all back out. I put the novel back on the shelf as Ruth asked,

"Are you alright?"

"I'm sorry…" I said, pushing past her and running out of the store. I ran across a street to my old blue Impala and jumped in, turned the key and sped away, screeching my tires as I fled the small oceanfront community of Sebrings Port.

"Maybe I won't have a boat here." I muttered as I hit the main road and was gone.

CHAPTER 5
BIG NEWS

Once I was on Highway 17 and started seeing the golf supply superstores and 24-hour pancake places I began to calm down a bit.

"My sweet Lord." I whispered to no one in particular, wiping the last tears from my reddened cheeks. I noticed my driving had been erratic as I swayed over the yellow lines for at least the seventh or eighth time. I pulled over in the parking lot of some jungle adventure putt-putt golf course and laid my forehead against the steering wheel. The horn sounded suddenly and startled me back up against the seat.

"Jesus!" I shouted, knowing if I hadn't peed myself it would be a full-blown miracle.

This got my heart doing aerobics again and I settled back and closed my eyes. Lighting a cigarette, I fumbled it in my fingers and almost dropped it trying to make my lips. A long, deep drag, and then another. God Almighty, where would I have been without my Kamels? Especially with my world turning upside down on a daily basis.

Was it real? Was it me? Was I going crazy? The questions deserved answers, but I had none. Was somebody trying to tell me something? No, it just couldn't be real. I had to see a doctor. Hell no, they'd think I'd taken that left to Albuquerque and put me away. This couldn't be happening to me.

I shook my head as if I could shake all the questions out like fleas. Crushing the cigarette in my overflowing ashtray, I restarted the engine. I wanted to go home.

Another mile or so and I was there, in the elevator on my way to the fourth floor. Victoria's red Stealth was in the parking garage so I knew she was up there. She could make me feel better, in a way that only she knows how. No one in my life has ever read and comforted me in the same way. Just seeing her would begin to turn my angst-filled afternoon around.

Opening the door, I was right. She was there, ready to hold me in her arms whether anything was wrong or not.

"Hi baby." She said before her tongue welcomed mine home. They had become very close friends. Her thumb and forefinger gripped my left nipple without fail, and again, the big scary world was a kindler, gentler place.

She still could tell something was different about me.

"What's the matter?" she asked.

"Oh, you wouldn't believe me if I told you. Don't worry, I'm O.K. now." I unsuccessfully tried to bypass her inquiry. She knew better of it.

"No, something's wrong. Tell me, honey. Come and sit on the couch."

I followed her to our couch, in the living room beside the sliding glass doors of the balcony. She had one of them slightly ajar, to feel the sea breeze we both treasured so. She sat next to me on her knees and wrapped her loving arms around my chest and neck.

"You didn't get the job?"

I smiled at her. Thirty minutes earlier I thought I would never smile again. But now I was smiling.

"You asshole!" she laughed and slapped me on the shoulder, "You had me going!"

"You want something to drink?" she jingled as she got up and walked towards the kitchen.

I watched her butt as she went. It was full and round and gorgeous in her black Capri pants. Not too big, but certainly not the ass of a skinny runway waif either. Just right.

She thought my feeling bad was an act to surprise her with the news of the mural. Maybe it was better this way, I decided not to tell her of the mysterious outing at the bookstore. Just leave it alone, I thought. She returned with a cold beer for me, opened it and put it in my hand.

"Well, I've got some news for you, too, sweet-*haht*," she said, mimicking Humphrey Bogart. She was so cute when she did that.

"What is it?"

"You ready?" She was approaching giddy, grinning from ear to ear.

She sat down next to me, again on her knees, facing me. She brushed her long red locks over her head, looked down, and then back at me.

"*What* already?" I asked, feeling comically impatient, but still enjoying the fanciful moment. She licked her bottom lip and then bit at it, looking down at the floor and then once again, up at me.

She was stalling, but didn't seem upset. Now I was getting concerned. Her hand touched my thigh and gently squeezed, then rubbed up and down. She parted her lips, began to speak, but closed them again. She pouted and then went straight to a full frown. Glancing up to the ceiling, she exhaled and brought her eyes back to mine. It was then I noticed she hadn't gotten herself a beer. She always got two beers from the fridge, without fail.

"Victoria…" I started, but she cut me off before I could I finish.

"I'm pregnant."

There was an awkward silent minute between us that felt like ten. A hush had fallen over the room, even the birds outside had gone quiet and the breeze stopped blowing.

She stared at me, awaiting a reaction, any reaction, but I just returned her stare. The images from Sebrings Port were creeping back into my brain, but they were more like photo stills now, in black and white. They wouldn't go away. I raised my hand to my mouth, and moved my fingers down across my chin. Tears welled up in Victoria's eyes and she fell into my arms; began to sob uncontrollably.

"Is it O.K.?" she asked, her head buried in my chest, "I wanted you..to be…"

"Happy." I whispered down to her, stroking her hair and holding her in a tight embrace. Her hands made fists into the sleeves of my shirt and she went on crying. I pulled her up to look at her again.

"It's O.K., baby. I'm happy." I assured her, wiping her tear-stained face, "I'm happy."

"Really?" she asked, sniffing hard at the air and trying to get herself back to normal.

"Really."

"I love you so much, baby."

"I love you too. Everything'll be alright."

"O.K." she said, "I need a tissue now."

I gave her my biggest smile and headed to the bedroom for her box of Kleenex.

Returning, she blew her nose and laughed at herself. We laughed together, kissed for a while. I went to get another beer, lingered in the fridge for a moment, and when I returned, she had just fallen asleep on the couch. I stood and looked at my wife, so peacefully napping, but wondered if everything would indeed be 'alright'. I tried my best to put the ghoulish, grisly scenes of the last two days behind me, and concentrate on the fact that I was going to be a father. I plopped down in the recliner across the room, drinking my beer and watching her sleep.

CHAPTER 6

MAD LUST

Since The Grotto didn't need me to start painting for another week until they closed for an inventory, the next few days were spent celebrating, laughing, and loving each other more passionately than ever before. We visited the OB/GYN and learned everything we needed to know about being pregnant. At night I put my ear to her belly and pretended I could hear something. It was a magical, wonderful time in our lives.

Aside from Victoria's past indulgences into alcohol and cigarettes, she was extremely educated on matters of staying healthy. She had her certification in massage therapy and was exploring the wonders (or claims) of Raiki. Sometimes it was strange, but nothing I couldn't live with. She started me on some kind of seaweed pill because she said there was too much yeast in my system. How she knew this I have no clue, but didn't mind. She would check the bottle every few days to see if I had been taking them, and let me hold it if she suspected I was skipping.

One morning she produced a book on seeing auras, and made me stand against the white wall in the kitchen. She squinted so hard she looked like a Chinese woman who had lost her glasses.

"It takes a lot of practice." She said.

"Well hurry up and see it so I can go to the bathroom!" I would answer, and she would be furious. But only for a moment, long enough to throw a roll of paper towels at me.

I loved her. I treasured every second I spent with my lovely Victoria; even the silly stuff was unforgettable.

She allowed herself a half glass of wine every night, either with or after dinner, when we cuddled and watched movies. These nights were my favorites. Or we'd just light some candles and talk, exploring each other's lives, past lovers, places we'd lived, anything and everything. She avoided the issue of her abusive brother, and never said another word of it. I supposed everything that could be said about that subject had been, so we left it alone. It was fine with me.

The mural went well and my new clients were very pleased. Nothing else moderately freaky had transpired in three weeks time and I was thankful for it. No Satanic newborns came rising out of any bowls of ravioli, or anywhere else. I became comfortable with it and found it hard to imagine it had ever happened at all. But in the back of my mind, hidden away like the horror section in Ruth's bookstore, I knew that it had. Whenever it came creeping up, I shuttered and squashed it back down, until it just stopped creeping and let me be.

The roar of my compressor and the faint yet annoying hissing of a small leak that I never saw about, were comforting sounds as I airbrushed away on the walls of The Grotto. It had been so long since I'd painted anything, it felt good to be working again; I'd always felt honored and privileged to be able to make money this way. And extremely lucky.

As it turned out, the D'Agastino family wanted images of all of Italy, not just Sicily as previously mentioned. I saw an opportunity to paint my Victoria, riding in a long gondola through the canals of Venice. She had on her big yellow hat, reading her book as if it were just another gondola ride. A light breeze picking up strands of her hair, that I made the original black, instead of the artificial red.

When I finished with this particular piece, I sat back in a booth, lit a cigarette and admired it. I thought of an old artist buddy of mine who had coined the phrase 'quickie whore-art'.

Compared to the old masters that I adored, Bouguereau in particular, my airbrushed creations resembled a preschooler's scribbling in a coloring book. Well, to me they did.

As ecstatic as my clients were, past all the looks of awe on their amazed faces as I threw these things together before their eyes, I knew inside that it was really crap. Quickie whore-art, selling your artist's soul for money. How I longed to be able to just paint what I wanted to paint, something nice, portraits of Victoria perhaps, in oils on professionally stretched canvasses.

One day.

I was pondering this issue in my head as I frequently did when I was working, when Momma D'Agastino appeared from the kitchen with a steaming plate of angel hair pasta, covered in their home-made sauce, with garlic bread on the side. It smelled so good; I could taste every herb through the air.

"You work so hard", she said with a thick accent, "making our place beautiful. Eat. Enjoy."

These were good people. I loved doing work for good people. I loved them more when she came back with the wine.

That night I surprised Victoria with a NY cheesecake from the nearby bakery. She loved rich desserts, and especially cheesecake. She loved a good steak, too, and I loved a woman who loved a good steak. I sat on the floor and massaged her feet with strawberry lotion while she ate cheesecake on the couch above. (She was the trained massage therapist, but it seemed *I* was always massaging *her.*)

"I have never been so content in my life." She said, letting a light moan escape. (I honestly didn't know if it was from me or the cheesecake, or both.)

"If anything ever happens to me, and I make it to Heaven," she continued, " I just don't know if any angel up there could rub my feet as good as you do."

I smiled, kissed her foot and kept doing my thing. She took another bite of cheesecake; closed her eyes and tilted her head back as she savored it.

"I don't think Jesus could rub my feet like you do."

Now that was a compliment, ladies and gentlemen.

"I don't know, sweetie," I said, " I think Jesus might surprise you."

She laughed.

I added, "And I don't think he's up there giving out foot rubs to everybody either."

"Well if he's not," she said, sucking her fingertips after her last bite, "I'll have to find a way to come back so you can keep rubbing my feet."

"Well, you just do that, baby. But I don't want you going anywhere just yet."

"Don't worry baby. I'm not goin' anywhere."

She curled her toes and blurted out, "O.K. That's enough! Time for bed!"

She grabbed my hand, literally dragged me through the condo, and we fell into bed together. She was like a wild woman, tearing our clothes off, and I noticed that look in her eyes again. She stripped my underwear off my legs in one fluid motion and plunged her mouth upon my chest, kissing and biting her way across it, and down my stomach. The pleasure/pain combination was different, and took me by surprise. When she sank her teeth into the tender flesh of my side, my torso rose off of the sheets and the hairs on my neck stood to attention.

She nibbled her way down to my 'candy' as she called it, and ferociously inhaled it, sucking until my erection met her approval. Mounting my hips, she rode it hard, slamming her bottom into my groin over and over, pinning my shoulders to the bed with her hands.

Her long thick hair hung in my face and she made low grunting noises with each thrust downward, reminding me of Monica Seles in a tough match at the U.S. Open.

She continued to impale herself relentlessly, grinding her teeth and now heaving in heavy breaths. Never this dominant or forceful before, she threw her head back and gasped for air.

"Come baby! Come now! Come NOW!" she yelled.

I could not have lasted any longer with or without her exclamation. We climaxed together; her fingernails scraped their way down my chest and dug in around my nipples.

"Oh, Jesus Christ!" she shouted at the ceiling, as she grinded. I watched her endure a powerful orgasm, and winced as her nails drew droplets of blood, as if she were trying to rip off chunks of my skin.

Then suddenly, she relaxed. Her head dropped, her fingers mercifully released, as she slumped over to one side. I slipped out of her as she rolled over to her side of the bed. We both lay there awhile, without saying anything.

"Baby...," I began, "you O.K.?"

Her eyes opened, but she appeared to be delirious. Before I could say anything else, she closed them again and seemed to be drifting off to sleep. I let her. The skin on my chest stung from her biting and clawing, and would be bruised the next day, I was sure, but I wasn't complaining too much. She never ceased to amaze me. I put my hand in hers and closed my eyes as well.

I decided I would bring cheesecake home more often.

CHAPTER 7
RONNIE

I awoke beside Victoria, who was still sleeping. If I lay very still, I could hear her faint, low snoring. Cute. In the bathroom I splashed cold water on my face and ran my wet fingers through my hair. Pulling on my favorite pair of blue plaid sleep pants, I stepped out onto the balcony for my morning smokey-treat. I always had my first cigarette of the day out on the balcony, but now I was having all of my cigarettes out on the balcony. Victoria had given them up since becoming pregnant, and I felt a little guilty that I could not. I was too far-gone. What I could do in the compromise is not smoke around her, though. I gave myself a little credit for being considerate.

My first step outside told me I needed more than just my favorite pair of sleep pants. It had finally gotten a little nippy on the old beach. I knew it was coming, sooner or later. Back to the bedroom for a t-shirt and socks, she was still sleeping. I didn't bother her and returned to my fourth floor perch over the ocean. We had a small white table out there then, and a couple of chairs. I sat down, lit a Kamel Red and noticed a great many seagulls just standing around on the wet sand, like they were having a dirty ol' sea bird convention. Suddenly they all started taking off in the same direction. An older couple down the beach had thought it would be nice to throw some bread to the birds that morning while taking their stroll. Had to be from out of town. They were then stars in their own version of an old Alfred Hitchcock movie, swarmed with hundreds of gulls and running for cover. You had to be careful; those dirty ol' seabirds around here took their breadcrumbs seriously.

When the elderly couple was out of sight, they all returned to their big pow-wow, to await the next exciting event of the day.

A long drag brought with it thoughts of my best friend Ronnie, who I realized I had not seen or even called since the wedding. He must have thought I'd dropped off the earth, or that I'd hated him or something. Ron could be very high strung from time to time and had a tendency to become emotional or flustered easily. We were very close, closer than I ever thought I would get to another man in my life. I could tell him anything, without fear of judgement or ridicule. It would be a good time to call my old friend, maybe he could help me sort out some of the nuttier things that had been going on as of late. I crushed out my cigarette and went inside to do just that.

When I came in the sliding door to the living room, Victoria was sitting there on the sofa, pouting.

"Well good morning, dear." I said, chuckling.

"I want a cigarette too." She whimpered pathetically.

"I know, baby, sorry." I said, sitting next to her and kissing her cheek.

She held the pout as long as she could before bursting out laughing. We kissed and shared a quiet moment together, lightly rubbing our cheeks, and basking in our love for each other.

"Good morning." She whispered, kissing my earlobe and neck.

"Was I...a little rough last night?" she asked.

I made her no answer, just pulled up my t-shirt to show her the damage. She gasped and began apologizing.

"No, no, it's fine." I said, "you got a little carried away, but it was the heat of the moment, sweetheart, don't worry about it."

"Are you sure?" she asked.

"I kind of liked it, actually," I admitted, "but not every night. You'd kill me." She laughed.

"What's on the agenda today?"

"Well, I thought about calling Ronnie."

Victoria had met Ronnie briefly at the wedding, but she knew what good friends we were.

"Better yet," she suggested, "you should go surprise him. I've got some running to do myself, so it'll be a good day for you guys to get together."

"Besides", she continued, "you've got to get sick of me some time."

"Not a chance. Shower with me."

She was happy to. An hour or so later I was cruising down Ocean Boulevard en route to Ronnie's house. I felt bad. I realized I had not told Victoria *everything* about Ronnie and I, after we had been so open and honest with each other. My guilty feelings were unwarranted, I thought; I had been through so much with Ronnie, it hadn't been intentional.

Ronnie lived in a small house behind the old Air Force base, which had been closed for some time now, and changed into neighborhood developments. I eased into the driveway, next to his old yellow Mustang. The rides I'd taken in that thing. I'd driven it many times as well, when poor Ron was too intoxicated to find the door handle.

Before I could knock, the door flung open and there he was, with the biggest smile I had ever seen on his face. The hug was long and fierce, and tears welled up in his eyes before he spoke.

"Where in the hell have you *been*?" he said sarcastically.

"Well, Ronnie, I..."

"Screwing that fat & sassy wife of yours night and day, day and night, I suppose."

We laughed and hugged again.

"Don't worry about poor Ronnie here by himself, he'll be alright." He continued, throwing his arms up in mock distain, "You want something to drink, handsome stranger?"

He headed into the kitchen to get my drink before I could answer. Didn't ask me what I wanted, he knew me too well.

I looked at the framed photos all around, mostly of Ronnie in drag, doing Marilyn or Cher in some pageant or another. He won most of them. Ronnie was the sexiest, most realistic drag queen I had ever seen; that's one of the things that attracted me to him in the first place, years ago.

Five now, I counted, since he made eyes at me in a Denny's on Kings Highway at four in the morning, sitting with six other 'girls', fresh out of the local gay bar, The Offshore Drilling Company. In this bustling resort city, it was commonplace for all sorts of interesting people to be out and about at all hours of the evening.

I guessed they were just screwing with me at first (This is how some ballsy, drunken drag queens occasionally get the living shit beaten out of them, when they screw with the wrong people.) but when Miss Veronica Valentine came over to sit with me, I was floored at how gorgeous she was. She said I was a cutie, and her friends had sent her over to see if I was gay.

I had always been impressed with these people, men who could transform themselves into women, and it was kind of magical when they could really pull it off. And then to go out in public, strutting their stuff for the whole world to see, that would take balls the size of battleship buoys.

She had on a spaghetti-strapped short black lacey cocktail dress, and a long curly auburn wig with a black bow tied in it. Silver-glittery eyes and the brightest cocksucker-red lips you ever saw.

I was lonely, I was bored, picking at a sausage and cheese omelette and hashbrowns at Denny's at four o'clock in the morning. I thought, what the hell? I can talk to this guy.

We talked for a while, and when his friends became agitated and ready to leave, he told them to go. We talked for another hour over coffee and Kamel Reds, and then I drove him home.

He was entertaining and funny and beautiful, but I got to see the person on the other side of that thick makeup when he began to show signs of sobering up at last.

I remember kissing him for hours on his couch, until the morning sun was on its way to becoming the afternoon sun.

I saw him every night after that, I started going to the clubs, watching him perform in contests that he rarely lost. He was good, a nice guy, and a nicer girl.

"Here you go." His voice called out as he reentered the room, "Captain and Coke for the long-lost artist."

"Thanks, Ron. You never forget."

"How could I?" He shot back. "You drank enough of them, I'd never forget."

He put the drink in my hand, with a napkin wrapped around the glass.

"You know," he continued, (Ronnie always did most of the talking) "That girl of yours, I finally decided who she reminds me of. It's 'Blair' on the Facts of Life, with black hair."

"It's red now." I answered, sipping my drink.

"Well goddamn, blow my observation all to hell! Blair with fucking *red* hair then."

I chuckled as he got frazzled.

"So tell me everything!" He said, sitting in a white wicker chair across from me.

"She's pregnant." I added.

"Oh Jesus Christ the Lord!" He exclaimed, "What else are you going to hit me with today?"

He looked so different out of character. For the first week and a half after we met, I only saw him as Veronica. It still seems strange to see this slightly skinny little boy sitting there with close to shoulder-length blonde hair. He was still pretty. High cheekbones, full lips, colorful on their own without enhancement, a pinkish-peach color and not a blemish anywhere. Ronnie really took good care of his skin.

"Ronnie, there's something bothering me, and I need you to listen to me. It's going to sound really nuts at first, but I'm not crazy."

He saw I was serious, and became silent and attentive, sipping from his glass of white wine on ice.

If the roles were reversed, and it was me listening to some crazy telling me about babies crawling out of womens' mouths, I would immediately deduce that the person had been smoking crack, and I'd start looking for a back door through which to beat a hasty escape. But Ronnie didn't. He sat patiently and listened as I spun tales of hallucinogenic horror that wasn't drug-induced. I told him of the terrible scene at the bookstore and how I probably looked like a fool running out of there the way I did. I told him of the panic I felt inside when my wife revealed that she was pregnant, and my speculation that maybe the insane visions might have been some dark forewarning of things to come.

I told him how I feared that something could possibly be wrong with the baby. I spoke uninterrupted for what seemed an eternity, just letting it all out, until I had admitted everything to my poor dear friend, who I figured by this time was pondering my sanity, or waiting for the Candid Camera guy to pop up from behind the couch.

Ronnie sipped his wine and glared at me, I suppose waiting for me to burst out laughing in robust guffaws, and let him in on the joke. When he realized that this wasn't going to happen, he spoke.

"Has she had an ultrasound done yet?" Calm.

His cool tone and concerned expression relieved me.

"Yeah. Everything was normal." I answered.

He looked away, lost in thought, like he had just been asked a really tough Trivial Pursuit question.

"I don't want to scare you anymore than you already are," he said, without looking back, "but I don't want to just tell you it's nothing, either. I think you have good reason to worry."

I just stared at him, waiting for him to say more; I knew there was more on its way.

"Something may be wrong with your baby, but it's not going to be a physical problem, that a doctor will be able to point out. It's deeper."

After a pause, he asked, "Are you sure that it's yours?"

"Of course," I said, "we've been inseparable."

He made a face, downed the last swallow in his glass, and placed it on the coffee table.

"I don't want to freak you out, but you have to be able to handle what I'm about to suggest to you."

"Please, go ahead." I said, "I need your opinion, I need someone else's input, no matter how bad it sounds."

Ronnie reached over to a cluttered end table and found his Tarot cards, pulling them out of a small black velvet bag. Without saying another word, he shuffled the deck and handed them to me. I cut them and placed them on the table. I knew to do this because Ron and I had done it a thousand times before, he had always been fascinated with black magic and the occult, and studied it extensively, which I guess is another reason I chose to confide in him, other than being my closest friend.

I had never made love with Ronnie, although he had endlessly tried to go beyond our simple petting. It was an odd time in my life, a time I don't regret, but was glad I had moved on, and that Ronnie had remained in my life anyway.

"Draw the top three." He instructed.

I slowly did as he requested, but the results did not ease my mind.

The Lovers.

The Devil.

Death.

"Well that's encouraging." I muttered under my breath.

Ronnie paused and said, "They are all major arcana, representing your past, present, and future. The Lovers represent you and Victoria meeting more than likely, your marriage and her pregnancy. The Devil tests this and injects temptation and strife into your happiness, The Devil can signify bondage or an addiction."

"And Death?"

"Death is an ending or a transformation. Your relationship has been tainted and will come to an end...from what the cards have revealed, and what you've told me...it doesn't look good."

"The secret lies inside of Victoria," he said finally, "I'm so sorry. Your suffering's only begun."

He sighed and we both just looked at each other, exasperated.

After an awkward few moments, I thanked him and moved to leave. Ronnie held me tight and kept telling me how sorry he was. He kissed my cheek and watched from the doorway as I started the old Impala's engine and backed out of the drive. As I sped down 17 all I could see was the three foreboding cards in my mind. The painted images burned their way into my memory. The passionate ecstasy in the eyes of the lovers, the sick cocksurity on the face of the devil, the cold steel of the reaper's blade. What could have been waiting in store for me and my precious Victoria?

⚔✦⚔

CHAPTER 8
DREAMS

I was sitting on a metal folding chair, the kind professional wrestlers use to bash each other's brains out. The room was completely white, like the house in that John Lennon video, but this one had no windows, doors, or even electrical outlets. Nothing but painted sheetrock. I felt a little lightheaded, but other than that, I was fine.

But I couldn't get up. I wasn't tied down, I just couldn't get up. My legs were paralyzed, even though I could still feel them. Why was I here?

Sobbing.

I turned my head to the right, and saw Victoria, she was nude and sitting Indian-style on the floor, terribly moved and the tears splashed her cheeks like a summer downpour. She was holding her stomach with both hands, and leaning over in obvious excruciating pain. I tried to call out to her, but I was mute as well, and had no voice, helpless. She groaned and let out a sharp, agonizing scream. She tried to call out to me, but could only mouth a word or two before gritting her teeth and snapping her head back against the wall.

I was then crying too, unable to move, forced to watch my wife endure this episode alone. I turned my head away, and before me were a man and woman, making love on the floor just ten feet from me and my chair/prison. The woman was writhing underneath him, trying to grip something, but there was only the hard ivory floor. Her knuckles were that color too, slender fingers trying their best to dig in somewhere, to no avail.

The man's skin and body was the immaculate form of a mythological Greek god, his ass rising and falling at a fevered pitch. She reached up and clawed at his broad shoulders. They were going at it like nobody's business, like two perfectly oiled machines, reminding me of my own sexual prowess years ago in college, in my youthful prime. Where had the years gone?

Suddenly I recognized the two lovers.

The Tarot deck.

It was the painting come to life in front of me. I was in awe of this revelation, until a stray disturbing thought ran through my mind. If the lovers could come to life...

I could not complete my own observation, when I looked up and saw the terrible form of Death, the ragged torn cloak, the sinister gnarled teeth were all the face I could make out under the shadowed black hood. The menacing sickle by his side. He stood above the oblivious couple, lost in their passion, as if he were waiting.... for....

The man quickened his thrusts, his pelvis moving at an almost blinding speed. The woman yelped, her breathing became wildly erratic. They were approaching their respective orgasms and I was screaming at them, but they couldn't hear me.

The reaper stood patient, unmoving, as they completed their lovemaking with a thunderous, draining climax. They never saw him, but I saw it all. His weapon fell like a blur, severing her head and sending it across the room like a bullet. Her blood sprayed across my face, warm and wet, I tasted her, sweet on my tongue.

I turned again to Victoria, but she lay silent and limp, her big brown eyes staring, but seeing nothing.

⭐

I sprang up in the bed shouting, my heart drumming faster than a Neil Peart android.

"Victoria!"

"Victoria!"

"Vic-"

"I'm in here." She answered from the bathroom.

I flew out from the covers and into the hall, to find her, bent over, puking into the toilet.

"I'm sick, praying to the porcelain god again, sorry." She said, before letting go with another turret of vomit into the toilet.

I was shaking.

"M...Morning sickness." I said.

"Yeah. I hate it!" was her reply.

"I had a dream, baby, a bad one, it's kinda freaked me out."

"Oh, I'm sorry baby, I...hold on..."

She coughed and spit, long strands of yellow drool cascading into the bowl.

"Hand me a..."

"Towel." I finished her sentence and handed it to her, and she wiped her face. She was pale, flushed red under her eyes.

"I'm sorry, baby." She said, holding me.

"It's O.K.," I said, "You gotta do that pregnant thing. I wish I could be more help."

"You've been awesome."

I hugged her there in the bathroom, squeezing her against me, trying to let the nightmare go. At least I had been in bed, and not out somewhere to make a fool of myself again. It felt so real, like I was *there.*

I sat on the couch and listened to Victoria's shower run. She was everything to me, my world. If Ronnie was right...I just didn't want to think about it. I knew some weird stuff was happening, but the baby, our baby...Ronnie had to be crazy. Ronnie *was* crazy.

I wished for Ronnie to be crazy.

Be crazy, Ronnie.

"Where's my cigarettes?"

CHAPTER 9
LABOR PAINS

The months went by and the chilling nightmares came and went, each one ending the same way, with my vibrant, loving wife wide-eyed and lifeless on the floor. I guess you can get used to anything, because I had to. I purposely had not contacted Ronnie again, and tried to make the best of things. I missed his companionship, and his sometimes-outlandish behavior, but I learned to live without it as I watched Victoria's belly grow outward with our child inside.

She was sick a lot and stopped taking massage appointments, sleeping quite a bit instead. It seems she had to make mad dashes for the bathroom a hundred times a day to pee about a thimble full. It was amusing to watch her curse with disgust each time.

I waited on her hand and foot, even though I didn't have to. I wanted to make her as comfortable as possible, I wanted to share every minute with her that I could during this memorable majestic time in our lives. To watch her literally waddle about the condo, and plop down on the sofa with a loud exhale, was in a way comical, but my heart went out to her every moment. Her bright shining eyes never lost that look of wonderment, that comforting look that said "I love you" each time their gaze crossed mine.

At night she would weep softly, confiding in me that she had had enough, and wished for it to be over.

I held her and in the most sincere reassuring whispers I would tell her, "Very soon…hang in there."

⇥⇤

I was painting a very long wall in an upper-scale pool hall downtown called "The Brass Rack". It was one of those interesting jobs, even though each one was interesting in its own way, I airbrushed famous players shooting at the tables; Minnesota Fats, Ray Mezzarak, Jackie Gleason and Paul Newman from "The Hustler". It took a few days to locate reference material on all the subjects, but it was coming together nicely and all preparation was worth it.

The owner was a large character named Vance (known affectionately to his clientele as "The Fat Man") who was ecstatically happy with the proceedings and took lots of pictures of me working.

Taking a break outside, it was warm and summer was beginning to creep upon us once more. A smoke, an ice-cold Pepsi, the sun on my face and Victoria on my mind seemed like a taste of Heaven. I closed my eyes and began to imagine a bigger picture. My heart had always been filled with romance, and I followed it wherever it would lead. But the demands of a cold society catch up with us all sooner or later, and I found myself thinking about health coverage and life insurance. It would be any day now, and I had to begin thinking about being a father, providing for a family and kids going to college. Maybe a real job would be in order, pushing my first love, art, to the side, to become a mere weekend hobby while I slaved in a depressing, demoralizing factory atmosphere. It's suited just right for some people, maybe for most, but having artists' blood in me, true artists' blood, it makes it so different, and so hard. Only others like myself could possibly understand. It's like we have a gift for the world, but sometimes the world just doesn't want it.

Unfortunately, some things in life are unavoidable, and no matter how deeply in love Victoria and I were, I knew that at some point there would be a change, when reality and money come together to play spoiler to true love's masterpiece. So many are driven apart by it, I only hoped that when it was time for us to face it, that we would face it together, with endless respect and support for each other.

I decided I was digging too deep into the philosophy grab bag and lit another Kamel. A skinny redheaded kid with baggy pants burst through the door, and told me to come quick.

I came through the door and it seemed that Vance had been right behind him, and we almost collided.

"Dude, the hospital just called. Your wife's there already! Go, man, go!"

He was yelling something else as I threw the Kamel butt and headed to the Impala. I assumed he was trying to tell me which hospital, but I already knew. I was sweating as I burned up a stretch of bypass 17 to the emergency room parking lot.

"No cops today, please." I muttered to myself as I pushed the pedal down.

The next few minutes were like a blur in time, I was in the elevator, but didn't remember parking my car. I followed the hallway signs to maternity, and found Victoria in a bed, with a hollow look on her face. When she saw me, she smiled.

"Hi, baby." Her sweet voice whispered out, sounding exasperated. She was pale and her hair was flat, dark circles under her eyes.

"You got here quick, I was…"

The pain of a contraction hit her in mid-sentence and she never finished it. She winced, gritted her teeth and let out a low groan. A nurse brushed by me and told me we were having a baby.

It all happened so fast, there were no twenty or so hours of hideously painful labor, it was time *now*. Another nurse, a tall black woman dragged me off into a room to scrub up and get into the funny green outfit, so I could attend the proceedings. My head was spinning and I felt faint. The nurse was telling me how the cab brought Victoria in barely an hour before, that I had made it just in time. I wouldn't have missed it for anything in the whole god-damned world.

Back in the room, the doctor was there and Victoria was huffing and puffing furiously, the first nurse trying to calm her down, saying something about her blood pressure.

Victoria looked at me several times and attempted smiles, but the agonizing situation wouldn't allow it. She was crying now, and I tried to dry her eyes with a damp cloth. I wiped her forehead and cheeks, and kept telling her how much I loved her.

I felt like I was high, the doctors and nurses clammering in what seemed some foreign language, Victoria shrieking and biting at the air. I breathed with her, doing my best to get a rhythm going, but she was taking it very hard.

The price God laid on woman for eating from the tree of life in the garden of Eden. Sometimes that sounded like such a crock of shit, and this was one of those times.

Victoria lifted up some and screamed at the nurses, first cursing them to Hell, and then begging for their help. To their credit, they shrugged it off and were very professional.

I felt so weak and helpless, everything we had done together for the last nine months was over, now it was all up to her, and I was reduced to a powerless bystander, with nothing to offer but a hand to hold and a damp cloth.

The doctor was barking out orders, telling her to push, and then not to push, then to push again. Victoria's eyes met mine, and she looked so sad.

"Please let it be over soon." Her soul cried out to mine without a sound, much like the night we met.

"I love you, I love you, I'll never leave you…" she mumbled over and over again, like she was now incoherent.

"Keep it together, baby. I'm here, It'll be over soon, hang in there."

Her head lashed from side to side, her hair was in her face and I kept brushing it aside, but it did little good.

"I see the head." The doctor called, and I froze.

Magdalene.

Heaven and Hell.

I shook the memory away, but a cold chill found its way through my limbs.

Heaven and Hell.

The bookstore.

Welcome to Eternal Damnation.

The Lovers.

The Devil.

Death.

No. I couldn't think about any of that. Forget it. It's all bullshit.

"O.K. Victoria, push for me one more time." I heard the doctor say.

"Doctor, there's a problem." said a very concerned nurse, staring at a beeping monitor.

The Lovers.

The Devil.

Dea...

"Push, Victoria!"

"Doctor!"

The doctor, looking up, ordered fifty cc's of something or other, as I began to panic.

Then I saw the baby. For a moment I was so relieved, a feeling of joy overtook me, a feeling like I'd never known.

"It's a girl."

In my daughter's first minute of life, we cried together. The black nurse who helped scrub my hands swept the infant away, and another nurse was pushing me aside. I looked down, and Victoria was white as a sheet, and unconscious.

"Please sir, take a step back."

My expression of joy was short lived, replaced again by panic. The doctor rushed around to the side of the bed and again began barking orders, this time at his nurses. I watched them scramble around. Something was wrong. Another nurse ran into the room and strapped an oxygen mask over Victoria's face. I could only watch in silence as they tried in vain to stabilize her. The heart monitor mocked them, unaffected by their efforts. Its steady hum where a beeping sound should have been only meant one thing, and they didn't have to tell me that my Victoria had died.

"No!" I yelled, or at least I thought I had.

"No, don't let…"

The doctor cursed aloud and put his hands over his face. Lowering them, he looked at me, and we just looked at each other for a moment, lost.

Finally, he found the courage to speak, and told me he was sorry, but they had lost her in the childbirth. He sniffed at the air and looked down, in obvious shame and disbelief.

"I'm, so …sorry." He said again.

I fell to my knees at the bedside, sobbing and stroking her hand.

"Victoria…please baby don't go."

"Please…..please…."

I held her hand to my face, and kissed her palm. My own tears ran down her wrist.

"Don't leave me baby, please…"

With her last words she told me she would never leave me, as she had promised so many times before, but indeed she had. My entire world had been stolen from me, and I wanted to die too.

"Goodbye." I choked out, my throat swelling with grief; I was almost blinded by my uncontrollable tears.

CHAPTER 10
GOODBYE TO ROMANCE

The funeral was in two hours. I sat alone in the front pew of the tiny chapel, just me and her. The casket was open; she was beautiful. Even in death, she was the most beautiful woman I had ever seen. Her mother had insisted they dye her hair back to its original black, which was fine with me, and I knew Victoria wouldn't have cared either. She'd probably have balked at the makeup, though; she was so meticulous about her makeup. Hardly ever left the house looking a cent less than a million dollars.

I had endured the bullshit "God has a plan, son" speech from an inept mortician with little fuss, and I was more than ready for it to all be over. Those past few days I had been nothing short of a walking wreck, and no one could comfort me. Not my sweet mother, who had graciously cared for the baby, who I had named Alissa. This was the first peace I had had, sitting in the chapel, looking at her, just lying there, like she was sleeping. It wasn't fair, but life isn't very fair. I'd like to think there is a God, but if there is, then I fear he'd have to be a complete asshole. Laughing at us. I didn't know what to think, really, it was too big of a philosophical concept to be concerned with at the moment, anyway.

My eyes remained transfixed on Victoria's slightly upturned nose, that I adored, and that little dip underneath, that part of the human face that no one knows what its called. Victoria's was perfect.

I got up and approached the casket once more. Another tear, it seemed one would run out of them after a while. I wiped my tired eyes and leaned over, kissing her red lips and brushing her cheek.

I'll never forget you, I thought to myself. How could I? She had been everything to me, my world, my life, my dream when we were apart. I was finally calm, but inside I was ready to explode like Mount St. Helens.

I heard careful footsteps behind me, and I turned to see her mother, and another man in a suit coming down the aisle with her.

Gold shoes, my God.

"She and I had our differences," she began, touching my shoulder, "but I'm glad we had some time to put them behind us, before…"

Her voice trailed. We shared an awkward moment before the man reached out his hand.

"I'm Danny, Victoria's brother."

He was about 5'10", medium build, and balding. He had an uncommanding chin, and a cheesy black moustache that was trimmed ever-so-neatly. It made me hate him more.

I hit him hard, right between the eyes. He stumbled backwards and fell onto the floor, not expecting my action at all. He began to get up again, but cursed when I kicked him in the head, and then again in the ribcage.

His helpless mother stood there in her gold shoes, her mouth hanging open, shocked into silence, as I dragged the poor bastard by his tie back down the aisle and out of the double doors. The funeral home had a large front porch area, and I held him down face first on the cold cement floor.

"You son of a bitch, I'll kill you!" I yelled, scrubbing his face back and forth as he screamed and cursed some more. I was sitting on his back, choking him with his tie, feeling a lot like 'Rowdy' Roddy Piper, when people from the parking lot started pouring onto the porch to break up our melee. I shoved a couple of guys that I didn't recognize that were attempting to grab and pull me, and stormed down the steps towards my old blue Impala, waiting on me like a cowboy's horse on a dusty street in front of a saloon.

"If you're at the funeral, yours'll be next!" I said, feeling stupid as soon as I said it. This wasn't the WWE, after all, and I wasn't cutting a promo for the pay-per-view next month.

I cranked her and drove away. I needed to get to the nearest pier and calm down. I couldn't believe he had the fucking nerve and sheer audacity to show up there, I suppose he thought his baby sister had taken the more colorful events of their past to her grave.

But she hadn't. I imagined her lips turned up into a satisfied smile if they could.

I pulled off the road at the Springmaid pier and walked out onto the wooden planks, all the way to the end. The sky was a gloomy lavender, forecasting the coming rain.

A deep exhale, and I watched two dirty brown pelicans diving into the sea for their dinner. I pulled my pack of Kamels from my jacket pocket and lit one. I had beaten somebody up in the chapel of a funeral home. A new low. I cracked a smile and shook my head at my own behavior. Boy, was it going to be embarrassing to go back in there. I wasn't concerned about police being called, because he had to have known what it was all about, after he had a minute or two to recover. He had to. And if he was that stupid not to, then fuck him anyway. I knew then that I would never be close to Victoria's family.

It was then that I saw her. I shook my head again, but she was too real, walking towards me on the pier. She was nude, smiling, and getting closer.

I was frozen with fear, staring at my wife's apparition, not knowing what to do. I was at the far end of a fishing pier; I wasn't going anywhere. My shaking, trembling fingers were doing their best to hold on to the burning cigarette butt between them.

She was a phantom, I could see right through her, and she kept moving until she was right in front of me and stopped. She stared at me, tilting her head from side to side, like an alien curiously studying a human for the first time. I could barely breathe I was so afraid. I dropped the smoke and pressed my body against the wooden railing.

"Alissa is a nice name." She said.

"P…please Victoria…" I stuttered, "please don't do this to me. I…I…I can't take it."

She smiled wider, showing her teeth, and then vanished.

I stood there, stone frozen, for a full minute, shivering.

"Jesus Christ!" I yelled, holding my chest. I took a few wobbly steps forward until I collected my bearings, and then sprinted the full length of the pier and back into the parking lot, where I fell in the gravel and scraped my palms. Getting up, one knee had been ripped from my pants.

"Damn."

I turned and looked back. She hadn't left me.

"I thought you'd be here, mister."

I spun around again to see Veronica Valentine, all in black, complete with hat and veil, dressed for a funeral.

"It was the closest pier, I kind of had a feeling. They told me what happened…"

I fell into her arms.

"Ronnie…she was here. She spoke to me."

"Who?"

"Victoria! I saw her…on the pier…" I said, pointing, "She swore she'd never leave me…she was on the pier…"

I realized I was babbling, and had started crying as well.

"It's O.K., honey." She said, embracing me, "Veronica's here. Veronica's going to make it all better."

"Ronnie, I don't know what to do, I'm scared."

"I know…"

"I'm seeing all this crazy shit, and now this….she spoke to me, Ronnie."

"What did she say?"

"She said Alissa was a nice name…that's it. I freaked out like a dumbass and she was gone."

"Well at least you know she's not in *hell*! Come on, dear, we've got to get you cleaned up."

We left my car there and took Ronnie's yellow Mustang back to the condo, where she washed my hands and applied some of those tiny-sized Band-Aids over my cuts. She sat in the living room looking at the last issue of some rag magazine that came in the mail while I found another pair of dress pants in the bedroom closet.

I stared at a collection of pencil drawings on the wall that I had done of Victoria.

"Oh baby, where do we go from here?"

CHAPTER 11

RONNIE AND ME

I didn't know how Ronnie knew how to change diapers, but she did. She taught me a lot of things about babies I didn't know. Burping, feeding, bathing, there was something new to learn every five minutes it seemed. My little Alissa had Victoria's brown eyes and a thick patch of black hair, just like her momma. Her momma. I felt her presence all around us in the condo. I knew she was there, watching and smiling as I fumbled with the bottles and Pampers.

Ronnie was there, too, everyday. She was my savior, babysitting on a moment's notice when I had to go meet a client, or picking up groceries for us on her way over. She had taken an avid interest in Alissa, but an even stronger interest in me. Ronnie came every-day in casual drag; capri pants, sneakers and t-shirts, but with her flawless makeup and hair. It seemed she was now living life as a woman, which was always Ronnie's private obsession anyway. Hell, she looked good enough to pull it off, so why not? Everyone has different dreams, some they talk about and some they don't, but if you get an opportunity to live one, the last thing to do is suppress it. He was always funny dancing around the room singing "don't dream it, be it" from Rocky Horror.

But Ronnie was also there to be close to me. I didn't see it at first, but as the weeks went by, I could tell exactly how much she had missed me those last several years. She told me, back then in her own special yet comical way how she had always just 'made do' with other 'queers', and had never been held by a real man's strong arms before. After she and I had our thing, she was hopelessly addicted.

One night we got Alissa off to sleep, exhausted after more than a few attempts, and sat in the living room together on the couch, having a beer.

"I'm so tired, Ronnie." I said, "I hardly sleep at all anymore."

"You poor thing."

"Thank you…for everything. I don't thank you enough."

"Stop it!" You know I'll *always* help you."

"I know."

We sat there for a minute or two just drinking our beers, watching David Letterman with the volume down, when Ronnie moved her hand to my thigh. She looked at me and I looked at her and when she felt no resistance, she put her beer on the coffee table and crawled into my arms, snuggling her head into my chest like a child. I held her, feeling her breath against me, and it felt nice. I missed Victoria so much, I would have gone insane then if it wasn't for Ronnie holding me together. It felt good to have someone to hold. Ronnie being there made me feel so less alone, and eased my grieving.

I thought about how easy it would be to just invite her to move in here with us. Ronnie was still a man under all that faux finish, and I didn't know if I could live that way. I could never take it as far as Ronnie hoped for, and that just wouldn't be fair to her. It felt so wonderful having her there, to help with Alissa and comfort me at the same time, to be a loving friend without equal. She was glad to do all those things, in exchange for being close to me, and occasionally a little closer in quieter moments.

I finished my beer and realized Ronnie had fallen asleep in that same position, much like Victoria had at times. I lifted her up in my arms (she was lighter than Victoria was) and carried her to the bedroom, carefully placing her on top of the comforter. I suppose I could have woken her, and told her to go home, but it seemed so cruel, after she had been so kind. I imagined myself falling into some sort of periless trap, but paid no heed as I slid off her Keds. I chuckled to myself as I thought Ronnie had pretty feet for a guy, the shimmering purple polish accented them nicely.

I fished another beer out of the fridge, careful not to rustle and rattle the bottles together, and returned to the couch. I briefly sorted through the mail on the table, remembering that I had some more papers to sign at the assistance office. My new 'single dad' status had qualified me for some insurance and health benefits for Alissa and I, and I was very thankful for that. Laying my head back and closing my eyes, I thought about how content and happy Victoria looked on the pier. I wish I had reacted differently, but seeing a ghost, anybody's ghost, can really get your dandruff up. I was sure she'd understood. At the same time, I really couldn't say whether I'd want to see her again like that. Maybe I wouldn't. Maybe it was a last farewell. Maybe she had come to see me one last time before she continued on to wherever she was going. I guessed she didn't figure on me almost shitting my pants, but I supposed it was the thought that counted.

My sweet Victoria. Fly to the angels, my love, if they're there, was my last thought before letting my heavy eyelids come down like the final curtain on my day.

⊰⊱

I awoke to the sound of my daughter's middle-of-the-night wail. I slid off the sofa and bumbled around the kitchen, half-asleep, warming formula. I thought about the little guy on that commercial, 'time to make the doughnuts'.

"Hold on Alissa honey, daddy's comin'." I would say, my eyes were slits like I was straining to see someone's aura.

Suddenly Ronnie appeared from around the corner with the infant in her arms.

"Here she is, ready for a midnight snack."

"Thanks, baby." I said, too weary to realize what I had just referred to Ronnie as. She winked and took the bottle from me and sat at the kitchen table, feeding Alissa, who was now silent. I leaned on the counter watching. Playing 'mom' must have made Ronnie feel like a real woman; she was getting off on it. I watched her burp Alissa and rock her back to sleep, like she was a natural. I followed to the bedroom where Ronnie laid the baby back in her crib. We stood there together, and she reached over and took my hand.

"You're going to be a great dad, buster brown." She said, squeezing my finger.

"We'll see."

I kissed her on the cheek and turned to leave the room, but Ronnie held on to my hand. I pulled her to me once more, and held her there in the darkness.

"I love you." She whispered in my ear.

"Ronnie…" I started.

"I know, I know…" she said, "sometimes I just have to say it, you know? You don't have to answer me, sometimes it's just too much to keep inside."

She backed up and hung her head.

"I'm sorry, I'll go." She said as a teardrop fell from her eye.

"No, it's alright, Ronnie." I said as I pulled her back to me, "You know I love you too, you know how dear you are to me."

"Yes."

"O.K."

I held her for another minute, and then returned to my spot on the couch, where I fell asleep almost immediately.

——+——

I was awake. I turned my head to glance at the digital clock on the wall in the kitchen. Three thirty-seven. It had only been a touch more than an hour since I closed my eyes last. I should have been dead asleep and dreaming, but I wasn't. I sat up and reached for my cigarettes and lighter. The lighter I grabbed was Ronnie's, it was pink and said 'DIVA' on it. I walked out onto the porch and looked at the ocean. It was peaceful tonight, only an occasional crashing wave, and then a slow fizzing sound, like opening a slightly shaken two liter. Then silence until the next wave finally collapsed near the shore. Sleeping gulls floated on the water like little white buoys, rising up and down with the current.

There were so many nights like this that Victoria and I would sit out there and smoke and talk. We would discuss any and everything, a lady's funny hair in line at Bi-Lo, to places our grandfathers had taken us for ice cream when we were kids. I dropped an ash into the little ceramic ashtray we used and realized there would be no more amusing anecdotes to share with her. I lived for those tiny scraps of information, how she loved Franken-Berry but hated Count Chocula. I didn't care for Count Chocula either, but it would do in a pinch. You couldn't pay Victoria to eat it, no way.

I remember mentioning the short-lived Fruit Brute to her and watching her stick her finger down her throat in disgust, and then laugh to beat the band. I crushed out my Kamel and lit another.

Then there was Tootsie in there, wrapped in the same white comforter that Victoria and I had made love underneath a thousand times. I knew Ronnie wasn't trying to replace her by any means, but I was becoming uncomfortable with where our current situation was heading. I had always been attracted to Ronnie, and still was. Even so I didn't think I could or should label myself bi-sexual. I was just an artist who appreciated beauty, in all its glorious forms. And Ronnie was beautiful. A small-framed boy with skin like soft woven silk. He had full lips like a girl, and natural high cheekbones, covered in Revlon the transformation was no less than uncanny. Piercing sky-blue eyes that could hypnotize if given the chance. Ronnie, Ronnie, Ronnie. I felt a hint of unease in my jeans and thought about crawling in bed with him, touching him, holding him close to me. Listening to his light breathing and faint heartbeat in the warmth of the bed, like I did nestled with Victoria.

I looked down at my cigarette, its cherry end glowing red in the darkness. I crushed it out and re-entered the living room through the sliding glass doors. Pausing at the couch, I pulled off my Levis and left them in a crumpled pile on the floor. In the kitchen I inspected the contents of the refrigerator, not looking for anything specific, just looking. I closed the door, and again in the darkness, took a deep breath and exhaled. Did I want *Ronnie*, or did I want *someone?* Someone to fill the void, to just take the pain away for a little while.

I eased into the bedroom and stood there, watching him sleep. The covers were pulled up to his chin, his profile pressed into the pillow. He had grown his shining blonde hair long so he wouldn't have to rely on wigs any longer, adding an amazing natural effect, and those days could pass for a girl anywhere. In my hungry eyes that night, he could have passed for a slumbering angel. So delicate and feminine. My fingers found his cheek, and brushed at his golden curls.

"Sexy bastard..." I whispered aloud, before I turned once more, tip-toed out of the room and back to the waiting sofa.

CHAPTER 12
FAMILY RESEMBLANCE

The weeks continued to roll past us like products on a factory's assembly line. Ronnie was spending more and more time with Alissa and I, and stayed over quite a bit. She was aware of my boundaries and respected them, but it had to have been difficult for her. It was difficult for me as well, because I was beginning to water down those same boundaries that I had set up. I found myself desiring her more often than not, though I remained silent. What bothered me the most then was an old photo album of Victoria's that I uncovered in a box one afternoon. It was an older album that I hadn't seen before, a collection of snapshots from her childhood. I was delighted in my discovery and saw images of she and her late father, opening gifts with a little scribble at the bottom of the page that read, 'Christmas '73'. I could see the love in her eyes for him, he was just as she had described him to me.

The next few pages were the disturbing ones; Victoria's baby pictures. At first I thought they were shots of Alissa, but that was absurd, why would they be in there? I had never seen that book before. I realized then that it wasn't Alissa, it was Victoria. I hurried into the living room and held the album up to the framed Alissa's I had hanging. I was stunned. They were identical. Same faces, same *poses*. Same black hair, same upturned nose, same expressions, same *everything*. I dropped the album to my side and rolled my eyes around in my head, searching for an explanation that didn't come. I suddenly became cold, that familiar chill finding its well-beaten path from one end of my spine to the other. My arms blanketed in goose-flesh, I took the short steps to the couch and flopped down. It was unbelievable for their baby pictures to be so damned identical. It was scary and downright weird. But in *my* life, weird things were happening on a regular basis. Only this time it wasn't something that only I could see. For the first time, I could show someone. I looked at the clock and saw that Ronnie would be there within the hour. Good. I opened the book again and just stared. Jesus Christ, they were wearing the same outfits. I closed it again because I was starting to get really spooked. I glanced onto the porch, then into the kitchen, then back to the porch, halfway expecting to see Victoria sitting there, smiling at me. But she wasn't. I hated feeling that way, just despised not knowing what I was going to see, the fear of losing contact with reality.

The visions, the dreams, and Victoria herself had scarred me for life, and I knew that I would always carry that odd new emotion with me, the fear of the unknown.

The time slipped away slowly. I sat there with the album in my arms, not wanting to look at it again. I watched the red digital numbers like a starving owl spying on an oblivious squirrel below him. I felt frozen, in limbo. Ronnie's voice was like a screaming alarm clock, jarring me back to life.

"I'm back, handsome! I stopped at Toys R Us and got those Spider-Man diapers you've been talking about for two weeks. They weren't *that* expensive, dear. Anyway, did you miss...." And her voice trailed there when she saw me with the scowl on my face.

"....me?" she finished.

"What's wrong?"

"Ronnie, I have something to show you. Please come here."

My calm yet uneasy tone made her hesitate before approaching me.

"Sit down. This is going to freak you out."

"Oh my god, did you...see her again?"

"No, no." I said, opening the book once more, to the baby pictures.

"Look."

Ronnie looked, first at the book, then back at me in bewilderment.

"What am I looking at here, dear?"

I looked down at the page and my stomach twisted in a knot that only Popeye the Sailor man could untie. They were different. Hair, poses, colors, expressions, everything.

"Goddamnit!" I shouted, slamming the book closed, just missing Ronnie's fingers.

I got up and yelled at the photos on the wall, " They were the same! They were the same!! It was Alissa, Ronnie, it was ALISSA!

"That is Alissa, Tiger."

"No, Goddamnit! In the book!"

I opened the book again, and tapped my index finger on the yellowed cellophane.

"They were the same!"

Ronnie glared at me in disbelief. I was delirious, and angry.

"Tiger, you're scaring me."

"Jesus, Ronnie, come on! Get your cards or something! What the fuck is going on?!"

I yelled in her face, and slung the whole book across the room, where it slammed into the wall over the television. I rubbed my palms into my eyes and began to cry, I was falling apart.

"Ronnie...." I fell to my knees in front of her, and embraced her. Her arms fell upon me and she held me while I got it all out, mumbling incoherently and sobbing. Then the nausea. I stumbled like a drunk into the bathroom and vomited into the sink. Wiping my mouth and standing in the doorway, I looked into the eyes of an angel. Her face was more beautiful than I'd ever seen. Her sad eyes focused on me, absorbing my anguish. There were no words.

I got up and took a turn around the living room, wiping my swollen eyes and sniffing at the air.

"This is all wrong." I said, "all wrong….can you stay here with Alissa? I've got to go somewhere."

Ronnie just nodded as I grabbed my car keys and closed the door to the condo behind me. This had gone too far, I wanted to know what the devil was happening to me. I drove from the north end where we lived to the south end, once again to the Springmaid pier, where I had seen her before.

I arrived and was astonished at how many tourists and fishermen were there. Mothers held up sunburned children to look through the big telescopes that cost twenty-five cents for what always seemed like twenty-five seconds of time. Her other sons screaming for their turns. Men cleaned fresh-caught flounder on little wooden tables. Lines of fishing poles were locked into place all the way down the pier, like street lights. Lovers in swimsuits and sandals held hands, pointed and waved to friends below on the sand.

The whirring sound of a taken line got mine and everyone else's attention, several men gathered around to see what would get reeled in next. A cheer went up when an older gentleman in a plaid shirt pulled up a footlong baby shark. He unhooked it and bid it farewell as he tossed it back over the side, as it was illegal to keep sharks that size.

I made my way further across the crowded planks, but I soon began to realize that Victoria appearing again under these conditions just wasn't going to happen. I felt stupid being there in the first place. I turned and followed my steps back the way I came. My heart skipped a beat or two when I saw a woman in a flowing white dress sitting in a beach chair reading a book. Her big floppy yellow hat obscured her downturned face, but the black strands of hair that peeked out from under it blew in the breeze and drove my optimistic imagination into a frenzy. I walked up to her and stood, silent, almost afraid to know. I breathed hard and swallowed harder as I worked up the courage to say her name.

Then, she looked up at me. It wasn't her, and my relieved exhale was like the sea breeze itself. She seemed in her fifties or early sixties, very dark, attractive for an older woman. Her skin told me she had lived here all her life.

"May I help you?" she asked.

"No, ma'am," I answered, "I thought you….might have been someone else, I'm sorry."

She smiled a kind, sweet smile and went back to her reading. I kept walking, but turned again to look at her. She was still there, head down and reading. She could have been someone's grandmother, looking forward to the weekends when she would bake cookies for her visiting grandchildren and take them out to play on the summer shore. I hoped she was treasured and loved by someone.

I turned to continue my way back to the parking lot and found myself face to face with Victoria, in broad daylight, in front of all those people. My bones locked in place and my blood ran cold. Tourists parted and made their way around us, or around me as I imagined they could not see her. She was the same as before, nude, smiling, staring at me. I had almost rehearsed it, knew what I'd say, but it was a mute issue, as I was dumbfounded once again. She reached out her arms and placed her hands on my chest, which was shivering like I was standing in a blizzard. I couldn't feel them, she was only a spectre, not a physical being anymore. She looked down, and then up to me, smiled, and was gone.

I stood there. Whispering to myself, I said, "Please baby, tell me what's going on...what's happening to me? What are you trying to tell me? God, please tell me...I miss you, baby..." and the tears came to me again. Somebody bumped my shoulder and I heard a trailing voice saying 'excuse me.' I bit my bottom lip and took deep breaths. I took a step, and then another, and then another.

CHAPTER 13
LATINO HEAT

"You need to get out."

I heard Ronnie's statement for the second time, but to me it sounded like it was echoing through a turnpike tunnel.

"Hello…."

I came back to my senses hovering over a sinkful of dishes, my hands soaking in the lukewarm bubbling suds. I had been standing there grasping a plate, lost in thought.

"Sorry, Ronnie, I was…"

"You need to get out and get drunk, that's what you need, mister. I'm going to call that sweet old Margie from 4-C that volunteered to baby-sit last week, the one you totally blew off, and tell her we need her to-night."

"Ronnie, I really don't feel like…"

"Stop it! I'm not listening to you anymore! You're going out with me tonight and that's final, I'm not watching you sulk around here anymore."

"Ronnie…."

"No, goddamnit, you sit out on that porch smoking and brooding like a vampire. And when you're not you're working on that damned card company thing. I'm sick of it. There's too much life inside you, *I* know."

"Not tonight."

"I'm calling her."

"No."

"I'm moving towards the phone."

"No."

"I'm picking up the phone...."

"Ronnie..."

"I'm dialing the number...."

She was playing and I fought with a slight grin but she was too much for me. I hung my head in defeat.

"O.K., O.K., but its got to be a gay club. I'm not getting in a fight tonight."

Ronnie shot me that shocked look that always made me laugh, then flipped me the bird while she dialed Margie's number. It *had* been a long time, and I was driving myself batty cooped up in there; my entire existence revolved around Alissa and work. I had been working like a slave on my big presentation for Crystal Vision cards, making it no short of perfect. An in-house illustrator position would be a dream job for me, and I decided to go for it with both guns blazing. But that night I supposed I would be the helpless captive of a flawless transgendered queen, buying me Captain and Cokes until I couldn't walk. I had a sneaking suspicion, though, it would end up being me carrying Ronnie back to the car.

Whatever, I thought. A break would do me good.

"She'll be here in an hour and a half." Ronnie was glowing as she headed to the shower.

⇒⟨+⟩⇐

I remember explaining everything about Alissa to sweet old Margie from 4-C in triplicate as Ronnie pushed me out the door.

"She's going to be alright." Ronnie kept repeating in the elevator.

Ronnie was dressed to the hilt, as glamorous as ever. She was also very much on, laughing and joking in the car all the way to our destination, the legendary Offshore Drilling Company. It just wasn't worth it to take Ronnie anywhere else, as good as she looked, it wasn't worth the trouble if anyone suspected her true gender and wanted to start something. People can be so stupid. Ronnie understood this and never pushed the issue, I always hoped she didn't take it as an insult.

We arrived and I could hear the bass in the dance mix thumping from the parking lot. Everyone seemed to know Miss Veronica Valentine, and we were greeted by many in the foyer. Endless clubgoers pawed over her, suffocating her in compliments, that Ronnie took in like oxygen, and then the pawing over me would begin.

"He's *my man*, you jealous bitch." Ronnie would playfully reprimand. It was a comical atmosphere, but enticing and exciting at the same time. I knew those other queens wished they looked half as good as she did, and Ronnie knew it too.

She was a dazzling vision that night, sequins glittering from her gold outfit, sparkling metallic makeup to match, and her blonde hair pulled up on top of her head, she was a knockout for sure.

We also didn't pay for the first three rounds of drinks either. Ronnie was well-liked in this community, and everyone treated her like she was queen of the queens.

"Miss Valentine, good to see you again." announced a rather large bartender with a huge handlebar moustache.

"Hello, Mel," she chimed back, "Captain and Coke and a Zinfandel."

"You got it, dear."

The rest seemed like a blur. Ronnie wanted to dance but I didn't, so I nursed my drink while she ran off to let the bass thump up her wazoo with everyone else. Mel played the concerned barkeep, checking on me every now and then, to make sure I was alright. Brooding like a vampire, she said. I felt like the Phantom of the Opera, lurking in the shadows, watching everyone else do their thing. I didn't want to have fun, didn't want to join in. The alcohol before me was to be my only companion that night, until a Latino princess sat on the stool beside me and told Mel she needed a Long Island Iced Tea and a man.

"Plenty of men in here, seniorita." Mel joked.

She rolled her eyes and replied, "You know what I mean."

"Not quite the right bar for that now, is it?"

" I know, I know, my friends dragged me along with them. I wanted to go to Studebaker's but I was out-voted."

They chuckled together for a moment and Mel got the drink to her in record time. He laid out a bright red napkin, placed the glass squarely in the middle, and with a sly gesture that we all saw, diverted his eyes in my direction and moved on to another customer at the end of the bar. So now I had her full attention without saying a word.

"I guess that was supposed to be an introduction." She said.

"I guess so." I replied.

"So...you here with anybody?"

We both laughed out loud as soon as the words left her lips.

"I guess not." she continued, still giggling.

"Well...sort of."

"Are you..."

"No, I'm not."

"You don't look..."

"Well that's good."

We laughed again and she told me her name was Maria, but everyone called her 'Emmie"

"Do you like 'Emmie'?" I asked.

"No, not really." She laughed again.

"Well then, Maria it is."

Her skin was bronze and sparkling with just enough of that gold glitter body spray. Her hair was dark and long, and she smelled so good, like vanilla. I had always carried a weakness for women who smelled like food. We talked for awhile, drank and laughed more. I felt like a million dollars. A Mexican mamacita to wash away all my troubles, if just for a little while. My optimism would be short-lived, though, as soon as Ronnie wandered back to the bar.

"What the fuck is this?"

I looked up, startled, to find Ronnie glaring down at us and already soused out of his gay gourd.

"He's *MY* man, bitch! You can carry your coochie-coochie ass on to the next guy!"

"Ronnie, what the hell…" was all I could stammer out before Maria got up and chastised me.

"Who is this? Your 'girlfriend'? Fuck you, asshole!" she said to me and stomped off to the dance floor.

"No! Wait.." I called getting up, but Ronnie stood in my way.

"Are you crazy?!" I yelled at him.

"I love you, Tiger." Ronnie said, trying to put his arms around me. I pushed him away and realized we were causing quite a scene.

"Why don't you love me, goddamnit?" Ronnie bellowed, grabbing my shirt. I pushed him out of the way and headed towards the door, but he was right behind me shouting outrageous things, embarrassing me like I'd never been embarrassed before.

Outside in the parking lot, I lit a much-needed Kamel and paced, listening to him rant, and wished I was anywhere but there. It was so childish and stupid, and for the first time, I saw Ronnie in a different light.

"I love you so much, baby! Please don't treat me like this..I love you!"

"Damn, Ronnie, get in the car. I'm not going to do this with you."

Ronnie started sobbing and I dreaded what was going to come flying out next.

"I help you with your baby, I do so much for you! I try my best to look like a woman for you! But you don't care! You don't care!"

Ronnie was just babbling then and a crowd had gathered which made me twice as uneasy.

"I'll take you home." I said, reaching out for his arm.

"No!" he screamed, "Fuck you! Go on and fuck that slut!"

Ronnie turned and walked back towards the bar, still shouting, at the moon then instead of me, I supposed. What a disaster.

"Ronnie, I'm leaving. Are you coming with me or not?" I implored, but received nothing in return but a tirade of drunken obscenities. I got in my Impala, hesitated for a moment, then cranked her and drove away. I did love Ronnie, but I should have known better than to let him so far into my life the way I had. Our friendship was then soiled, I didn't think I'd see Veronica Valentine again for a very long time, at least, if ever.

I was still in shock and out of sorts when I arrived back at the condo. An unusual crisp breeze found me as I stepped out of the elevator. I dismissed it, coming to the conclusion that we may have a morning rain. It would have been welcomed, if anything to cool the beach down a little.

Inside I settled with Margie and thanked her over and over again as she left, always smiling. It seemed Alissa had been no trouble, sleeping the evening away while Margie had watched what could be found on late-night television. I made some coffee and pulled on a sweatshirt before heading to the balcony for a minute's peace. I could almost see Victoria playing in the water. My desperate and disgruntled imagination was doing its best to add to her ghostly appearances. I closed my eyes, then opening them again, finding myself wishing she would be there, kicking at the waves and laughing under the moonlight. If she had been on the pier, why couldn't she be there? She *was* there, I could feel her, that slight presence.

I imagined her leaning on Alissa'a crib, watching our darling daughter dream on without a care.

The phone's incessant ringing interrupted my fantastical dream sequence as I cursed it aloud and picked up the receiver. Oddly enough, it was Mel from the club.

"Miss Veronica, she's been attacked." He recanted in a slow, bothered tone.

"Attacked?" I repeated.

"Yes, I know you two had a blow-up, but I know she would have wanted you to know."

"Mel, tell me."

"After you left, she went..." Mel paused, catching his breath, " she went back outside to have a smoke and look for you. She thought you may have come back."

"And what happened?"

"She was rolled. Some guys beat her up and robbed her. She was devastated, it was awful."

I was shocked and just held the phone for a moment, not saying anything. In her state of mind, was this some sort of game to get me to come back? No, I thought, Mel was too broken up. That or he's a great fucking actor. If so, he'd really missed his calling.

"Where is she?" I asked.

"She wouldn't go to the hospital. I put her in a cab, she'd be home by now."

I didn't speak then. I thought of poor Ronnie being kicked and punched by some of those local homophobic thug types who routinely prey on the innocent. I thought of how scared and humiliated she must have been. How utterly destroyed, if this story were true.

"Thanks, Mel." I said, before putting down the receiver.

I glanced down the hallway to where Alissa lay in her bed, and took a sip of decaf from my "World's Best Artist" mug, remembering Victoria buying it for me at the flea market for a dollar, the same day she found her beloved yellow hat.

I felt confused and lost, concerned and awkward. I decided not to go, even though I knew it meant leaving a part of my past behind me for good. Ronnie would never forgive me, and would move on with his life as I would. I knew from experience that you can never say never in life, but in this case, I decided to take my chances, and bid farewell to another beautiful friend.

CHAPTER 14

ALISSA

Alissa and I sailed along together, and the more she grew, the more she looked like her mother. The hardest thing I ever had to do besides saying goodbye to Victoria was saying goodbye to the sacred grounds on which we met, and moving on to Charlotte and my new job at the Crystal Vision card company. Leaving Turner's Island, the condo and its unbelievable ocean view, its stirring memories, and the backdrop of the best times of my life was difficult. I had sent numerous portfolios and promo packs to my new employer and had an impressive collection of rejection letters, but something in the last one sparked their interest and we were on our way to the Queen City.

I rented a small house a short distance off of Independence Boulevard, a three bedroom, enough room for Alissa and I, and a little studio, where I would cover many canvases with the buttery smelling oils that I had so longed to work with, and become a legitimate artist with something to contribute to the world besides quickly-airbrushed murals. Even though mine were always a step above your average quickly-airbrushed mural, they remained so, at least to me. I was hungry to create more.

I studied our new living room, envisioning where everything would go, when Alissa stumbled through the door struggling with a large suitcase, gripping the handle with both hands.

"Dad!"

"Sorry, honey." I said, taking it from her and placing it against a wall, "Why don't you concentrate on the smaller ones, sweetheart?"

"But I wanna help more." she whined.

"You are helping, baby, believe me."

"O.K."

I watched her sulk back to the rented truck and knew everything was going to be alright. I really had no idea of the twisted road we were about to take, and the effect it would have on my soon-to-be mangled psyche. At that moment I was exuberant and optimistic. The coming years would change all that.

"Is that her, Dad?" Her quiet voice asked from the doorway, "... Mom?"

I looked away from my painting to see my daughter, barefoot in her purple nightgown. No answer was required, Alissa knew she was all I painted.

"Shouldn't you be in bed, sugar?"

"I couldn't sleep. I heard you talking again." She mumbled, rubbing her eyes.

I had a terrible habit those nights of engaging in imaginary conversations with my Victoria as I brought her back to life, one brush stroke at a time. I suppose it was the first signs of madness.

"I'm sorry, baby. I'll try to keep it down. Why don't you head back to bed?"

"Do you think she hears you, Dad?" Her question struck me and I invited her closer.

"Does she hear you?"

"Yes, sweetheart, I believe she does."

"She's so pretty…and she looks so real. It's really cool, like she's really here with us."

"She *is* here, sweetie. She's watching us, all the time."

"You paint good, Dad."

"Thanks, sugar…now can you get back in bed for me?"

"Sure, Dad," as she kissed my cheek and hugged me, "Can I get some water first?"

"Sure."

I watched her pink bare feet pad back down the hallway. God, I loved her so much. She was my eternal link to her. So much like her…so beautiful and perfect. I was in love all over again.

Sitting down on my stool and lighting a Kamel, I stared at my night's work. A few more hours and that one would be done. She looked back at me with those luscious brown eyes, filled with endless untamed passion.

"I miss you…" I whispered.

She didn't move or answer. Just glared back at me, almost demanding more color, here, and here, and there.

"Dad?"

"Yes, baby."

"When I grow up, I want to be just as pretty as her, so you can marry me and be happy again."

We smiled at each other, her childish gesture sending some much-needed warmth over my battered heart.

"Goodnight, sugar."

"Goodnight, Dad."

She turned and disappeared into the dark corridor once again. I smoked my cigarette to the filter, crushed it out, and lit another.

Alissa is a nice name. Alissa is a nice name.

If I thought too much about it, it would end up moving me to tears. Sometimes there was no way to stop them.

Alissa is a nice name. Alissa...

I would go back to work and lose myself in her. Lost in her was a comfortable place to be. It was like having her back, an intimate visit from her if just for a few hours. Just me and a 6x6 canvas, bringing Victoria back to life. I thought of Ronnie and his foreboding predictions, of how something was supposed to be wrong with my daughter. It seemed so absurd. We had a new life, no more insane dreams, no more freaky visions, and Victoria lived only in my heart and in my paintings. Still, you can't make love to a painting, and I was very much in need of some type of female companionship. Should I have continued to punish myself?

The feeling of gratification when a piece is completed is something only the artist can experience. That moment when the final detail brings the whole damned thing together. I stared at my wife, wrapped in flowing snow white lace, her full black mane falling free across her angelic features. Was this enough? I glanced around my studio, from Victoria lounging naked in aqua sea foam, to Victoria in an early hour's moonlight, to Victoria stretched across the hood of her blazing red Stealth. I didn't want to betray her, but perhaps it was time to take a much-needed step forward with my life.

I just couldn't keep on living that way. No matter how much I resisted letting go, I knew deep inside that at some point, I had to.

CHAPTER 15
JESSICA

I couldn't concentrate. I got up from my work table and again stepped to the large window that looked out upon downtown Charlotte. I was on the twentieth floor, and the people scurrying around on Trade Street looked like tiny beetles. Crowds on every corner, waiting on crossing signals. Decorated busses and hotdog vendors with their carts gave the city a very grown-up New York feel, only cleaner. Charlotte was so pretty, the perfect blend of an artsy-fartsy community while still maintaining its southern flair. And of course, a big money town as well. I had come so far, I reflected, slipping my tie between my fingers.

Back at my table, I grimaced at the line-dancing 'get well soon' skunks I had drawn. I didn't usually let my personal issues get me down at work, but that day the events of the last few years were weighing in heavy on my overloaded brain. I sat down and doodled a little portrait of Ronnie. I knew his face so well, as well as my own. I missed him, but realized I couldn't let that get me down. He was gone, and I had let him go. I was just so lonely.

"Who's that?"

The voice startled me and I buried the number two into the paper, breaking off the tip.

"I'm sorry, oh god, I'm sorry," she said, "I didn't mean to…"

"It's alright." I said, turning to meet my assailant.

She was an impeccably dressed brunette in a black business suit, Lisa Loeb glasses and razor-sharp bangs ending evenly above her eyebrows.

"I've been working here two days now, and I can't for the life of me find that smoking area they keep talking about. I didn't want to ask, but I'm getting pretty flustered over the whole thing."

She looked too smart to not know how to find the smoking area, but I enjoyed her forwardness and went along with it.

"I could use a break myself." I answered. "We could go together if you don't mind."

"That would be great. Thank you."

I grabbed my Kamels and lighter out of the top drawer under my table and we started towards the elevators.

"I really appreciate this."

"No problem."

There was a silence in the elevator on the way up, almost as if she were waiting until we got there to resume the conversation. A little awkward, but we *had* just met. The twenty-fourth floor had an outside balcony, very nice with lots of plants and benches. On a pleasant spring day it was very relaxing and enjoyable, a great place to unwind.

Glancing over the shiny modern skyscrapers and Ericcsson Stadium, a marveled again at my new home's beauty. I had been to northern cities like Baltimore, and Columbus, with their old brick buildings and deserted factories that seemed so grey and gloomy compared to Charlotte. I felt lucky.

I lit my smoke and then hers. It was a thin menthol Capri 120, a very feminine cigarette. She inhaled the first drag with a passion, like she had been dreaming of that moment for hours. I respected that.

"That's so much better." She smiled, "I'm Jessica."

I introduced myself and we had a quick laugh over the broken pencil.

"Who was that you were drawing anyway?"

"Just somebody I haven't seen in a while."

"O.K.," she replied, "I'll leave that one alone."

She winked at me and continued, "Everybody's got one of those I guess. Those skunks were cute."

"They're trash."

She laughed again and asked, "Are most artists as hard on their own work as that?"

"Yes." I said, "If they're true artists. If it's in their blood."

"I thought that breed died off long ago, like the dinosaurs."

"No, there's a few of us stragglers left, dreaming of using our talents to become a little more than just servants to the world."

"Hmmm…bitter."

"No, not really," I said with a reassuring grin, "What do you do, Jessica?"

I'm in the marketing department," she said, blowing white smoke into the breeze, "boring shit."

"Are you sure you couldn't find the smoking area by yourself?"

I went for the kill and her cheeks turned six shades of crimson.

"O.K., O.K." she admitted, looking down now. "I wanted to meet you, and I knew you smoked, so…"

She was cute as she was irresistible, that con-artist from marketing, and I didn't let her suffer long. I was flattered and immediately asked for her number. Jessica went back to work and I returned to my dancing skunks, who sang 'being sick stinks', and seemed to look a bit better to me then. Happier. Refreshed. As happy and refreshed as dancing cartoon skunks could look I supposed. I wanted to leave my car at work and fly home, exploding inside with anticipation. What an interesting turn of events. I couldn't wait to tell Alissa.

I came in the door to find Alissa sitting on the couch with Cornelia, our babysitter. Alissa was reading to her from my thick hard cover edition of *War and Peace,* of all things. I had never read it, for God's sake. She saw me and ran to me, wrapping her little arms around my waist.

"You're home." She swooned.

"She was very good today."

Cornelia was a sweet eighteen year old from down the street. She came over every day at three to get Alissa off the bus and stayed with her until I got home. I was fond of her, a thin, pale girl, your average teenager really, but much on the responsible side, which is hard to find in a teenager to tell the truth. And Alissa was crazy about her. I paid her and asked if she could stay late on Friday or Saturday, that I may have a date, and I'd call her with the details. After she left, Alissa stood staring, overhearing our conversation.

"How was school today, sweetheart?"

"What do you *mean* you have a *date*?" was her direct response, not intending to let that one go without a fight. She was so adorable standing there so matter-of-factly with her hands on her hips.

"I met a nice woman at work today, honey. I'm going to take her out to dinner."

"What about Mommy?"

I took a deep breath and dreaded the talk I was about to have with my little girl.

"Alissa, sit down here on the couch with Daddy a minute."

She crawled on the sofa with me and waited for my explanation like I had done something unforgivable.

"I met a nice lady at work today, sugar. She was really nice and really pretty…I get lonely without Mommy sometimes, baby…well, all the time…I want to…"

"As pretty as Mommy?" she interrupted.

"No, baby, nobody's as pretty as Mommy was, O.K.? But Mommy's not with us anymore. I miss her very, very much. I…"

"You said she *was* here. You said she was. That she's watching us all the time."

"Baby, I know Mommy wants us to be happy. I want somebody to hold on to, like I used to hold onto Mommy. There's nothing wrong with that."

"But you'll forget about her."

"No, sweetie, I'll never forget about Mommy, ever. I promise."

She sat glaring at me, mulling all that together in her mind.

"What if…"

"What if what, baby?"

"What if… what if Mommy comes back one day?"

"Sugar," I started, my eyes beginning to well up, "as much as I'd like that, she's just not coming back. I'll love her forever, and I'll never forget her, but there's a time when you have to move on…"

My voice got shaky, and trailed, hoping she would understand.

"What's her name, Daddy?"

"Jessica. Jessica's her name. She's real nice."

Alissa breathed a long sigh and got up.

"Where are you going, sweetheart?"

"I'm gonna go play in my room, O.K.?"

"O.K."

And it was over, just like that. How much of it sunk in I couldn't tell right away. Besides, it would only be dinner. I wasn't expecting some wild romance to begin on a first date. But sooner or later I knew I would meet someone, someone who would indeed take her place and become a part of our lives. I hoped Alissa would be able to handle it when that time came. Jessica would be a good test subject to get Alissa used to the idea that Daddy was lonely. God, I didn't want to hurt my daughter, but

I couldn't continue to live that way, crying over my wife who had died several years before. I lit a cigarette and slipped off my shoes. The vision of Victoria playing in the ocean flashed through my head as it often did. I'd never forget her as long as I had Alissa with me, she was a 24/7 living reminder of the exquisite woman who bore her in her last moments in this world.

Then I started thinking about what Alissa might want for dinner. Should I go balls out and make that meatloaf, or throw in a pan of chicken nuggets? It seemed she would eat anything I made, and it didn't make much of a difference to her whether I slaved in the kitchen for hours or popped something in the microwave. She was just six. Dining together at night was our time, where I learned about mean Miss Graham and the annoying boy who sat behind her and threw spitballs during math. I treasured every second.

My overhead lamp put a spotlight right on her face. I sat in the pitch dark, my canvas the only thing illuminated. It was finished and I sat back staring at her. The white lace in strong contrast to her sun-kissed flesh.

"How do I let you go?" I whispered to her, almost anticipating an audible reply. The red-orange glow of my cigarette's lifeforce was the only other break in the sea of black nothingness that enveloped us. This one, I thought, would be the last. Would I continue painting her and painting her until I was old and feeble? Talking to Alissa about Victoria, it seemed I was trying to convince *myself* that she wasn't coming back. Goddamn, she was gone so fast, she never even got to see her. So fast. It wasn't right. Alissa's birthday was coming up, and it was always a bittersweet affair. A death and a new life, all in the same instant. After nearly seven years it remained a difficult pill to swallow. I supposed it always would be.

Putting out the light, I walked down the hallway and stepped into Alissa's room. She slept soundly. I sat on the edge of the bed and brushed my fingers across her soft cheek.

Alissa is a nice name.

I looked up, almost as if the words were placed in my mind deliberately. I saw silhouettes on her dresser of all the Barbies I had gotten her. She only wanted the ones with black hair so sometimes it was tough. I had become a veteran toy hunter, scavenging stores in search of the right dolls. I would have done anything for her, though. I crawled up and lay behind her, draping my arm across her torso as she dreamed on. I held her close and kissed her hair.

My sweet little Alissa. And there I fell asleep as well.

CHAPTER 16
FEELS LIKE THE FIRST TIME

The days went by and my anticipation grew as I bumped into Jessica at work, by the Pepsi machines or in the smoking area, feeling the warmth in her smile, the hunger in her eyes for the weekend. Friday night I drove to her apartment on Providence Road, a very impressive upscale residential area, listening to an old Meatloaf tape and feeling like a kid again. It had been so long since I was that excited over anything. I recall trying to make out the numbers on the buildings and experiencing newfound respect for pizza delivery people.

At the door she was magnificent and took my breath as soon as our eyes met. A stunning deep blue dress, open-toed heels, and those glasses were still slaying me. Jessica was refined, full of style and grace, yet goofy enough to laugh with over the smallest things. And we did.

She preferred a Merlot with dinner and I was more than glad to oblige. I was having a ball. Everything forgotten save she and I and the romantic atmosphere of that small yet elegant candle-lit steakhouse, Picasso's I believe it was. I was lost in the moment when she asked me about Victoria.

"So you were married before?"

"Yes."

"Well, tell me something…anything."

"She died."

"Jesus. I'm sorry…I didn't know that." She stammered out, I thought she would spit her wine across the table when I said it.

"I'm sorry I hadn't mentioned it before. I'm just trying to get over everything, it's taken a while."

"I can imagine…how…" she paused, "no, if you don't want to talk about it, it's O.K."

"No, no. You asked. It's alright."

I took a breath and a sip of wine and said, "She left me giving birth to our daughter. It was a bitter pill to swallow…it's been seven years."

"You poor man. I'm so sorry."

"I want you to know how much tonight means to me, Jessica. It's been long overdue. Thank you."

Her sweet lips curled into a smile as she looked at me.

"I'm having fun," I admitted, "I'd almost forgotten what fun was like."

She reached across the table and touched my hand.

"I'm having fun too."

If there hadn't been a table between us, I would have kissed her right then. The moment was lost anyway when the waiter appeared, inquiring about dessert or coffee.

"I know a place on Central that has the best desserts," she said, suddenly becoming animated, "the cheesecake is five or six inches high."

"Well, my god, what are we waiting for?" I quipped back, following her fanciful lead.

I paid with my Visa and we struck out in search of the biggest piece of cheesecake in Charlotte, or in existence for that matter, according to her. It started misting rain on the windshield of my Impala, just as she reached over to put her hand on top of mine in the seat between us. It was still a first date, but we somehow felt so connected at that moment we bypassed the usual pleasantries to realize we weren't teenagers after all, we were adults, lonely adults, and we both needed that. What I didn't need was a month or two to tell me that I genuinely liked her.

She gave me directions to a place called The Landmark, and upon walking through the foyer I was taken aback by the extensive pastry case, maybe even more so than the blue dress. She was right about the cheesecake, and I thought about the old 'kid in a candy store' adage, mesmerized by all the confections and pies.

Jessica laughed as she dragged me back to earth and to the booth, where the hostess was waiting for us with menus. A pretty girl, foreign and a touch exotic, I believed she was Greek.

"I told you, didn't I?"

"No shit."

The menu was crazy, everything from blueberry pancakes to Surf n' Turf.

"I've got to bring my little girl here to see those cakes, maybe tomorrow."

"How old is she? Oh crap, I'm sorry. She'd be seven wouldn't she? You told me that at the restaurant."

"Well, she's six. Her birthday's coming up."

"That's got to be hard."

An awkward few seconds were interrupted by our coffee, and we drank it without saying much, just gazing at each other. The artist in me saw every strand of hair, every glisten of her lipstick as she moved.

"I'd love to meet her." She said.

"You will." I answered, then added, "I hope you will."

"I will."

We smoked and talked some, and it was raining harder as we trekked back to the car, hurrying to get inside. She ran her fingers through her dripping hair and stared at me.

"This has been really great." she said, clutching my hand tighter this time, "Rain and all."

Our lips met as if by instinct, and I kissed her with fervor. Her hands were over my ears then, our mouths melded together with a passion I hadn't known since discovering Victoria years before.

When we came apart, we were silent as she brushed my forearm up and down, pausing for an occasional light squeeze.

"What are you thinking about?" I asked.

"You're going to think I'm some kind of floozy." she said.

"Never." I whispered.

"I haven't been with a man in a couple of years myself...I've needed this as much as you have. I just wanted it to feel right."

"Does it?"

"Would you make love to me, if I asked you to, tonight?"

"Are you sure?"

"Yes...please. I've never wanted anything so much in my life."

"I have to go home," I said, "to pay the babysitter."

"I'll go with you, if it's alright."

"Alissa should be in bed by now," I said, going against my better judgment. I wanted her, and I wasn't going to let that golden opportunity pass me by.

We rode without saying a word. She held my arm as I drove, snuggled against me like a child. She was so beautiful, so divine.

I couldn't wait to get home. I paid Cornelia and sent her on her way, thanking her too many times. Alissa was tucked into bed, and I crept in to see her myself. A little angel, her eyes closed, she looked so peaceful. Satisfied, I took light steps back into the living room and to Jessica.

"Everything O.K.?" she asked.

"Yes. Are you alright?"

"Yes."

We fell into each other's arms, and I held her tight for a bit before taking her hand and leading her to my bedroom. It was dark, and her kisses tasted as wonderful as they had in the car.

My hands found her hips, I grasped two handfuls of blue material and brought it up and over her head. My clothes found the carpet and her sexy glasses found the nightstand as we explored each other's bodies with the wonderment of children and the longing of starved prisoners. The smooth skin of her thighs gripped my ribs like a human vice, her teeth gnashed and it seemed her big brown eyes never closed, taking in everything. Her big brown eyes, the eyes of Victoria. She was staring at me through Jessica's eyes. I was unnerved for a moment, and shook my head. I looked down again, and it was her face looking back at me, it was Victoria. My heart pounded like a machine gun and I was scared.

"Don't stop, Tiger."

Her words rung in my ears as I made love to my wife with a furious urgency. I was soon sobbing as I did so, my tears falling and splashing onto her face. She was real and I was inside of her. She was here with me and I was making love to her.

"Honey, what's wrong?" Jessica's voice came blazing out at me like a freight train.

"You're crying…my god, did I do something wrong? Tell me."

I stuttered out something unintelligible.

"You're shaking! Oh, baby…" she said as she wrapped her arms around me like a comforting mother.

It was Jessica, and I had hallucinated, I had to have. It was so real, she was there.

"I'm…sorry…" was all I could say, and I had to get away.

"I'm going outside for a smoke and some fresh air," I said, not realizing at the time how ridiculous that sounded, "please, just give me a minute or two, O.K.? Something really weird just happened."

She was confused but understanding, and I worshipped her for it. How more embarrassing could that have been? Jessica snuggled under the covers as I threw on my pants and made my way out the front door. I lit a Kamel and smoked it in the yard. I wandered to the mail box and back again. The grass was wet from the rain and it felt cool under my feet as I paced. I didn't just see her ghost on a pier that time, I felt her flesh again, she was there with me, she spoke to me. I began to cry again and plopped down on the front steps. I was going mad. I should go to a doctor, I thought. But no, I couldn't. I'd lose my job when they committed me to an institution. Damn. Damn!

"What the fuck is going on?" I said out loud, between my sobs. I knew I had to go back in, so I choked them back as well as I could. I had Jessica waiting for me, I didn't know how I would recover from this, or what I would tell her. I opened the door and stepped back in. What I saw then I would never forget.

I stepped back into the bedroom and saw Alissa first, standing by the door with a dripping carving knife. She glared at me, holding the weapon out from her little body, almost as if waiting for my inspection of what she had done. I saw Jessica's fingers, and then her hand and arm draped over the side of the bed, and then saw Jessica herself, drenched in her own sweet crimson blood, the sheets, the pillows, the floor, as if someone had thrown a paint can against the wall and splattered a gallon of red latex around the room. Alissa and I stared at each other, speechless, a hellish scene for our backdrop.

"Alissa…"

"How could you do this to us?" was her response.

"Do…"

"How could you?"

"Alissa…"

She was crazed, her eyes not her own. Her voice, the tone of her voice, not her own. I didn't know what to do, I wished I was still in my front yard, smoking, the moisture of the grass soothing under my feet. Her nightgown was soaked,…Jessica. Oh God, Jessica. Alissa.

Alissa is a nice name.

I took a step back, and another. I stepped back into the hallway, and into the living room. I reached down and placed my hand on the telephone but did not pick it up. I was sweating then, my eyes searched the room for a miracle answer that would tell me what to do.

"I had to do it, baby." The soft voice found me.

"What do you mean you had to do it?! Why? Why, Alissa?" I screamed at my daughter, finding my voice.

"You betrayed us! How could you bring her here?!"

"Alissa! You...you hurt that woman."

"No, baby, I killed her. I KILLED HER!"

Insanity. I grabbed my face and forehead, attempting to wipe it all away, but it didn't go away, and Alissa was still there, yelling at me.

"I killed her for *US*! To save *US*! Wake the fuck up!"

It was the first time that I had heard my six year old use the word 'fuck', which seemed petty then in lieu of the circumstances. She wasn't making any sense, and at some point during her tirade I had picked up the phone and pushed the three magic numbers.

"What is your emergency?" the man asked.

I didn't answer him. He asked again and again. Alissa and I stood and looked at each other in silence. Then she began to cry.

"I did it for us..." she whispered.

She dropped the knife and moved towards me but I moved away. I hung up the phone and sat down on one end of the sofa, Alissa sat on the other.

"Oh Alissa..." was all I could muster, in disbelief.

She sat and said nothing more. We were in the dark, except for the street lamp light, filtering through the windows and across her blood streaked face, making a pattern of light and shadows against her body, reminding me of another time and place a million years in the past.

CHAPTER 17

ALONE AGAIN

"Last name?"

"Morrison."

"First name?"

"Jim."

"Heh, like in The Doors."

"What?"

"Like the group, The Doors."

"Yeah."

I had been kidded through school about my name, but no one had made the connection in a few years. The officer wrote it down without mentioning it again. I sat at his desk with some black coffee in a little Styrofoam cup. I loved coffee but hated drinking it out of those damned little cups. I wanted a mug, with a handle. But you can't always get what you want. I had learned by that point that you couldn't have a lot of things that you wanted from life. Not even a normal life. They had questioned me endlessly at the house, and it continued there at the station, even though it was quite obvious what had transpired. They just kept shaking their heads, saying things about never seeing anything like that before.

"How long did you know the victim?"

The victim.

"She has a name."

"Yes sir, we know. But for all the intents and purposes of this report..."

"Alright, sorry. I met her last week. We worked together at Crystal Vision cards downtown."

"Has your daughter ever had or shown any violent tendencies, maybe at school?"

"No."

"And you were outside when the incident took place?"

"Yes."

A hundred more inane questions and he finally said, "Sir, we are not charging you with anything at this time, but pending an investigation, will you be available for further statements?"

"Yes, yes of course."

"Do you have any family or friends you can stay with?"

"No, not really...I'll get a hotel though."

He then told me to 'hang tight' and headed off into the station somewhere with the folder full of papers. I looked around the station without seeing the station. I was far away, pondering Alissa's words to me. She didn't even look scared when they put her in the police car and told me something about a juvenal detention center. I didn't know when I'd see her again.

⊨+ +⊨

I couldn't go home, it was a crime scene and I wasn't allowed. I had no clothes, no toiletries, no car. I knew I probably wouldn't make it to work that week. I wondered if I ever would. I was distraught as I checked into a room at The Inn Town Suites, a nice enough place with efficiency apartments and a weekly rate. I collapsed onto my new bed and imagined what would become of me and my miserable existence. I didn't know if or when I'd see Alissa again. I had been given the basic rundown by a detective, descriptions of mental institutions with children's wings, alternate variables and possibilities. I lit a cigarette, taking in the view of my new quarters. My mind was racing. Jessica's face, her shocked face, her last emotion before…Christ, that was too much to handle. My muscles quivered for a moment, as if I had some kind of miniature seizure. I shook it off and began pacing the room. Smoking and pacing.

I stopped at the window and pulled the drab mustard colored curtains open. The window had a calming effect, I could look out and see the parking lot, all the cars, the Krispy Kreme across the way, just off of 74. I pressed my forehead against the cool glass and shut my eyes tight.

Alissa…

It seemed as though nothing would work out for me and my life was doomed to tragedy and failure. I was a brilliant artist, but no one cared. Victoria's mother certainly didn't care. Sure, you impress some folks along the way just being an artist, but unless you're a successful dollar bill-shitting artist, society just doesn't give a damn.

Hence the term 'starving artist'. The card company job was providing a pretty good living for Alissa and I, but I wanted to sell my paintings.

Then I thought about Jessica's family. I didn't know if they had been contacted, I didn't know anything, really. I had had no sleep at all. I crushed out the cigarette and lay back on the bed. To that point, my brain was trying to take the gold in the hundred meter relay, but somehow I managed to drift away, and dream of my Victoria, and a time when everything made sense.

CHAPTER 18

CABIN FEVER

A week in the room and it had become my world, my universe. Smoking endless amounts of Kamel Reds, eating endless servings of delivered dinners, and staring out that fucking window. Victoria's mother's calls were relentless. I told her everything over and over, but she just kept calling. I knew I had to get out of there before I lost it. I remembered a quaint sports bar about a mile away in a shopping center and called a cab.

My driver's name was Paul, a bald man of Italian descent with a big black moustache like one of the Mario Brothers. Very pleasant fellow, and the first real human being I had conversed with since leaving the police station Saturday afternoon.

"Where you headed, brother?"

"That sports bar up the road, in the shopping center, the one near the Super K-Mart." I didn't know what it was called.

"That's the Game Day. Game Day Café. Nice place."

"Good place for football?"

"Oh, hell yeah. Everybody watchin' the Panthers today...'ceptin' me."

I apologized for his luck and he laughed.

"No worries, brother. I'll be off if they go to the Superbowl again, though, guaranteed."

"Can't be worse than what I've been through this week."

"Yeah? What'ch you been through this week?"

"You wouldn't believe it."

The conversation ended there for the moment, as I stared out the taxi's window. Hell, I didn't believe it. We reached the bar and I asked Paul if he knew of anything exciting going on later that night in Charlotte.

"You should look in the Creative Loafing, Bar'll have one."

I thanked Paul and paid him. Between Alissa and work, I hadn't been anywhere or done anything in years, except with Jessica.

Jessica...

The place *was* nice. I sat at the bar, ordered my usual, and lit a cigarette. There were a lot of TV's, Jake scrambled out of the pocket and barely got a pass off to Davis before getting hit. Davis was also hit, stopped for a loss behind the line of scrimmage. Three guys at a nearby table groaned in unison.

I needed to get my head out of that horrible place it was in. I loved football, but I had a sinking feeling that even Jake Delhomme wouldn't be able to pull me out of that funk. I saw a Creative Loafing magazine at the end of the bar and reached to get it, as I pulled it over Jake dropped back, the pocket collapsed and he was scrambling again.

"Come on, Jake..." I mumbled under my breath, frozen in the moment.

Getting rid of the ball as he was tackled, he hit Muhammad in the end zone for a miraculous touchdown. The three guys jumped up cheering and toasting their draft beers together.

Thanks, Jake.

I sorted through the nightclubs, the band listings, and what finally caught my eye caught it hard. A club called Scorpio's was having a drag cabaret show, the special guest of honor would be the reigning Miss Gay North Carolina, *Miss Veronica Valentine.*

I read the name again and again, rubbed my fingers over the ink. Just a few minutes ago, I had been thinking that my week couldn't get any crazier, but indeed it had. I had to see Ronnie. She having any interest in seeing me would be the actual deciding variable. I'd sit in the back, she'd never have to see me, I thought. I'd just see her. Just for a little while, dear God, just for a few minutes. That old yearning welled up in my heart and I bit my bottom lip hard to keep the emotions in check. I had to see her; there was no way around it.

I moved my fingers over the ad again, and it hit me harder than Kevin Greene planting a hapless quarterback in the turf.

Ronnie's cards.

She told me before Alissa was born there would be something wrong with the baby, that Victoria was carrying evil inside of her. Ronnie tried to tell me. The Lovers, The Devil,…my hand began to tremble and I felt cold. Cold and a little sick. Suddenly there was nothing more Jake could do to make me feel better and I asked the bartender to call me another cab.

Scorpio's parking lot was packed, and the number of people in line was astounding. That was a big night, and all manner of patrons were anxious to get inside. I saw drag queens of all shapes and sizes, but none that could ever match Ronnie's finery and grace. As I moved closer to the entrance, I became nervous, thinking of her. Who would I be to her then? If I did find the courage to approach my old friend, what kind of reaction would I receive? Oh, fuck it, I thought, I'd find out soon enough.

There was a ten dollar cover after showing my I.D. to a gruff portly woman inside the foyer, and then suddenly I was inside. I noticed upon entering the main room that it was very dark, so dark you couldn't really see other people at all until they came close or passed you by. I wasn't crazy about that, but assumed they would illuminate a stage area for the show. I needed a flashlight like a theater usher. The bar seemed the best place to remain low-key while awaiting the festivities, so I made my way through the shoulder-to-shoulder sea of gay humanity and found it. And there I sat for four hours, drinking, smoking and waiting.

><++><

She was drunk! She was *very* drunk, I kept repeating to myself. She wanted too much from me, she wanted what I couldn't give her, at least not then. From guilt to longing to pity and back to guilt, my emotions were running the full gauntlet while I cultivated my rum buzz like a veteran gardener caring for his prized tomatoes. The dance floor lights passed over the crowd, red, purple and blue, revealing flashes of people in love, moving slowly, cheek to cheek, kissing and cooing over each other. True love is a beautiful thing, no matter who the participants, I supposed.

Damn, Ronnie had embarrassed me that night so long ago at the beach, the fight had played over and again in my mind since then, every word. Perhaps her explosion was untimely, not to mention unpleasant to endure, but there was a genuine anguish behind it, a squelched desire to be with me, that couldn't have stayed bottled up another minute.

What a fool I seemed to be then, losing the love of a lifetime, and refusing another, handed to me on a silver tray. I couldn't help thinking that I had betrayed poor Ronnie, that it must have been torturous to spend so much time with someone you adored, but kept stifled at a distance by the object of your affection's unsure confusion. I had always loved Ronnie, but my stupid reservations kept us apart, when we could have been reveling in each other's company to the fullest, instead of tip-toeing around that sensitive issue.

So Ronnie was a man, he strove with all his determined mind not to be. I saw him as a divine creature, devoid of gender, until the most intimate of moments, when no matter the amount of smoke and mirrors could hide the fact that Ronnie was a man, and I wasn't ready. I was scared, and I'm sure Ronnie knew it. He tried so hard, and I kept pushing him away, living some kind of fantasy life there in the condo. Mine and Victoria's condo.

My forehead found its way to rest in my palm. I closed my eyes and saw an image of my poor Alissa, locked in a room somewhere, more scared than I could have been then, or ever had been. How could things have gotten so bad? What in the hell had happened to my life? A draw off my Kamel gave me a tiny bit of reassurance, but it only came in small increments. My friend nicotine was always there to comfort. It didn't say much, but calmed my wired nerves better than anything in those twisted days.

The dance music faded into the theme from 2001 and my first conditioned thought was to see Ric Flair come through the curtain in a sparkling robe. What did come through that curtain wasn't the Nature Boy, but it sure sparkled. A bright spotlight revealed a heavy-set female impersonator, glittering from head to toe, informing us all that it was 'showtime'.

I became uncomfortable, my chest uneasy as my eyes locked onto the stage, anticipating the guest of honor. The string of performers were amazing, one more divine than the last, lip-synching and collecting dollars from the front row patrons, cheering them on.

Seven or eight came and went, changed outfits, and came and went again, with the shiny plus-sized hostess introducing them until finally she spoke the words I came to hear.

"O.K. all you boys and girls out there in queer land, the moment you've all been waiting for, our special guest performer of the evening, the reigning Miss Gay North Carolina, the beautiful, the glamorous, the flawless, the incredible...Miss Veronica Valentine!"

The spotlight made a circle of white on the black velvet curtain, a light breeze blowing across the bottom of the material's folds, a hidden fan I guessed. Those seconds dragged by as I heard the beginning chords of the music, and saw the backdrop part. A living breathing goddess of a woman stepped through and I was left breathless at how much Ronnie had changed. Her hair was so long and full, she was so graceful and perfect. A flowing blood-red gown and gloves, it was almost too much to take. An adoring fan ran up with a dozen roses and presented them to her. She kissed him on the cheek and waved to everyone, her diamond tiara reflecting every glimmer in the building.

My heart was close to palpitating as I watched her every move, as if she were Elizabeth Taylor floating across a silver theater screen.

My God.

She lip-synched her way through a couple of slow, classy numbers, then disappeared again as quickly as she arrived, smiling and blowing kisses, that crowd worshipped her. My elation in seeing my friend after all that time turned to gloom when she was finally gone and the show came to an end. An emptiness set in, a self-loathing and an overbearing sensation of loss. I sat there, finishing my seventh or eighth drink and smoking cigarettes until the bartender announced last call. My mind was blank as I stared at what was left of the ice cubes in the bottom of my glass. They were melting away, with my sanity and my hopes of ever having any manner of normal life. I purposed that perhaps there was no such thing as a normal life, that there was just life, and we to make the best of what we'd been dealt. Maybe I'd heard it in a movie, but it applied.

I also purposed that I should get back to the hotel and go to sleep before I started having inclinations of ending my misery by ending my own life.

The house lights came up and I saw the entire bar for the first time. It was bigger than I thought, and messy, napkins and bottles littering the floor, with men making their way towards the exits, hand in hand or arm in arm, to some soothing Enya provided by the deejay. I followed, through the lobby, across the wooden deck, down some steps to the gravel of the parking lot. I remembered falling in the gravel outside of the pier years ago, looking up and seeing Ronnie there to comfort me. A heavy sigh and someone pushed by me. I then felt like a fool realizing I had come in a cab, and turned to head back inside. I was good and toasty drunk, thoroughly cacked, but at the top of the stairs I heard a voice that would have awoken me from my deathbed.

"Jimmy?"

She was now in a pink top and sweats, with a ball cap, her blonde ponytail protruding from the back, but her lips were still a brilliant red as they had been in the show. We stood a moment, just looking, like we were both in some type of unbelievable dream state.

"I...just came to see the show, you know...I wasn't...going to bother you..or nothin'." I stood stumbling over my words.

"Oh, Jimmy..." was her reply, falling into my arms.

I held her, there on the patio. We wept.

"What are you doing here? Oh my God!"

"Ronnie, I..."

"Getting drunk and checking out the queens? I know all your tricks, mister."

"I wasn't going to..."

"Oh my fucking God in Heaven, if you would have left here without...Oh, I don't even want to think about it!"

"Ronnie, listen, can we talk? Do you have a few minutes...to spare an old friend?"

"Honey, bring your long lost ass back in this club right now and talk to me."

It was Ronnie no doubt, still on. She dragged me through the doors and back to the bar. There were guys sweeping up and collecting empties from everywhere, rolling large cans through the room and tossing the bottles in, crashing them against the others.

We sat and she continued, "O.K. Tell me, what brought you down here?"

"I saw you in the paper, Ronnie. I had to see you." I answered, my head a little off kilter from the booze, "I missed you."

She was so pretty, as always, and she answered, in a rare serious tone, "Oh Tiger, I missed you too."

"It's been a long time, look, about…"

"Oh Goddamn, forget that. I was *so* fucked up. I've never forgiven myself for that crazy shit."

I reached to touch her face. She didn't resist. I caressed her cheek as her bottom lip trembled just a bit and a tear fell from her eye.

"No, no." I said, "You'll ruin your makeup."

"I missed you so much…" she said twice, the second one a whisper, "I missed you so much…I'm sorry…"

"Ronnie, its my fault, I didn't see. I lost you, and now I've lost… God, Ronnie, you wouldn't believe it."

"Veronica! Your cab's here!" a guy called out from the next room.

She did her best to dry up and asked, "Were you going to call a cab?"

"Yeah."

"Well I've got one. Come on."

I helped her with her bags and we returned to the deck, and into the waiting yellow automobile.

She kept saying, "I can't believe its you."

I said, "Believe it."

⤙┼ ┼⤚

We carried on like kids at a birthday party until we reached her hotel room that the club had provided for her in the Adam's Mark, a very nice place uptown. What a night! It was in the elevator that the pit of my stomach felt queasy and reality returned to me, stopping on a dime at my feet. I became quiet and Ronnie misinterpreted my silence as a romantic mood change. She kicked off her shoes and plopped down on the edge of the queen-sized bed, very fitting considering the circumstances.

"It's real soft, bubby." She said, waving her hand around as if she were showing off what I could win if my price was right.

I moved next to her, and began to relive a portion of what I never cared to think of again.

"Ronnie, something bad happened."

"How bad?"

"Really bad."

"Is Alissa alright? What is it?"

I hung my head and pulled a cigarette from the other constant in my life, a box of Kamel Reds. Lighting it, I continued, "I don't know. They took her away…"

I began to break down right there, never getting it all out, and Ronnie enveloped me into her ever compassionate arms.

"They…took her away…" I repeated, my words choppy and filled with pain.

"Who took her away? Tiger, tell me, its alright."

When I didn't answer right away, she began to guess.

"DSS? Children's Services? Not the grandmother! I never liked that old sun-dried bat!"

"Me either." And a giggle broke through the ice.

I looked up and through my watery eyes saw an exquisite friend. How could I have allowed those years to get away from us? I felt like a fool and I kissed her on her lips, with all the tenderness I could conjure from my wounded and bandaged soul. We fell together onto the top blankets, and made out like teenagers with their loins afire. How far would I let it go? My answer was as far as our re-kindled emotions would carry it, to infinity. I dropped the smoke into a crystal ashtray resting on the bedside table and pulled her pink blouse over her head. She nestled back into the pillows, she had no breasts, but at that moment among the loveliest visions ever laid before me. I slid her sweats from her legs and over her bright red toenails. I was kneeling over her body, Ronnie reclined and touched herself, touched the thing, restrained only by the thin material of her silky red underwear.

"Jimmy, I'm yours…" she whispered, "I've *always* been yours."

I dimmed the lights and removed my own clothing, she watching my every motion. I crawled up to her, and we reveled in each other as never before, touching, kissing, and adoring one another without remorse or fear, without boundaries or restraints. I had always loved Ronnie, and it was time to show her how much.

CHAPTER 19

REUNIONS

My eyes opened at 9 am, and snuggled beside me was my Ronnie. The front desk's wakeup call came, ringing moments later, waking her as well. I thanked them and turned to face my precious companion. Her gentle morning fingers made trails across my torso.

"Hey." She whispered.

"Hey."

"you were amazing, Tiger. I waited so long to get to know you, in the Biblical sense."

She smiled and suggested a steamy shower together, I told her to start it and I would be there. She slid out of bed and stood nude, her hands in her hair, an uncircumcised appendage perfectly sheathed, and not a tan line in sight to obstruct her body's slim luxurious smoothness.

"Sure you're coming?"

"Wouldn't miss it."

She winked and turned the corner, and I had no regrets. I knew I had razed a wall that I had built some years ago, but I didn't care. I felt free, and so natural. I felt complete. I vowed to never hold myself back again, I would follow my heart to the corners of the globe, open and honest, and enjoy life to its fullest fruition.

I called my hotel for any messages, and was delighted to learn that not only could I return to my house, but I could see Alissa, and I jotted down the address. Yes! What a piece of news! In the bathroom the mirror was already fogged over, and I peeked around the curtain to view Ronnie washing herself. I climbed in, holding her hot soapy body against mine. In a dream I couldn't have enjoyed her more. In a dream I couldn't have been happier.

⇒⊢⊣⇐

We checked out of Ronnie's hotel and took a cab back to mine, and then on to my place. It was a disaster, the cops had left it a shambles. On the way over I had tried to prepare Ronnie for what she would see when we arrived, but even I was aghast forgetting how much blood was on the walls. Jessica's blood, now dried to an umber color. She didn't deserve it, the poor girl. Jessica…

Ronnie was speechless, no doubt for the first time since I'd known her, as I inspected the ransacked rooms, finally stepping into my studio, relieved to find my paintings intact and where I had left them. I showed them to Ronnie, one by one, my Victorias. She was shaken from the remnants of the murder, but managed to tell me how beautiful they were, and asked if I would someday do one of her. I promised to do many, one every day if it were possible, and I held her.

"I've always loved the way your arms felt around me." She said, sounding content.

"I know," I said, "a real man to make you feel like a real woman…I remember. I remember everything."

"I love you, Jimmy."

I called the juvenal center for more details and we headed down South Boulevard in my car. I was nervous about seeing my daughter, and confused about what was to happen next. What would become of her? I asked myself over and again as we approached the building.

Ronnie lit a cigarette and said she would wait there, on a bench. I was scared, wondering if my little girl was alright, terrified of losing her. I met with an officer and filled out some forms, and followed him down ochre and pumpkin painted hallways, ugly.

I was lead into an office and told someone named Dr. Edwin would be in to speak to me. I scanned his wall and read his degrees, George Edwin, Bachelor in Psychology, Masters in Child Psychiatry, University of South Carolina. On the desk were photos of his kids in their little soccer uniforms, freckled and grinning. Another frame held his trophy wife, smiling and lovely with pearls adorning her slender feminine neck. I wondered if she was a good wife, if she really loved him, or did she salivate over the good physician's salary? So many people find out too late that they have been living a lie most of their lives, to please or comfort undeserving others instead of themselves. Oh, the wasted years.

I was lost in thought when he finally entered the room.

"Mr. Morrison?"

"Dr. Edwin?"

We shook hands. A pleasant man, yet serious, began to tell me about my estranged daughter, and I clung to every scrap of information I could get like a starved prisoner being thrown a chicken leg from the king's table.

"I can *see her*, right?"

"Oh, of course. But there are a few things you should know. I want you to be prepared. Alissa hasn't spoken a word to us the entire time she's been here, and she's barely eaten. The only emotion she exhibits besides her indignation is a seething hatred for myself and my staff."

"What about other kids?"

"She's been kept in an isolated room, until her mental evaluations are being completed. I imagine you're dying to see her, but you'd be smart not to expect a whole lot."

249

"I understand."

"How are *you* holding up?"

"I just got back in my house today. Ran into an old friend, took my mind off of it for a little while, thank God. Other than that, I've been a wreck pretty much, pacing a lot and fearing the worst."

"Alright. I can't promise you its going to get better anytime soon. Honestly, she may be here quite a while. It's going to be tough."

"Please. I want to see her."

We walked through a visitors day room and up to a series of chairs in front of narrow windows. My God, they weren't going to let me touch her! I had to speak to her through a goddamned piece of glass! He explained something about violent offenders and safety, but I only heard bits and pieces, zoning him out, staring at the window.

I sat five minutes, psyching myself up, wondering when they would bring her. And then I saw her. Another guard led her to the chair and on the other side of the pane, but to me it might as well have been the other side of the world. She was pale, with no expression really, her black hair tangled and matted. She was in a little orange gown, and my heart sank to the floor. Her eyes were sleepless and red, and they burned into me as she took her seat. I was moved beyond description, and with meek apprehension, I picked up the receiver to my right.

"It's Daddy, honey…pick up the phone."

She did, but said nothing.

"Alissa sugar, are you alright, baby?"

Her silence was unnerving, but I kept up the banter.

"Baby, I've been worried sick…I miss you…I'm going to try everything I can to get you out of here, to make you better…so we can be together again, OK sweetheart?"

"Jimmy…" she growled, "you sound like a damned fool."

"What?"

"Get me out of here."

"Well, Alissa, sweetie, I'm going to try, honey. It's not that easy after..."

"No, Jimmy," she cut me off, "that's not good enough. Get a lawyer and get me out of this shithole."

"Alissa, you were talking like this the night they took you away, do you remember why they took you away?"

"Yes I remember!" she was irate, "I killed that bitch girlfriend of yours, because you didn't wait on me!"

"Wait on you? What are you..."

"You just couldn't wait, couldn't wait until I grew up?! I thought you loved me, Jimmy! Don't you see? Can't you *SEE ME*, baby?"

I was stunned, the terror resounded through my bones as she let out a shriek and slammed her forehead into the glass partition, cracking it. Her head plowed forward, hammering into the window, five, six times, her blood spattering it and running down her cheeks. The guards came sprinting, grabbing her arms just as she smacked the glass a final time with her face, shattering it.

Shards flew everywhere, my little girl's features transformed into a contorted crimson mask, screaming, "DON'T YOU *SEE ME*, JIMMY?" as they dragged her away from me, and back down the corridor she had appeared from minutes earlier.

I sat in awe. The window destroyed, its remains coated red in my lap and all around the tile beneath my feet. I thought the unthinkable. I imagined the unimaginable, and said only to myself, "I see you."

Hanging my head I began to cry as Dr. Edwin and some attendants attempted to clean me off with towels, and swept up the broken pieces, apologizing. I wondered who was going to sweep up the broken pieces of me.

⤜⧓⤛

When I staggered out of the facility, I must have been white as a ghost, Ronnie jumped up.

"Give me a cigarette."

"What happened?"

"Just give me a cigarette… please."

She did, and I continued, "Ronnie, do you still have your cards with you?'

"What, are you a comedian now? Of course I do."

"Good. Come on, let's go. We have to talk."

CHAPTER 20
REVELATIONS

"Tiger, tell me what's going on. You're acting crazy."

"I feel like I *am* crazy, Ronnie. Please, the cards."

"O.K.! God! Don't blow a gasket, fella!"

Ronnie pulled her set of Tarot cards out of a small leather bag containing personal items she had assembled for her trip, and laid the deck on the coffee table.

"Do you remember the last time we did this?"

"Yes, at my place at the beach."

"Do you remember what you told me then? Do you remember what the cards were?"

"Yeah..."

"It's all making sense now...as much as I hate it, its coming true."

"Sweetie, that was like, seven years ago."

"I know, but look what's happened. Look what's *happened*!"

Ronnie glared at me without moving.

"Ronnie, please baby, humor me."

"O.K., but just because you're so handsome, getting all worked up over there." She blew me a kiss as she shuffled.

"Cut them."

I split the cards and stacked them again.

"Draw the top three. Concentrate on what you're concerned about."

It was all about Alissa. My right hand hovered over the deck, I was hesitating.

"Ronnie?"

"Yes?"

"What if it's bad? What if it's as bad as last time? What'll I do? I'm already at the end of my rope."

"Then don't draw them. Talk to me, baby, calm down."

"Ronnie, you've studied this stuff, you have ever since I've known you."

"What is it?"

"Did you believe everything I told you back then? About the visions, the nightmares, seeing Victoria on the pier?"

"Yes, hon, I did. I know that shit happens."

"Well do you think that what's happening now with Alissa is linked to that stuff back then? Honestly."

"Jimmy, I've always known that something strange was going on, that something freaky was going to happen, and it involved Alissa. It's finally playing out."

"Do you believe a person could…"

"Could what?"

"Could…"

"*What?*"

"What do you think will happen to Alissa now?"

"Draw the cards, Jimmy, *they'll* tell you."

I did, and as I turned them over I felt my very soul clawing to get away, to hide, but there was nowhere to run, it was left out in the cold, shivering naked in a miserable January downpour.

The Lovers.

The Devil.

Death.

In dumbfounded silence I stared at the same three cards I had drawn seven years prior, laying there lifeless yet mocking me with a renewed zeal.

"I see you..." I whispered to them, whispered to her.

"You see who?" Ronnie asked.

"Ronnie, when Alissa spoke today, and that night, it...it wasn't her." My voice was slow and cautious, as if even I couldn't believe the words that were passing my own lips. Ronnie sat and let me talk.

"I did it for us...I did it for us..." I repeated, getting a smoke and tossing the pack back on the table. I stared into space for a moment before lighting it.

"Ronnie, that can't be Alissa in there, it can't be."

A deep exhale and I wiped my tired eyes.

"Who is it, Tiger?"

"Alright, everything I'm about to suggest to you is going to sound totally cracked, O.K.?"

"It won't be the first time."

"She's...she's...trying to...Oh Jesus, no, it's too fucked up, it can't *be*."

"Tiger, come on. You're the one who talked to her. Tell me what you're feeling."

I hesitated again. A drag from the Kamel, and another, and mental images of my Victoria passed before my eyes. She was blowing me kisses and laughing, her black hair floated free with the summer breeze, like a Bettie Page photograph.

"She promised she'd never leave me. With her last breath she swore it."

I lowered my head and scratched my scalp, waiting for Ronnie to tell me how insane it all was, how it just couldn't be. When I received no response of any kind, I raised back up to see her wide-eyed and stunned with a touch of horror accenting her features.

"Oh lord I need a drink!" she exclaimed and headed for the kitchen.

I sat alone and mulled over Alissa's outbursts.

"I see you." I thought. "Now what do I do with you?"

I gathered up the cards, shuffled the deck, cut them and placed the pile down again. I turned towards the kitchen, Ronnie was still in there. I drew the top three.

The Lovers, The Devil, Death.

⊱⊰

I wandered into Alissa's room, her dolls were strewn across the carpet. I picked them up, one at a time, and placed them back on the dresser. Sitting on the bed, I remembered where I had acquired each one. Barbies, Bratz, My Scene, Zodiacs, Goths, Wonder Woman; she only wanted the ones with black hair. I saw her face on each one, Victoria's face, and to my dismay everything was becoming clearer by the minute. I had no idea what to do, or where to go from there. I heard a creak, and turned to see Ronnie, leaning in the doorway. She spoke, but it wasn't her natural tone, and she was visibly shaken.

"I...couldn't find anything to drink in your kitchen. Never thought you'd live anywhere without a bottle of rum somewhere."

I just looked at her, and after a moment she continued, "I put on some coffee."

"Thanks."

She turned and made her way back down the hallway.

CHAPTER 21

CONFESSIONS

The years were welcome friends to Ronnie and me. I had matured as an artist, and our relationship had matured along with that. She was my best friend, my lover, my enduring companion. She became my business manager and my agent, secured me many gallery showings in Charlotte, and my paintings of her spawned their own greeting card line, that we packaged ourselves and distributed nationwide, drawing from the experience I acquired at Crystal Visions. I quit that job soon after our business took off, and never looked back.

We started small, selling assortments to local bookstores and adult novelty shops, but their popularity grew and my work found its way into the pages of several national magazines, and I was happier than I ever imagined I could be. It's safe to say every aspect of my life had been altered. We moved to a much nicer home in the South Park area. Ronnie was on her way to becoming one of the more recognized female impersonators in America. Life was grand. Of course, we had our dark secret that after many nights of torturous soul-searching we decided best to lock away in the nether reaches of our minds. She convinced me that no good could come from it, it was unnatural and evil. It nearly destroyed me emotionally to abandon my daughter, but scores of doctors and specialists all told me the same sad story, that there was no hope. An unexplainable mental affliction had gripped her and its hold was unrelenting. They couldn't explain it, but I knew what had happened. It still made me shiver to think about it. Visiting the hospital was draining me, and after a time, Ronnie assured me that it was best not to return.

Those days, those glorious days of my success couldn't have been possible without my ingenious and devoted Veronica Valentine. We traveled and saw the world, kissed atop the Eiffel tower, made love in the quaint bed & breakfasts of Scotland, laughed and rolled in the sands of Key West. I never wanted it to end, and there was no end in sight.

There was an evening in Paris, in the fall of the year, we were having a glass of wine outside of a cafe' on a narrow cobblestone street, when she dropped the bombshell that floored me.

"We've come so far together." She began.

"I know." I answered, my cigarette in the air close to my face, the smoke twirling and twisting upwards in the air, as free as my spirit felt at that moment, and every moment since I freed myself from my worrisome bondage and depression.

"Tiger, would you care to go a little farther?"

She hesitated before speaking again.

"We have so much now, I feel a little guilty telling you there's still something else I want."

"Tell me, baby. Tell me anything."

She glanced across the street, a boy on a bicycle shouted up to someone leaning out of a window who waved back at him. The garçon arrived with fresh wine and a smile.

When he was gone, she looked at me with those eyes, aglow with desire, and said, "Jimmy, I want to marry you."

"You want to…"

"I want to be your wife."

She was as beautiful as any woman alive, more so even, I just looked at her, seeing all the details of her flawless elegant features.

"I know...we can't, Jimmy. Not like this...but for years now I've had a dream, a dream to be on the outside what I am on the inside, what I've always been."

"You mean..."

"There's a reassignment surgeon...in Frankfort..." Her voice broke and she lowered her chin as the first tears came.

"It's all I ever wanted..."

I pulled my chair around the table, sitting next to her. It was something she'd never eluded to before that day, and I could see she was frightened to tell me.

"I don't want to lose what we've got." She said, "I don't want to change anything if it means losing you."

"Ronnie...please, sugar, if that's what you want, it's what we'll do. You won't lose me, ever."

She held on to me, and mumbled into my shoulder, "I was afraid to tell you...but I just couldn't hold it in anymore."

"It's O.K. baby, It's O.K."

She looked up and wiped her eyes with a napkin. Our lips pressed together for a moment and she wanted to go back to the hotel. It was a few blocks up and we walked, holding hands and talking.

It was an enjoyable mild night for a walk in Paris. Me and my girl. I had eliminated everything negative in the immediate world around me, and nothing mattered more to me than making my Ronnie happy. I recalled the same feeling, eons ago, strolling hand in hand with Victoria down the Boardwalk in Turner's Island. She was nothing more than a distant memory, almost as if she had never existed, just an elaborate dream I had awakened from, like it never really happened, those strange days at the beach.

"What are you thinking about, Tiger? You gonna share with the missus or what?"

I grinned, still moving forward.

"Denny's."

"Jesus Christ." She replied, as we stepped into the elevator in the lobby, "Don't even go there."

⫘

As Ronnie showered, I stood in the room in front of a mirror, studying my face; my hair was a little thinner, and a few new wrinkles had appeared. Lines under my eyes, and my complexion wasn't what I had grown accustomed to seeing. I felt like the pressure and stress of the last few years had aged me a bit, and as much as I tried to put it all behind me, it was still there, recoiled into a far closet at the end of a lonely, dimly lit hallway in my brain. I didn't speak of it to Ronnie anymore, it made her so uncomfortable. After all, we had it made. Everything was good, except that memory. I sat in the chair, which was also very uncomfortable, and thumbed through my sketchbook, going over drawings I had done of Ronnie earlier that day in a park. I had gotten used to the way she was, and who she was, but I so wanted her to have everything in the world she desired. It was our last night in Paris and I was ready to get home, back to my work.

"Would you paint me?" she asked from the bathroom.

"I have, dear."

"No…" she said, coming into the room, still nude, reminding me of how much I loved her openness, "I mean, with breasts…and without, you know, just to see."

"Yes, baby."

She put her arms around me and kissed me with a wet smack.

"Thank you! Thank you! Thank you! I can't wait to see it."

I smiled as she bounced back into the bathroom. I heard the blowdryer and a peace came over me. Even though my life hadn't worked out exactly as planned, to say the least, for some peculiar reason I felt like everything was going to be alright. As usual, I was dead wrong again.

END

To be continued in *'CHILD OF RAGE'*

To be continued in the 'Turner's Island' book & film series by
Michael Tisdale

Love Me Two Times
Child of Rage
Disturbing the Priest
To Hate or Be Hated
Turner's Island
Blood of the Vagrant Damned
Bride of the Hunter
Deeper in Darkness
The Great Picasso's Hot Tamale
Call of the Sea Siren
Dan Lee
Visits From Ariel
The Grim Reaper's Bedside Manner

www.partsunknownpro.com
www.facebook.com/turnersislandmovie
www.facebook.com/lovemetwotimesbook
www.facebook.com/disturbingthepriestbook
Contact the author: turnersisland@gmail.com

Cover photo: Michael Tisdale
Model: Tara Stewart
Author photo: Kristine Johnson
Back cover photo: Michele Johnson

 Michael 'Sheik' Tisdale was born in 1966 in Killeen, Texas. A son in a traveling military family, he lived abroad and saw most of Europe and the States at a young age. A graduate of The Art Institute of Atlanta, he spent summers drawing and painting on Myrtle Beach's Ocean Boulevard, as well as continuing to travel, creating unique life experiences as his prominent priority. He began writing *Love Me Two Times* in 2002 during a dramatic, turbulent time. The main character is a relatable artist, following Stephen King's valuable advice in his book, *On Writing.* In 2007 a friend suggested that a good preacher battling an evil vampire in the Old West would make a great movie, and that planted the early seed for *Disturbing the Priest.* After receiving the blessing to run with the concept himself, and after completing the screenplay for the independent film *Turner's Island,* he began writing that story in 2015. His plans are to connect all tales within the realm of the continuing *Turner's Island* book series.

'Sheik' is a writer, artist, actor, indie filmmaker, photographer, and retired pro wrestler. He enjoys selling art prints of his 'gourmet celebrity caricatures' at various comic cons, festivals, events and shows, and lives near the ocean in South Carolina.

Made in the USA
Lexington, KY
09 August 2017